A QUESTION OF MERCY

STORY RIVER BOOKS

Pat Conroy, Editor at Large

OTHER BOOKS BY ELIZABETH COX

Familiar Ground
The Ragged Way People Fall Out of Love
Night Talk
Bargains in the Real World
The Slow Moon
I Have Told You And Told You (Poems)

A QUESTION OF MERCY

A Novel

ELIZABETH COX

Foreword by Jill McCorkle

The University of South Carolina Press

© 2016 University of South Carolina

Published by the University of South Carolina Press
Columbia, South Carolina 29208

www.sc.edu/uscpress

Manufactured in the United States of America

25 24 23 22 21 20 19 18 17 16
10 9 8 7 6 5 4 3 2 1

Library of Congress Cataloging-in-Publication Data
can be found at http://catalog.loc.gov/

ISBN: 978-1-61117-722-0 (hardcover)
ISBN: 978-1-61117-723-7 (ebook)

This is a work of fiction. Names, characters, businesses, places, events, and incidents are either the products of the author's imagination or used in a fictitious manner. Any resemblance to actual persons, living or dead, or actual events is purely coincidental

This book was printed on recycled paper with 30 percent postconsumer waste content.

This book is dedicated to all my students in Special Education classes during the 1960s. They taught me about living out of the heart.

To my Aunt Pearl,
who died in the Milledgeville asylum in the 1950s.

Here is the shadow of truth, for only the shadow is true.

Robert Penn Warren, "A Way to Love God"

The weight of this sad time we must obey,
Speak what we feel, not what we ought to say.
The oldest hath borne most; we that are young
Shall never see so much, nor live so long.

William Shakespeare, King Lear, act 5, scene 3

FOREWORD

The writer Elizabeth Cox has an accomplished literary career built on the solid foundation of giving voice to those who, for whatever reason—class, race, accusation, affliction—have been denied an adequate opportunity to speak. This was true in her stunning debut novel, *Familiar Ground* (newly reissued by the University of South Carolina Press), and the compassionate and memorable portrait she painted of a mentally challenged man known as "Soldier." Though he was not the central character in that novel, Cox's astute attention to Soldier drew him into the fabric of a place and time in ways both necessary and important. This vision that captures all the members of a family or society, drawing the lines that both connect and separate them, is one of Cox's greatest strengths as a writer. She has successfully explored divorce, rape, prejudice, and injustice without sounding topical or climbing on a soapbox or into a pulpit. Rather, she allows those unheard voices—the children, the accused, the mistreated and betrayed—to tell their own stories with great clarity and satisfaction.

Cox's novel *Night Talk* won the Lillian Smith Book Award for its attention to racial issues and inspired conversations about race in churches both in Cox's native South and in New England where she was living at the time. The award is one given to a book about the American South with emphasis on racial and social conditions with "a vision of justice and human understanding." Cox shares this honor with other highly accomplished literary and socially present authors, among them Alice Walker, Ernest Gaines, Will Campbell, Cormac McCarthy, and Henry Louis Gates.

This new novel, *A Question of Mercy*, once again brings to the page that *vision of justice and human understanding* as Cox takes us into society at a time when there were institutions for the "feeble-minded" where prison-like conditions were not unusual, nor were compulsory sterilization and other surgical procedures to render these people, deemed not suitable for society, harmless and easy to manage. This is a troubling history that appears occasionally in the news but in many ways has remained a dark secret closed off and avoided. With this new novel, Cox is opening that door and venturing in, and beyond writing a powerful novel about family ties and abiding love, she has also created yet another forum that I hope will once again spur important and necessary conversations about the moral ethics of our society. I met Elizabeth Cox when her first novel came out and I have had the great honor over the years of both teaching with her in the Bennington College MFA program and hearing her read and speak on many occasions. Any student who has ever worked with Cox has been encouraged to venture into and explore those places in their fiction that they fear or that make them uncomfortable. They have likely been told they need to go into that dark hole and stay there until they see something, learn something, find comfort within the discomfort. Cox is a master at this great feat and her awareness of the most fragile and fleeting aspects of life is what propels her fiction.

When we first meet young Jess Booker in *A Question of Mercy* she is being interviewed in a law office and we are presented with a mystery. What happened to her stepbrother, Adam Finney?

Then Cox takes us back in time to the day Jess runs away to escape what has just taken place. It is 1953 and Cox paints that era vividly—the music and dress and language of the time. Jess's journey, hiding in the woods, seeking rides along the way, provides ample time to learn more about her history, her mother's early death, her father's remarriage to Clementine Finney, and her meeting and growing attachment to her stepbrother, Adam, a boy we are told people crossed the street to avoid, mothers warning their children not to wave or speak. Jess's physical journey through this vivid landscape not only establishes Cox's love and mastery of the kind of intricate storytelling familiar in the southern literary tradition, but also sets the course for a personal odyssey that leads her to confront and deal with matters of the heart. Throughout the novel, she is writing letters to her sweetheart, Sam, a young man serving in the war who is forced to question his own sense of mercy. Jess's destination is a boarding house she once visited with her mother, and that place and her mother's friend who lives there provide a safe landing spot, a respite for Jess, if only for a brief time. The boarding house also provides the reader with a colorful cast of characters and wonderful comic relief in the midst of this tense and suspenseful journey.

No one writes children better than Cox and she has a special affinity for the voices of young boys. She grew up with brothers and on the campus of an all boys' school so perhaps that is the source but it is a strength she has perfected. The young boys Jess encounters in the boarding house, Shooter and Ray, bring humor but they also serve as foils to Adam's childhood and all that has been deprived him. These boys are orphans and have endured extreme unhappiness and yet, compared to Adam, we see them as lucky in their current circumstances.

This novel places the reader right in the heart of an ethical situation, weighing out right from wrong—the human heart and the laws of society in conflict with each other. It is about extreme practices and ethical questions in the broadest sense, but it is also about trust and faith and compassion—the guiding factors that tend to lead Cox's characters forward. There is romantic love. There is familial love. There is humor. There is grief. Ultimately, it is a novel about mercy and a level of love and devotion worthy of sacrifice.

Jill McCorkle

PROLOGUE

Jess Booker already knew how life could change in a moment—a car disappearing over the crest of a hill or sunlight slipping behind a dark cloud—she knew this, but did not know what lay ahead for her. She sat close to her father in the lawyer's office, a long, narrow room with shelves of books that rose high to the ceiling. For a moment, Jess studied their shapes and the patterns of their colors and their placements, and wondered about the sheer volume of information they must contain. Yet she also knew that the answers to the questions that brought her and her father into this office today would not be found on those pages.

The window of Mr. Strickland's office was open and a small breeze folded curtains back from the sill, letting in a frail morning light. The room smelled of peppermint.

In a moment Mr. Strickland came in carrying a cup of coffee, still steaming, and placed it on a stack of papers. His feet shuffled across the floor in this otherwise mute afternoon. He spoke to Edward Booker first, then turned toward Jess. "I want you to tell me whatever you remember about being with Adam Finney," Strickland urged. "Nothing is too small."

"Adam wanted to go to the river one more time. You know, before he had to go away." Jess told him. "It was the end of April, but the river was cold. He had on his jacket."

"Did he say he wanted to go *into* the river?" Strickland asked.

"Yes. I told him it'd be cold. He didn't want to be sent away. He hated the thought of going to that horrible place." She couldn't say its name.

"The Cadwell Institution," her father said. "Adam was leaving the very next day, but I'm not sure how much he actually understood about it."

Jess turned toward the window where she heard a swarm of bees in a ligustrum bush. "But he *did* understand," she said. One bee had squeezed under the screen and walked onto the windowsill. "He begged us not to take him there." Her shoulders fell forward, her arms and face going loose. She thought she had forgotten how to cry.

Her father put his hand on her back. "That was Clementine's decision to make, Jess. Not yours." He looked at James Strickland. "Adam's mother thought it was best that he be sent away. I married Clementine Finney a little over a year ago. Adam had never been quite right, you know." He cleared his throat. "We loved him."

"This is what I'm saying." Strickland spoke slowly so that Jess and her father would understand. He told them that Clementine Finney had made accusations, and that Jess could be charged with negligence or manslaughter. He said something about the possibility of prison.

The room grew quiet and Jess became aware of her own breathing. Her father kept looking at his lap. "The fact that you ran away, Jess," Strickland said. "It makes you look guilty. So what can you tell me about that?"

If she closed her eyes, Jess could see the way Adam had been found, the way the stranger had described it: the sloped riverbank, torn pants and muddy green shirt, deep cuts on his face, his whole body bloated like a sack of grain and dark round sockets for eyes.

"They found Adam's jacket by the river," Strickland said. "And your sweater too. You had been with him. You were the last one to see him alive. Is that right?"

"Let me think a minute," she said, or *thought* she had said. Her hands in her lap looked dead, gloved; and Jess turned again toward the bees. Another one had crawled under the screen. The swarm continued to sweep in and out of the ligustrum blooms. She couldn't stop looking at them. Even without closing her eyes, Jess could see Adam's jacket folded where he laid it on the grass. He had said, "You'll save this for me?"

She didn't know what to say to Mr. Strickland. Beyond the window a distant thunder threatened rain. She could smell it in the air. She wanted to speak, to say everything. She wanted her voice to break calm and measured with the truth. Church bells chimed the hour and Jess looked directly at Strickland. She could feel the heat of her father's presence beside her. "Listen," she said, then let her eyes settle again on the windowsill. It was dirty and had streaks of rust. Bees thumped against the screen, and their humming sound tore at her mind like a tiny saw.

"Listen." Both men turned toward the window. They thought she meant for them to listen to the bees. "Nothing about this is right."

MISSING PERSONS

— 1 —

On the day Jess ran away from home, she stole forty dollars from her stepmother's purse. She had never stolen anything before that day, and it felt odd to be doing so now. When she came home from the river, her pants had been soaking wet and she squeezed out the water before opening the back door. She hoped no one would be in the house. In the dining room she stopped, listened. No cars in the driveway, though she saw one parked across the street. She felt hurried, but stopped at the refrigerator to pour a glass of milk, then ate a piece of raisin toast left over from breakfast. She was not hungry and the toast stuck in her throat.

She went upstairs, lifting her father's satchel from the hall table, and slipped on some dry pants, all the time stuffing the satchel with clothes, photos, a spoon, and a thermos of water. She knew she would leave, but did not know where to go. She tucked a pack of letters from Sam into a side pocket, and one picture he had sent with a soldier standing beside him— somewhere in the Korean landscape. The other soldier had his arm around a huge gun.

She passed Adam's room and looked in, as though she might find him there, then pulled a large raincoat from his closet. His bedside lamp, shaped like a baseball, was still on. The fact of the lamp brought tears to her eyes. Everything that had happened at the riverbank hovered over her like some-one else's memory. She wanted to make the world go back to what it had been—before today. She was only seventeen and, already, it was too late.

The thought of leaving home left her heart in rags; and her mind strug-gled with the decision to leave. Her father would be home soon. What could she tell him? As she left the house, she snatched a loaf of bread and three pears from the kitchen table. She didn't know when she would be back, but she knew that darkness would close down in a few hours, and Jess hoped to put open miles between herself and Goshen, North Carolina.

At breakfast her father had reminded everyone that they would go to the picture show that night. She and her father, and Adam and her stepmother would sit in a row and eat popcorn. The show was one that Adam had chosen, and started at seven-thirty. It was four-thirty now. She lifted her father's satchel, put on her coat, and closed the door tight behind her.

She walked across the yard past their dog, Hap, who tried to come with her, and into the nearby woods. She looked toward their neighbor's yard, to see if Mr. MacDougal was outside, or if Emily was playing in the sandbox. Nobody. She felt strangely lucky. Across the street a car was parked, a man sitting in it. She thought he might be asleep. She lifted the satchel onto her shoulder and rushed into the woods. The air was chilly and she clutched the coat around her neck, then pulled the hood to cover her head. That one simple gesture, pulling up the hood, felt final; and when she heard a truck turn onto her street, she didn't look. She went toward the French Broad River that ran through town, heading toward Asheville. It was the end of April. The year was 1953.

After several hours of walking, Jess ate two slices of bread and a pear. She knew it must be almost nine o'clock. A gray spectral light was turning into such a sweeping dark that she could barely see her hand in front of her face. Her head felt swollen. By now, her father would have called the police. He and Clementine would be frantic. Angry. Maybe they would find her even before she woke.

Finally, she settled against a big tree and covered herself with Adam's raincoat. The woods, without starlight, seemed to have no end. Every sound on the ground was magnified by the dark, and Jess rocked back and forth to make the night less palpable. She pulled the raincoat tight around her and remembered when her father had bought it for Adam. The coat was long and Adam had liked the way it billowed behind him when he ran. He wore it everywhere—on some nights he even wore it to bed. She closed her eyes and hummed, until she entered a world where darkness knew its place.

The next morning Jess woke beside a stream. For a moment she couldn't remember where she was. She sat up. Sunlight straddled her body as the first rays shone through the trees. Her back felt sore from sleeping on the hard ground. She had awakened several times during the night, thinking that she heard footsteps and smelling the acidic odor of rotted leaves. Each time she woke she imagined going back home.

Across the stream a family of raccoons sipped water and scurried off. Water dripped from their mouths, and the largest one hissed fiercely. Jess walked to a shoal where she could bathe, but kept her eye on the family of raccoons. If they smelled her food they would steal it.

Her mind felt fractured. She could not stop remembering the sense of ease she felt at home—sitting at the kitchen table in the morning, making her bed, blinking against the dim light as she studied in her room. She was hungry and ate a whole pear and three more slices of bread, then moved slowly to the stream and sipped water. Already, she felt removed from her life.

The yellow porch light was not on when Edward got home that night. He wondered if it had burned out, but the fact that it was not on unaccountably disturbed him. He called out, to announce that he had come home early. Jess would be packed to go back to school and Adam ready for his new home at the Cadwell Institution—though he had begged every night not to be sent away. Edward wondered how Clementine would explain the trip to him.

The house was still. A half-glass of milk was on the kitchen counter. Edward called out again and the silence that came back sent a shiver down his spine. He heard Clementine's car pull into the driveway and looked out to see if Adam and Jess were with her, but she got out alone. She saw him at the window and waved.

"Where are Jess and Adam?" he yelled.

"I don't know. They're not home? I told them we were going out tonight. What time is it?"

"Just five-thirty."

"Well." She shrugged. "They probably went to the drugstore for ice cream."

Upstairs, Adam's door was closed. They looked in to see his bed unmade and his closet door open. Jess's bedroom door lay open wide and, though her bed was made, she had strewn clothes around the room. Her bags were only partially packed.

Edward washed his hands in her bathroom, but didn't know why, then went back downstairs. "Something's wrong," he said. "I feel like something's wrong."

"You worry too much. Adam won't miss that cowboy movie tonight."

"But he knows we're taking him away tomorrow."

"Don't say that. 'Taking him away.' It sounds heartless."

"No. I don't mean that. I just mean . . . he cries every night."

"I know. I know. Don't." Clementine took a deep breath. Her legs grew wobbly. "We have to do this. It's for the best." She had repeated that phrase many times over the past week.

"I wonder if he's run away." Edward kept looking around as if he might see Adam at any moment.

"Where would he go?" Clementine grew very quiet. "You mean you wonder if *Jess* took him away?"

"They should be here, it's almost dark."

Clementine called out the back door, then went to the front yard, still calling. Hap was barking.

"We could call the police," Edward said. "That dog knows something."

"Don't be silly," Clementine said, but her face looked worried and she took Edward's hand. They stood in the yard listening for anything. Next door, Mr. MacDougal came out onto his porch.

"Are Jess and Adam over there?" Edward called.

"No. They haven't been here today," then added, "I saw them going toward the river earlier."

Edward and Clementine waited, separate as statues. The street and other houses bustled with suppertime, with people coming home, and kids in the yard. Their own house stood vacant and they could feel the emptiness of it behind them.

"We'll laugh about this later," Edward said in a matter-of-fact tone.

"They'll be here soon," Clementine's voice sounded like a thin line to nowhere. "Where are they?"

For days Jess kept close to the river, slogging through helms of marsh-weed. She hated marsh-weed. She hated sleeping on hard ground, and being afraid. She avoided the main roads, where she sometimes heard sirens racing toward an unidentified destination. Whenever she heard them, she cowered and slid out of sight. Yesterday she fell over a log, cut her leg and didn't notice the cut for hours. She never even felt it. Her body felt separate from her life.

After a week she couldn't remember the taste of good water, only the slaking that came when she drank water from a stream. River-water made her sick. She hoped to get a ride. She was aware of the highway close-by, and knew she was moving in the direction of Asheville, going south.

After ten days, Jess ate without discretion. One day she ate about a cup of grass. She did not know hunger could feel like this—a flat gnawing in her gut and the back of her throat. She knew that in these woods even small mistakes became large: the smell of food attracted animals, a tear in her jacket left her unprotected from the cold and rain—everything mattered. She began to carry a large stick and stay alert to the sudden appearance of coyotes or barking dogs.

Soon her clothes began to hang on her body, like big pajamas, and she wrapped her waist with a rope to hold up her pants. She had left the French Broad River, going on back roads until she could walk no more. She had asked directions a few times and knew she was covering many miles. She used daylight hours, since she was afraid to walk at night and, for two days, she walked through a cold rain. She was young, but if she kept up this pace, she'd be old in a year.

She sneaked through orchards and swampy marshes, drinking from a spigot behind a farmhouse. Her hair, usually lustrous and dark, grew knotted and grainy. She tried to interpret signs around her: the long look of a deer, the shape of a tree in the distance, scribbling on a stone. She wanted to read the signs. She wanted instructions. And though she was surprised at her superstition, what surprised her even more was the discovery of her own fortitude. Her main work lay in the effort to stay alert and hidden, dry.

She stole shirts and jeans from a backyard clothesline, and ate from a sack of raw potatoes left on someone's porch. After stealing forty dollars from her stepmother, these lesser crimes seemed as incidental as necessary. The order of her life was completely random. At night she found shelter in an abandoned car or an empty store, or slept under a tree with low branches.

Last night Jess had awakened in the middle of a dream, or rather she was still asleep, but *dreamed* she was awake. She saw her mother, still alive, opening the bedroom door. She heard her say, "Breakfast is ready, Sweetie." She saw her father, younger and smiling. Clementine Finney was not there, though Adam was sitting on the front porch. When she woke, the dream seemed perfectly reasonable. Jess heaved a sigh and shivered.

The next morning, waking completely, Jess wanted to bring back the happy dream. Make it true. She bargained with the day: *If I can find some food or a safe place to stay, I'll go back home.* She wasn't sure it was a bargain she could keep. Already she was a thief, a scavenger, a missing person sleeping under trees. She ate the third pear, two more pieces of bread, and a raw potato. Her life had boiled down to food, shelter, and trying not to be found.

She startled, when she saw a gray fox sniffing her shoe. She remained very still, not wanting him to go away—the small, young fox with its bushy tail, his eyes like tiny fires, steely in the early light. He stood for only a moment, then turned and was gone. Had she imagined it?

At home, sometimes, Jess might hear a door slam, or a flop-flop sound, like a fish inside the wall, and she imagined her mother's voice in another world trying to speak to her. Or sometimes she heard a movement down the hall, or saw a piece of light, something going around a corner, and expected to see her mother again.

But the fox was gone, and so was her mother's voice. All that was real was here. Jess put her face into her hands. Her palms smelled like burned ground.

She thought of her mother, what she would say to her. Before the illness, their life had been easy and sure. If her mother were still alive, none of this would have happened. If her mother had lived, Jess would have a different life now.

That's when it all started—her new and unimaginable life: with her mother's sickness, the smell of medicine in the house, those days of feeding her with a pewter spoon, then the funeral, the empty house, her father's quiet grief—and later, the entrance of Clementine Finney and her teenage son, Adam.

— 2 —

Jess was only ten when her mother's illness began with a persistent cough. At night, when the coughing would not stop, Jess heard her go into the guest room, not wanting to keep Edward awake. Some nights her mother didn't even bother to go to his bed, and the guest room quickly acquired her accoutrements: hair brush, powder, lipstick, DuBarry Cold Cream, and the Este Lauder smell of her mother's skin. Edward believed she had bronchitis and urged her to rest.

As Daisy began to lose her appetite, fatigue formed around her eyes and mouth and Dr. Willingham came to the house to listen to her lungs. He prescribed penicillin and urged her to stay in bed; but she stubbornly persisted. She was trying hard to get well, pretending that she was already well—rising to prepare dinner for Jess and Edward. During those days everything Daisy Booker did felt like pretending.

In the late afternoons Jess sat in the kitchen with her mother, copying recipes. She loved to look at her mother's high forehead, her small mouth, and round blue eyes that put people at ease, her long arms and legs that moved like a dancer. Daisy had a delicate beauty that stunned anyone who saw her. Even without makeup her face glowed, and she walked with the confidence of someone who had been beautiful for most of her life. Jess hoped some of that beauty might rub off on her.

The recipes were kept in a brown box spattered with grease and food stains. "Edward likes a lot of pepper on his chicken, but not on his steak." She told Jess to write that down. "Having meals together makes things seem normal," her mother told her. She lifted a large ham and brushed it with a paste of orange juice, mustard, and brown sugar. She handed Jess the brush to baste the ham before placing it in the oven.

After several weeks, when the cough did not improve, Daisy went to the hospital for tests. The diagnosis came late on a Tuesday afternoon. Dr. Willingham arrived at the house to deliver the news in person.

"You have cancer," he said. "It's leukemia. But, Daisy, it's progressed too far. Stage four." Jess sat on the arm of her mother's chair, and as the doctor spoke, her mother did not look up. "Leukemia is a disease of the blood and bone marrow and, though sometimes we recommend treatment, this has moved beyond our ability to control it. I am so sorry." The doctor looked embarrassed.

"What do you mean?" Edward said.

"It's just that we can't do anything for this kind of cancer. Maybe someday. I wish I could give you more hope."

Edward dragged his gaze from the back door to the doctor's face, as though he might not have been listening. "I don't understand."

"Edward," Daisy said.

"I want to know what he means."

"I can't give you much hope." Dr. Willingham touched Edward's shoulder. "She probably has six to eight months." He paused. "That's just an educated guess though. It could be longer."

Edward stood up. "Are you saying we can't do *any*thing?" He didn't believe the doctor. "It was bronchitis. That's all."

"Edward," said Daisy, some irritation in her voice.

Edward could not stop. "I know you're not telling us to just give up. Are you?"

Dr. Willingham looked tired. "I'm afraid that the disease has spread too far. I'm sorry."

Daisy nodded and kept nodding. "I don't want be in the hospital," she said. She turned and leaned her forehead against Jess's arm; and Jess's life, at age ten, began to crumble and shift. Edward sat on the floor and put his hand on Daisy's knee. Dr. Willingham rose to leave, but suggested that Edward hire a nurse to help them at home.

For the next months the nurse, Joan Landry, came to the house. She cooked and cleaned and tended to Daisy. On many days Edward found excuses to stay at home, but when people in town began to call, the constant sound of the telephone drove him back to work.

One day a childhood friend of Daisy's, William Brennan, called. Daisy had let him know about her illness and Jess heard her mother say, "No, don't come, Will. It would be better if you didn't." That night, Daisy told Jess to call Mr. Brennan *when the time came*. Jess never told her father that Mr. Brennan had called.

Before leukemia was diagnosed, when Daisy's coughing was just a nuisance, Jess and her mother had taken a trip together to visit William Brennan, who lived in a boardinghouse in Lula, Alabama. They had visited him when Jess was four, then when she was seven, and again when she was nine. Edward usually objected to their going. He felt suspicious of Brennan and accused the man of being in love with Daisy.

"He's like a brother to me," Daisy said. She said it every time. "He taught me how to drive a car and made sure I dated the right boys." She laughed. Her face turned bright whenever she talked about William Brennan. "Everybody in school knew he was my protector, not my sweetheart."

"Doesn't mean he didn't *want* to be," said Edward, but Jess and her mother took those trips anyway. They invited Edward, but he refused to go.

On their last trip Jess and her mother rode in their new Buick sedan with the radio playing. They sang songs and ate olives from a jar, keeping the windows rolled down, and following the yellow line from morning to night. They spent one night in a motor hotel. They had an Orange Crush for breakfast. When Jess thought of it later, that day seemed more dream than reality.

The first time Jess saw Tut's Boardinghouse—a tall, shaggy, nineteenth-century structure with turrets on four corners—she thought it looked haunted; but, inside, rooms bloomed bright with sunshine and cheerful curtains. Miss Tutwiler, the owner of the house, greeted them with an attitude of both welcome and suspicion. Jess believed that she, too, was doubtful about the relationship her mother shared with Mr. Brennan. Jess wondered if her father had been right.

Jess and her mother usually stayed for two nights and three days in an upstairs room. A Latin teacher lived in the room next to them and they shared a bathroom with a lady who always checked to make sure they did not leave makeup on the sink or a towel on the floor. At the end of the hall a mother and father lived with two little boys. The parents were always arguing about something.

Jess could see her mother's fondness for William Brennan, and Jess felt fond of him too, like a favorite uncle. He got up early to make breakfast for them, calling from the bottom of the stairs: "Waffles!" or "Bacon and eggs!" and they came down in their bathrobes. At night Jess heard Will and her mother talking late into the night. She heard them laughing.

On the way home she asked her mother if she had ever had a date with Mr. Brennan. "Not like that," her mother said. "But he was always around." She smiled.

Six weeks after their trip to the boardinghouse, after the coughing took a firm hold and Dr. Willingham made his bleak pronouncement, after Daisy took to the bed and Joan Landry came to the house every day, Daisy began to look thin and weak, slipping away in both body and mind. Jess fed her rice with butter every day, or sometimes applesauce with cinnamon, from her mother's favorite spoon.

Edward, though, came unraveled. He sat in Daisy's sick-room murmuring her name over and over, as if that ritual might bring her back. He yelled at the nurse about the fact that Daisy wasn't eating enough. He wanted Daisy to sit up and not lie down all day. "She'll get bedsores," he said. He propped her up with pillows until she told him to stop. He blamed Joan for everything, but this nurse was seasoned and expected to be blamed. She told Jess that her father's grief process was beginning.

Then Daisy began to see visions, or hear voices that weren't there. There were whole days when her eyes grew round, void of all recognition. She called out for people whose names Jess, or even Edward, had never heard.

"Medications dull her mind as well as her pain." Joan sometimes stayed all night. She moved through the house like a competent, invisible person, disappearing when Edward and Jess needed to be alone with Daisy. She had seen all of this before.

On that last night, Joan slept downstairs on the couch. Jess offered to feed her mother. "Please Jess," Daisy said, "I'm not hungry tonight. Just let me sleep." So Jess laid her head on her mother's small, flat breasts and let her sleep. The next morning she was dead. Edward found the bowl of rice beside the bed, saw the applesauce uneaten, and he cried. Jess thought she had done something terribly wrong, but no one ever blamed her for anything.

For weeks after the funeral a smell of stale and soured flesh lingered in her mother's sick-room, thick as smoke. Nothing could air out the odor. Edward tried to infuse the house with normal talk; but at night he walked through rooms like someone in a dull stupor. He stared at the dark blue fabric that was the sick-room's bedspread and whenever Jess passed the room she saw him sitting in the dark. If she entered, a voice came out of the chair: "Don't turn on the light."

Jess did not know how they would survive their sad new world. She felt more alone when her father was talking than when he was quiet. Windows everywhere were closing, and she felt like the doorknobs on all the doors in the world were gone. That's when Jess learned to live in the lonesome corner of her soul, that's when she began to seek the companionship of the French Broad River that ran along the edge of Goshen, North Carolina.

Jess was born in that river. Daisy Booker had believed that river-birth insured a prosperous life and, with the help of a midwife, had squatted in the river-shallows to give birth. Her own mother had done the same, as had her grandmother and great-grandmother. Edward objected with bitter arguments about this kind of birthing; and, in fact, when Jess was born he hired an ambulance with a doctor and nurse to stand-by in case anything went wrong. Nothing went wrong, and Jess moved easily into the French Broad River. Even now, she claimed a clear memory of that birth: one long tunnel moving into open water and bleary-eyed fish who saw her first, and muddy broth to breathe. At birth, that river was her first mother, and, at ten, her only one.

So Jess visited the river every day and, with the absence of Joan Landry, began to take over her mother's chores. She made the beds, washed clothes, cooked dinner, and went to the grocery store with her father. Edward went down the cereal-oatmeal-grits-tapioca aisle and Jess chose the vegetables, fruits, and milk. She liked to imagine her mother's long arm reaching for a peach or a quart of milk from a top shelf.

— 3 —

For the first two weeks, Jess stayed close to the French Broad River. She stumbled, skinned her arm, and thought of her friends in Goshen, coming home from school, putting on pajamas. Her head was spinning and she felt nauseated. But the thought of the river, and what happened there, drove her each day until she dropped—tired enough to sleep anywhere. She did sleep, leaning her back against a tree; but, all night, she woke to strange crackling noises and whooshings above her. She tried to determine what to do next. She had begun to mark each day with a small pebble she carried in her pocket, the growing weight a reminder of time and distance traveled. She had been gone sixteen days, and all she could think about was what she would say if someone found her.

The next morning, she ate the last piece of bread, but wished for another pear. Most of the food stored in her satchel was gone, and she tried to eat as little as possible. At times, she couldn't remember why she wasn't at home; at other times, she heard sirens and her body grew rigid. That far-off screaming was more like a feeling inside than a sound outside. She walked all day, trudging through brush, the sun rising high in the sky—her clothes stuck to her body, her shoes filled with mud. She would need to scrounge for more food.

She took out one of Sam's letters, and his picture. She never liked to think of Sam fighting in Korea, but, instead, pictured him in his fireman's uniform—the way she first saw him. Each night, before sleep, she looked at his face and chose a letter to read. The letters stayed in the satchel's side pocket, but a few had gotten wet and muddy. She picked one written January, 1953, when he had been over there only a few weeks.

Sweetheart,

Got two letters from you today. I keep them in my pocket and read them over and over. It makes me feel good to read them. What do you think of this war? I don't know what to think. We had a three-hour mortar barrage yesterday. Two hit our bunker, but didn't penetrate. Our crew was okay. I hate those big mortars. You can't hear shells coming until seconds before they hit. You get so jumpy that any kind of noise makes you go flat on the ground. I have never been so cold.

On the day we landed at Inchon, we got on trains. When the trains stopped, we saw all these poor people with pots. They hang around the stations begging for food from the GI's. We gave them all our C-rations. We couldn't help it. They looked so hungry. That night I volunteered for patrol just to keep warm, moving around. There is so much noise, or else it's too quiet. And so damn cold.

Nobody sleeps much at night. Some things I can't write about, but I want to tell you everything. I can tell you this: we spend a lot of time just waiting, then things happen all at once. When I'm waiting, my knees shake until I think I can't stand up—then I do. Right now is pretty quiet or else I could not be writing and thinking about you. I'll try to sleep and maybe dream too. I look at your picture—your long black hair and your eyes, big like plums.

Love,

Sam

Night was closing down and Jess couldn't read more in the dark. The air grew thick around her and she could smell her own sour breath. She slept holding Sam's letters. The next morning she walked to a shoal where she could wash herself. Out here, time flowed more easily: minutes, no longer connected to clocks, kept pace with the sun and stars in a normal rhythm of sunrise and moonrise. But Jess did not feel normal.

She pulled off her shirt and splashed water onto her face and neck. Her body stank of sweat and rotted leaves. She needed a destination and thought of Tut's Boardinghouse in Lula, Alabama. She knew the general direction, and maybe could catch a ride for part of the way. Those early visits made Jess think that Mr. Brennan would welcome her. She washed her feet, rubbing cracked mud from her toes. She dried her hair in the sun, then followed the stream to a clearing, where she saw a shopping center with a Woolworth's, two grocery stores, and a bakery shop.

Jess walked the aisles of Woolworth's, putting matches, a pair of scissors (wanting to cut her hair), a can opener, toilet paper, socks, and a bar of Ivory soap into her basket; but she stole a toothbrush and two tubes of toothpaste, and she slipped a package of new underwear, aspirin, and a wash rag into her satchel. She had to make her forty dollars last. She decided that every time she bought something in a store she would try to steal a few things as well.

At the checkout counter she waited in line. A man, standing with his son, motioned for her to go ahead of him. But she wondered if this man had seen her steal the items hidden in her satchel. He might turn her in. She looked around to see if anyone else was noticing her. The lady at the cash register counted up the items, and put them into a Woolworth's bag.

When a bell went off above the cash register, Jess screamed.

"You're the 100th customer this week," the cash register lady said. Her voice carried through the store. "You win a carton of Dr. Peppers, a jar of Peter Pan Peanut Butter, and a loaf of Holsum Bread. Congratulations!"

The man with the boy complained good-naturedly. "If I hadn't given you my place in line, we woulda got that prize ourselves. See, Tommy? We just gave it away." Tommy looked confused.

"Here," Jess said. "You take this carton of soda."

"No, ma'am," the man said. "You won that fair and square. It's yours."

"At least let me give a soda to your boy." Jess leaned to offer a cold bottle to Tommy.

"I won't deny him that," the man said. He looked at the boy. "We thank you, young lady."

This conversation was more interaction than Jess had had in over a week. She left the store feeling elated and somehow connected again to the outside world. As the man and his boy drove away in their truck, the boy waved goodbye. He was drinking the Dr. Pepper.

Later that evening, feeling empowered by human conversation, Jess stole three cans of food from a grocery store: Vienna sausages, pork and beans, and a can of soup. She still had thirty-three dollars left in her satchel. At the moment thirty-three dollars seemed like a lot of money, though it was disappearing fast. Jess Booker was a thief now. She felt an icicle growing inside her chest, that same kind of chill she had when her mother died, and again when her father married Clementine Finney.

The third week of May was beginning, so Jess collected pebbles to count the weeks now instead of the days. She had left the place of grocery stores, and hoped to find a stream before nightfall. Nights were getting warmer, and she liked sleeping to the lullaby of water. Three nights ago she had slept in a gully and dreamed she was being cradled.

But tonight, she lay back on the ground trying to hear the sound of stars jostling above the trees. She recognized patterns: the Bear, Orion's Belt, those sisters, and one constellation that her father (when she was five) had named Jess's Good Hat, and another one he called Mama's New Shoes. Jess slept that night, closing her eyes to familiar stars.

— 4 —

The year Jess turned twelve Edward took her to Niagara Falls—mainly because her mother had always wanted to see it. The next year they went to New York City and saw a play. *Harvey* had a character who believed he was followed around by a tall, invisible rabbit. Jess hoped they might take a trip every summer; but when she turned sixteen, her father began to pursue Clementine Finney, and their trips together stopped. Instead, he began to bring Clementine and her son, Adam, home for dinner.

Jess felt startled the first time she saw Adam come in the door. He was nearly six feet tall and had unruly hair. Clementine said that he had never been enrolled in school, except for one semester in the first grade—after which he was asked not to return.

Jess had seen Adam before at Greenwood's Grocery Store bagging groceries. She thought he acted goofy. She did not like having him in her house, and could not fathom what her father was doing with Clementine Finney. She was strong, sturdy, maybe even handsome, but not pretty like her mother. The woman's best feature was her thick red hair that cascaded down her back, or lay in a large braid on top of her head. For years she had worked as a seamstress in town. Even Daisy had ordered a few dresses and skirts from her over the years.

During those early months that Edward spent courting Clementine, Jess began to have a recurring dream of a pendulum swinging from a high place with a man standing below telling her to jump onto the blade and swing up high. So Jess swung high in the dream, but when she looked again at the man standing below he was staring down at his feet, as if he did not want to be held accountable for what happened next.

When Jess woke, the window was open to bird calls and she felt a soft breeze on her face. She sat on the edge of her bed and wondered if her father had thought about the consequence of bringing Clementine and Adam into their family. Each time she had the dream, she could not escape the feeling that she was gliding along the pendulum's long blade.

Edward had met Clementine on a September day when the church service went too long because Adam had to be baptized. Adam loved baptisms, with water dripping onto his head and face and shirt front. He preferred sprinkling to immersion, and had been baptized in so many churches that one minister had refused multiple baptisms, claiming that the repetition was becoming a joke.

On the day of his third baptism in Goshen's Methodist Church, Clementine stood on the lawn after the service. She and Adam were surrounded by members of the congregation. As Jess approached them, she heard Clementine talking about baseball. Apparently, she was an avid fan. She knew who played shortstop for the Cardinals, who had pitched a no-hitter, and what year. She even quoted batting averages. Edward lingered, listening to Clementine long after the others had left. Clementine laughed at everything Edward said, and Jess looked at her father in a shrewd, critical way, as if to say, *Don't be stupid!*

That day Edward asked Clementine to go with him to a game between the Chattanooga Lookouts and the Atlanta Crackers. They left the next weekend for Chattanooga and Adam went with them. Clementine wore a yellow dress that swished around her legs. She had large breasts and hips, but a small waist. She wore her hair loose that day. Her arms and face were nicely freckled. Edward Booker teased her about her freckles, but she didn't mind. Jess declined to go with them, choosing, instead, to stay overnight with a friend.

The next Monday evening, after supper, Clementine arrived at their house with Adam. She and her father lived on the corner lot of a tree-lined street, named Dogwood Avenue, with a wide lawn and gardeners who kept it cut and trimmed. The French Broad River flowed behind the house and a large oak in front had a swing from one of the high branches.

Clementine arrived with lemon cake and a cherry pie. They all sat together in the kitchen and ate dessert. Adam picked at his pie, too shy to eat. Jess wanted to leave the table. She ate slow bites and, without comment, carried her plate to the kitchen sink. She saw the way her father looked at Clementine, and suspected that he had already kissed her.

Adam left the table too, and was told he could go out to the tree swing, where he sat twisting and pushing with his legs until he went high. Jess watched him from her window. The whole yard looked lonely with him in it, and she felt a dull tugging at the back of her head. She imagined that if she counted backwards from a hundred, she might possibly wake to a better world.

Her mother's bathrobe hung on the back of her closet door and she put her face into it. At times, she could still smell her mother in the folds of the material and, for a moment, bring back her presence. But not today. And, in the quiet of where Jess lived, she knew her mother was slipping away, and that the scent of her skin would soon be forgotten.

Clementine and Edward came out to stand beside the oak and talk to Adam. Edward had his arm around Clementine's waist and she leaned into him. Adam was laughing hard.

Yesterday, Jess had told Clementine, "My daddy won't ever get over loving my mother, you know." She watched for a reaction.

Clementine had answered, "You're probably right."

That's when Jess felt that the lines between the two families were becoming inextricably tangled, and she wished for a map to guide her, or a hand to pull her back from the edge of something. She had already lost her father once, when her mother died, though they had grown close again through grief. Now she would lose him again—not to death, but to marriage and a slow brother she didn't want.

— 5 —

At first, Clementine had not been physically attracted to Edward. He was not an overweight man, but he looked thick, with the beginnings of a paunch. He was partially bald, and his head, already round, looked rounder without hair in front. He dressed each day in a sport coat and a freshly ironed shirt. His feet were large for his small frame so his shoes looked almost comic; but she admired his eyes, which were deep blue and shiny with kindness, and she liked the way he teased her, taking teasing in return.

Besides, Clementine missed sex and welcomed the thought of intimacy returning to her life. Edward was quick to hold her hand, or reach an arm around her waist. He kissed her tenderly and made her heart jump with expectation. And she loved the sound of his voice. She could listen to him talk for hours. And when Clementine saw the way Edward looked at her, she realized how a new life might be possible. She believed she could make Edward happy, and knew he could ease her financial burden, which would only grow larger as Adam got older.

After ten months Edward mentioned marriage, apologizing in case Clementine thought the suggestion premature. Clementine smiled and told Edward yes, but she had not shown the surprise or eagerness Edward hoped for, so Edward said that because of Adam and Jess he knew they could not plan a real honeymoon. He suggested they arrange a weekend away together. They could go to a nice hotel in Atlanta. Clementine agreed to hire someone to stay with Adam. Jess stayed with a friend.

In Atlanta's Francis Hotel, Edward and Clementine, alone for the first time, were amazed at their own excitement—anticipating an intimacy they already felt. They ordered dinner sent to their room, but could not finish dinner before getting into bed. The sheets were blue and silky and Clementine wore a yellow nightgown, her red hair curling around her shoulders. She slipped under the covers with Edward. She heard him moan when she took him in her hand.

"Wait," he said, his voice raspy with desire. He pulled her gown from her shoulders and down over her hips. "I want to see you." She pulled back the covers to let him see the fullness of her breasts and hips. She responded to his touch, his voice, his scent, and felt a lovely secret blooming between them. Both were hungry for each other. Their bodies turned in the sheets, and they were caught in awkward flexing and swaying of legs. Edward trembled with strands of desire until he fell back exhausted, and slept.

Clementine woke around two a.m. in a memory of what they had found together, and knew Edward was awake too. He said he felt like yelling for joy. He reached for her hand to hold it. Clementine had not said anything, but was staring at the ceiling.

"What is it? What's the matter?" he said.

Her words came calmly out of the dark. "I need to tell you something." Her voice was full of tears. "You may not want me anymore."

"What do you mean? Why would you even say that?"

Clementine sat bolt upright in bed, moving her fingers to smooth the sheet that covered her legs. Edward reached to touch her arm.

"This isn't right. You are such a good person." She couldn't go on. Edward was patting her shoulder. "I need you for the wrong reason." Clementine hid her face in her hands. Edward grew still, as if he were refusing to see what she meant. Everything around them lay heavy with mysterious meaning. He had thought she loved him. Was she saying she didn't?

"I *like* you though," she said. "I really do like you." It sounded like a final apology, but she did not pull away. She stayed near him and leaned her face into his neck. Edward sat on the edge of the bed and seemed vaguely insulted, ambushed by her tender honesty. She sat beside him. The whole room rang with aimless and momentary regret.

"Well," he said. He sounded short of breath, but moved to put his arms around her. They sat like that for a long while until, finally, he lay back and she put her head on his chest. The tension between them drained slowly away.

More than words, Clementine became aware of the rhythm of her own pulse and the weight of her head on him, and she caught a glimpse of the stream of days beyond this night. Then, before they went back to sleep, Edward told Clementine that everything would be okay. He said that he still wanted her, and she laid her head on the pillow beside his. Even in the dark she could see the frame of his face, his eyes looking at her.

He kissed her. "So," he said. "Maybe you could *learn* to love me."

At that moment she did.

After that weekend, Edward mentioned the wedding plans to Jess. She knew her father wanted to marry Clementine, but until he spoke to her directly about the plans, nothing about this new life had seemed true.

Three weeks before the wedding they sat together in the back yard looking up at only a rumor of moon. "You know things are going to change," he said. He hoped Jess might join his happiness. His laugh, when he spoke, sounded nervous.

"Yes," she said. "I know. How could I not know?"

"Well? Do you object?"

Jess had not expected him to even consider her objection, but told him that she felt wary of Clementine and suggested that she might be marrying him for his money.

"I don't agree," he said sternly. Jess suspected that he had already considered that possibility, but knew he was lonely and that the need for companionship would prove stronger than anything else. "I believe she'll be good. For *both* of us." He sounded apologetic now, even pitiful. "We need a woman in the house, Jess."

"But why do they have to *live* with us?" she said. "I liked things the way they were."

"That's what married people do," he said. "Live together." Edward was pleading.

She knew she wouldn't change her father's mind, but she asked anyway. "And what is wrong with *him*?" she said. "He's so retarded."

"I know. I know. But we can give him a real home. Help keep him out of trouble."

"Trouble?"

"Sometimes kids are mean to him. You've seen it."

Jess had seen her friends make fun of Adam. She was glad her father didn't know how often she joined them. "Uh-huh," she said.

They sat awhile without speaking. Her father placed a hand on her knee and Jess felt a trace of old comfort. The moon, shaped like a boat, shone through the trees. The yard looked milky with haze and they heard piano music from a neighbor's radio. This new life had no instruction book.

— 6 —

To her surprise, Jess had grown proficient in the art of stealing. She could smile and gain the trust of salespeople, engage in conversation, and ask questions about the merchandise—some things she bought, some she just stuck in her satchel. She grew proud of her talent, but not happy with her pride.

Today she had walked along the cinders next to a railroad track. She could see wide fields spreading out below, and birds meddling in the corn. She imagined catching a train, riding maybe to Mexico, or California. She sat down to rest and lifted a letter from Sam out of the satchel. She wanted to think about him.

Feb. 1953

Dear Jess,

I got the fudge you sent. It was gone so fast, but I shared some with the guys. C-Rations are our only food supply here. The cartons all have 1947 stamped on them and the Chesterfield and Camel cigarettes are so dry that, when you light them, they flame up just an inch before the fire goes out. Chocolate crumbles when you touch it.

It's been raining for twelve hours straight. We were flooded and our water supply was screwed up for a couple of days. We move out tomorrow. There are so many times when I'm in the field and I really need to talk to you—like tonight after everything is set up and in position, I don't have anything to do but lie here and think. Last night I pulled guard with a guy named Billy Keifert. Sarge told us that somebody in our unit had seen some Chinks hiding down in the valley. Saw them coming up the gully close to where we were. We had a telephone, a 30-caliber machine gun, and hand grenades. Then Sarge ordered us to spray the area with machine-gun fire. Billy started firing. He panicked and didn't let up on the trigger until all his ammo was used up. I was shaking so bad, I couldn't load the next belt. We switched positions and Billy loaded and I fired. We shot so much that the barrel got hot and bent. Tracers fell right on the ground in front of us. The next day, when patrol went out, they didn't find anything. We cleaned the machine gun and had to put on a new barrel. All this to say I'm still okay, but my head feels full of firecrackers.

We move again tomorrow, this time to a reserve near Inji. Word is out that we're getting inspected by Colonels and Generals. We'll be there for about a week, then we're going back to the front. I can't tell you where that is. I got a pair of leather combat boots when I came. Now the soles are loose from all this rain and my feet get wet. It's been raining every day—won't ever stop, seems like.

This inspection will give us time to shave, take a bath, and brush our teeth. We'll have real showers in big tents with boards on the floor. I haven't washed my face and hands or changed clothes in 13 days! You couldn't stand to be near me right now. I wouldn't even let you kiss me. Well, maybe I would.

Jess smiled. She imagined more letters from Sam being sent to her home, and knew her father would keep them for her. She imagined her father sitting in his chair, waiting for news about her. Clementine would not be able to comfort him.

Jess had already finished the peanut butter won for being Woolworth's hundredth customer. She reached for a can of Vienna sausages and a few crackers, and noticed how hunger had heightened her ability to see and hear, like a predator—or prey. As the sun went down, she sat on a wide log, and ate, then took three photographs out of her pocket. The first one—of herself, age nine, with her mother and dad—was taken at the farm where she boarded her horse, Buckhead. On the day the picture was taken, she had won a blue ribbon. Her father held it up high and could not stop looking at her. Her mother had placed one hand on Jess's shoulder. Jess could still feel the weight of that hand.

Another photo showed her mother and father when they were young, in a way that Jess had never seen them in real life. Her mother wore a small feathery hat and a silky dress. Her father wore a World War II uniform, and though he never spoke much about his days as a soldier, he did speak endlessly of famous generals from the war. The third photo showed Adam, fourteen years old. He stood by himself, without his mother standing near, though she must have been snapping the picture. He had dark hair, curly around his ears and forehead, and round blue eyes. His lips lay slightly open.

She studied each photo before tucking them into her back pocket, where they grew bent and cracked; then she leaned back, trying to remember Adam's voice in her head. She heard, instead, a noise in the woods—the breaking of sticks and brush around her. She startled up.

Someone was coming. Coming fast. The dulled sound of footsteps on leaves. She hoped it might be an animal; but in only a moment two men stood in the open space before her. It was almost dark, but she could see their size as well as their faces. They looked surprised to see her there. One man reached and grabbed Jess's hand, pulling her up from the log. He was young, not much older than she. The other man was older, maybe the boy's father.

"Put your hand over her mouth," the older one said. He was short, his nose bulbous, legs thick as tree trunks.

"She's not even screaming," said the boy, who was mildly pleasant to look at.

"You got any money?" the older man asked.

Jess shook her head, her hands trembling. She wondered if she should break away and run. She was afraid they could catch her.

The young man stood close enough for her to smell the odor of his cigarettes and sweat. He was a little taller than the old man, and his shirt, too small, reached above his pants buckle. The cuffs of his pants were rolled once and muddy, his shoes caked with thick dirt clods.

"Maybe we should take her with us," the boy said. He grabbed Jess's arm.

"We can't fool with her. We got to get going." The man had a gun in his hand, and he kept looking around. Someone must have been chasing them. "We got to go, Hull."

Jess abruptly disengaged her arm from the boy. She pulled the pair of Woolworth's scissors from her pocket and swung towards him with the sharp end. She cut his hand, not bad, but enough to bring blood.

"What's she got? A knife?" the older man yelled.

"Scissors," said the boy. He stepped back from her and held his arm. She still had not said a word or made a sound.

"What's the matter with her?" the boy said. "She can't even speak."

"Just as well. A retard." The older man turned to Jess. "Can you speak?"

Jess shook her head no. Her hair lay flat, knotted and full of brush. She opened her mouth to make a deep hollow sound in her throat, imitating what she had heard animals do in times of stress. She couldn't help the hacking coughs that followed.

Both men moved away from her. The older one spat deliberately. "Leave her," he said.

The boy seized Jess's wrist again. "We could . . . "

"Don't be a fool, Hull. No telling what kinda disease she's got. C'mon, or I'm gonna shoot you, too."

As they hurried off, Jess was aware of the quick flicking glance the boy gave her before he moved in step behind the older man. She was aware of her lack of strength against these men, and knew she had to move more quickly toward somewhere safe. She took a long breath.

They had thought she was like Adam—without a good mind—and they were frightened. She thought of people in Goshen who had been frightened of Adam, who crossed the street to avoid him. A mother warning her child, "Don't wave at him. Don't look at him," as they passed Adam's eager face.

Now, she had frightened these men with her silence. Adam's way had saved her. Thank you, thank you, she said to no one. She gathered up everything she owned. She could see some blood on the scissors, wiped them clean on the grass, then stuck them into her coat pocket.

Jess felt that she had opened a dark window and climbed out into a foreign world. She prepared to leave. She had to put more distance between herself, these intruders, and what she had left behind.

— 7 —

On the day Adam was born, Calder Finney passed out cigars like a carnival barker. He bragged to everybody that Adam weighed eight pounds, four ounces. He told complete strangers.

Clementine had lost her first baby (also a boy) when the umbilical cord wrapped around the neck of the fetus. The baby died only a few minutes after birth; but the birth of Adam was long and arduous until, finally, the doctor used forceps to pull him out and Adam's head, for a few days, was misshapen. Nobody mentioned brain damage at the time.

Adam was a beautiful child, with long lashes and a mop of dark hair. During those early years, Calder took him everywhere; but as Adam's lack of progression grew evident, Clementine took him back to the clinic where he was born.

A doctor suggested that Adam be tested and have some X-rays. Adam was three. They stayed several days in a motel, and both Clementine and Calder went with Adam to everything, pretending it was all a kind of game. On the third day the doctor said that they had found some brain damage. "A subdural hemorrhage—probably at birth, or maybe even before." He said that Adam would always have the mind of a child. He could never live independently. Another doctor urged Calder to make financial plans for Adam, so that he would be cared for if something happened to them. But Calder refused to admit that Adam wasn't going to be a normal boy. He continued to take him fishing and to ball games. He even coached a Little League team, and let Adam play.

For six years they struggled to teach Adam how to walk and talk, how to drink from a cup, and eat with utensils; and though Adam achieved some success, the learning curve had been steep. When Calder coached the Little League team, he worked every day that summer teaching Adam to hit the ball, catch, and throw.

"Look, he can run. Clementine, you're worrying for nothing. He'll do fine in school. You wait and see. He loves for me to read books to him."

"Calder, he doesn't understand what you're reading."

"You don't know that."

But Clementine did know. Adam's body was developing into a healthy specimen, but his mind lagged behind; and though he entered the first grade in September of his sixth year, he attended for only one term.

The first grade teacher taught the children about rivers (with turtles, catfish, and bluefish) and about oceans (with whales, sharks, starfish, and crabs). That fall Adam began to dream about the sea. He imagined he could live on the ocean floor, put on his socks and shoes, and run around underwater, chase bluefish and turtles—make them do tricks like a dog. He believed that someday the ocean would live inside him, inside his head and arms and legs. He thought he could grow into that bigness. He had dreamed it. When Clementine said, "No, it's not like that," Adam insisted that he could swallow the ocean whole, eat it like a cookie—all the fishes and conchs, all the starfish and tiny shells. He knew that rivers went to the sea. He thought his dreams were true.

When Adam came home talking about ocean life and fish that lived in rivers, Calder grew hopeful, even excited. "See? I told you. He's getting the hang of it." But the hopefulness was brief. By the middle of the semester, the teacher, as well as the principal, reiterated what the doctors had told them years earlier. Only then, did Calder accept the truth.

Christmas that year came and went, and Calder moved around the house like a ghost. Just before the New Year began, he explained to Clementine that he could no longer live in the house.

"You're leaving us?" Clementine panicked.

"I can't do this," he said. He didn't know what else to say. "I've left enough money in the bank for three months, and I'll send checks to be deposited every month. I'll take care of you both. I've found a job . . . " He stopped. Calder had worked for a company selling sports equipment to schools. He was successful and could find work easily.

"Where're you going?"

"I'll call you." He did not tell her more.

"But . . . "

He did not say if he would ever come back.

The night Calder went away, he sat on the edge of their bed and told Clementine good-bye. She wouldn't beg. He left, going towards Adam's room. She heard the door close downstairs, softly. She heard the car start, then a long pause before it pulled from the gravelly driveway onto the road.

For many years Clementine hoped for Calder's return. She loved him. She hoped he would miss them and that she might wake up one morning to find him sitting in the kitchen; but, as hope faded, she learned to accept her lonely days. She applied for a job in town, finding sitters for Adam during the day. The sitters, though, could not handle Adam's unexpected tantrums, so Clementine took in washing and sewing, and worked from home. She felt chained to her life with Adam, and on certain days thought she could not continue. She needed to do something where she could meet people in the community. She joined the church.

One day as Clementine was telling a woman from church how hard it was to raise Adam, the woman told her about a state hospital where "someone like Adam" could live. "People would care for him," she said. "It's a hospital near Raleigh. Cadwell. You should look into it." The woman felt sorry for Clementine.

Cadwell, an institution with a large campus of buildings and grounds, housed brain-damaged children, as well as schizophrenic and psychotic adults. When Clementine went there for a visit, the rooms smelled so bad she held her breath to keep from retching. Patients walked the halls as though they were lost; others stood in locked rooms, staring out of small, barred windows. Several were yelling. Everyone looked unwashed. Clementine drove away knowing she could not leave Adam in such a place, but felt the strain of long caretaking days, while the prospects of her own life dimmed.

There were no other choices and, in the dark secrets of her mind, Clementine began to imagine the freedom she would have if Adam were to die suddenly—in a car wreck or maybe he would get sick and die in a hospital. Something innocent, quick, not painful. She hated herself when she dreamed of his death, but for several years those imaginings pursued her. She never told anyone about them, and felt monstrous when she thought about her desire to be free of him.

Adam, who trusted everyone and expected people to like him, was a lonely child. He sought out friends at the park, but as soon as other children recognized his strange behavior, they avoided him. Still, nothing stopped his overtures for friendship, and Clementine began to admire his perseverance. She developed routines with him—taking him to the park, the grocery store, to church; and, by the time Adam was ten, his open-heartedness had won the favor of many townspeople. Mr. Greenwood hired him to bag groceries, and others from church stopped him on the street to ask about Adam's beloved hubcaps that he had begun to collect from garages around town.

Clementine earned the reputation of being an excellent seamstress, receiving more orders than she could fill. Her own clothes, as well as Adam's, were made of fine fabrics. With the money she earned, along with the money from Calder, she started a savings account for Adam. Their life together had taken a turn, becoming more settled, until Adam began to exhibit an interest in girls. He looked at magazine pictures of pretty women. He liked seeing pictures of girls in swim suits.

Then, out of the blue, Calder returned for Adam's twelfth birthday. Clementine woke to see a truck parked in front of the house. Calder was asleep in the front seat. She approached the truck. "Calder? You could have come in," she said, as though no time had passed, as though he had not been away for five years.

"I wasn't sure if I'd be welcome." Calder stepped out of the truck, thinner than she remembered, and his face looked angular, very much like Adam's.

"You are," she said, and hoped he had returned for good, but didn't ask. During those first two absent years, Calder had phoned Adam every Sunday night; then the calls became less frequent. Now he was here.

When Adam woke and found his father sitting at the kitchen table, he ran to hug him. "Hey!" Calder said. "You're going to be twelve in a few days." Calder buried his face in Adam's shoulder. Clementine looked away. "And I'm taking you to buy a new bicycle. You can pick it out. Whatever you want!"

Adam's face looked lit from inside. He could not stop smiling. "We can play ball," he said. "I can throw now." Clementine understood that Adam suspected his father had left because he couldn't play ball like the other boys. "I can throw good," he said.

During those weeks at the house, Calder and Clementine lived as man and wife, and the house hummed with regular family life. Calder played ball in the yard with Adam and taught him how to ride a bike. In spite of everything, Clementine believed that Calder loved Adam, that Adam was the heartbreak of his life. But a day came when she saw his restlessness return, saw how he still wanted to deny Adam's real self. She knew he wouldn't stay.

"I want you to see who he is," Clementine said. "Your son is a fine young man. He has a job at the grocery store, and he has friends. He goes to church; and people, at least some of them, are very sweet to him."

"You've done a fine job with him, Clementine. A good job, but . . . " Everything in his face said he would leave.

Four days later Calder left for the second and last time. Clementine did not believe she would welcome him back again, but for a long time she would miss him. The family was a unit of two now. Adam was hers and she would forget how the rhythm of her days had been disturbed or how she had once dreamed of a different kind of life. In a few years Clementine signed the divorce papers so that Calder could remarry, and she no longer thought about what she had wanted before Adam; she knew only that she wanted Adam to enjoy his life and to have a memory of happy times. She didn't know what patience or strength it might take to give him that memory; but she knew that everything seemed easier now, without Calder.

Adam waved to his mother on the sidewalk when he rode his bike—a royal blue Schwinn B-6 with big ballooner duck tail fenders, black wall tires, a six-hole rack, chain guard, and leather grips. He wobbled, but kept his balance. Clementine watched him ride all the way to the end of the street.

Adam

Blades of grass came up between his toes. He played a game with the other kids who called his father Coach. When the other boys hit the ball it flew in the air like a bird, then his daddy waved for Adam to pick up the bat and take a turn. His shadow had a bat too. His shadow swung its bat and the ball whizzed by him like a bee.

"Let him hit it," somebody yelled. "Let him get a hit." So the boy pitching threw the ball slow and easy and the catcher behind him said "Swing," so Adam did, but too late and missed again.

"Run anyway," someone said.

"No, he can hit it. Let him hit," Coach yelled. And with the next swing Adam tapped the ball and it bounced plop, plop a few feet in front of him, and he could see a squirrel run across the field and somebody yelled, "Run, run, Adam." Adam ran like the squirrel. He imagined he was running very fast. He didn't know why he had to run, but he knew where first base was and he ran past first base and everyone cheered. Adam smiled at the cheering and headed back to sit on the bench, but the first baseman told him to stay there and pointed to second base telling Adam, "I'll tell you when to run."

The sun was hot and Adam's father came to first base to pat him on the back and say "Good hit." The bright sun and shadows, as well as the fun of running, kept a place in Adam's memory. At the right time Adam ran to second base, but he kept on going, straight out into the back field, running while the other boys kept waving him toward third. They finally laughed, so Adam laughed too. Adam's father was not laughing as he walked Adam back to the bench. "Sit here," he said. "This'll be over in a little while." And the dark shape of his father's back got smaller and smaller as he moved further away. And it walked away more times after that day.

His father was gone one winter day and Adam caught the chicken pox. Spots popped out on his body. His Mama dotted him with pink lotion. "Don't scratch. Don't," so he scratched when she wasn't looking. His stomach and feet and toes and arms all had splotches. His face in the mirror had them too, and his ears. He laughed in the mirror. He thought his daddy would come home when the red spots were gone, but it was a long time.

When his father came back home, time had gone away. Adam was twelve and had a chicken pox scar still visible on his arm. His mother made a yellow cake with chocolate icing. His father bought him a bicycle. Now he could ride like the other boys on the sidewalk. But he wobbled and fell and kept falling until he could hold the handlebars straight and pedal very fast. Then his daddy said he had to leave again. Adam knew it was over, but didn't know why. He straddled his bike rubbing the long curved handlebars, and tried to think of ways that he could be good enough to make his father stay.

A few days later, before light, his daddy said goodbye again. Adam got up in his pajama bottoms and followed him to the door. "Don't get up," his father told him. "Go back to bed." But Adam followed him to the door. The house was still full of night. When his father opened the door, a cool air hit Adam's chest. He curled forward with the chill. "Go back to bed," his father said. The air was wrong and his father's voice sounded off-pitch, and throaty. Wrong. Then the door closed with a soft sound, and the black air inside the house smelled like pennies.

As Adam climbed into bed, the door kept closing and closing before his eyes, and the dark air seemed like a door itself, until he was asleep. He dreamed, remembering the shape of his father's back and head—walking away. Leaving always felt cold.

He woke to hear his mother crying.

— 8 —

During those first weeks Jess caught a few rides, and though they never took her far, she was aware of easy miles going by, and grateful for the relief in her legs and feet. Some old boots found in a box by the side of the road—waterproof, with no holes in the sole—were too large for her feet and rubbed blisters, so she used soft rags to pad the empty spaces. At least they kept her dry. She had seen signs for Chattanooga, and the map she found in the garbage showed that Chattanooga was close to the Georgia line. She was headed toward Lula, Alabama. She felt lucky when she crossed into Georgia.

She had seen the car again today. A muddy brown and white two-tone Chevrolet with a dent in one door and a sticker on the back bumper that said: I Like Ike, though part of the sticker had been torn off and it read instead *ike* Ike. She had seen a similar car on the day she left home. It had been parked in front of her house, but not in the driveway. People hardly ever parked on the street, so she noticed.

Then, a few days ago outside Albertson's Grocery Store, near Ringgold, Georgia, a man driving that same car had pulled up beside Jess and stopped, but she kept walking. She thought she saw the car again this morning, same man, wearing a hat with the brim pulled down over his eyes. She had been stunned to see the ike Ike sticker on the bumper. That's when Jess became more vigilant, and wished she had something better than just scissors.

At a garage repair shop near Dalton, Georgia, Jess used the restroom to wash thoroughly with soap and water. She chopped off her hair to barely shoulder length and pulled it back into a short ponytail. She decided to buy crackers or chewing gum but, as she rounded the corner of the station, she saw a state police car and two troopers talking to the owner. They stood with feet apart, looking staunch and immoveable. They blocked the door to the station.

Too late to turn around, she thought. *I need to go in, as though nothing is wrong.*

She squeezed by the men and walked toward the rack of crackers and gum. The men looked her over—with pleasure, she felt, more than suspicion. She was wearing a pair of jeans and a man's plaid shirt from somebody's clothesline. Her hair, still wet, was clean, and she smelled like soap.

"You're new around here," one trooper said, smiling.

"Just passing through," Jess told him. "I'm staying with some folks down the road." She hoped they wouldn't ask for a name. On the wall calendar, next to the phone, a girl in a red bathing suit sat on the hood of a car. She held a Coca-Cola bottle near her breast. The day was May 29, 1953.

The owner was listening to a radio broadcast, and turned it up.

The body of a young man was found in the French Broad River fifty miles from his home in Goshen, North Carolina. The cause of death was drowning. The man, identified as Adam Finney, was almost twenty years old. His body floated downriver for four days before he was found by a passer-by who said that he saw the young man's body lodged against a tree. His clothes were torn and he had lost one shoe.

"Could I :

The mother, Clementine Finney, claimed that the boy was retarded, and that he had disappeared the day before he was being committed to the Cadwell Institution, near Raleigh, North Carolina. When asked if the death could have been a suicide, Mrs. Finney said no, she did not think so. The young man had been with his step-sister, Jess Booker, who has also been missing since that day. Miss Booker is seventeen years old. The police are searching for her now.

Jess wondered if this day might be the end of her running. She felt slight relief at the thought of regular food, or shelter—even in a jail cell.

The cause of death was drowning, but the coroner is looking for any other signs of trauma. No suspects have been named. Anyone knowing any information about this incident, please call your local police station.

As Jess paid for the packs of gum she could not make her hand let go of the two nickels, then she dropped them; but as she leaned down to pick them up, her eyes went blind for a moment. She brushed her hand on the floor to find the nickels; then stood, not even blinking. She handed the man the change and reached to take the packages of Juicy Fruit. She opened one stick of gum and moved it to her lips. While tasting its sweetness, her sight came back; but her mind quivered. As she left the repair shop, she felt herself moving quickly past the two troopers; but, in truth, she moved deliberately, like a turtle—one slow step, then another.

She imagined Adam's shy face floating above the water. She saw his muddy shoes, his hair fixed flat against his head. Then her mind saw him

36

running down the stairs to dinner, hiding in the yard with his dog, or letting a blue balloon float across the river. Her mind held images like a box of coins.

A woman drove up in a large Studebaker with the engine smoking and the car making a grinding sound. She screeched to a stop in front of the troopers. "Looks like you got some work ahead of you there, Charlie," one said, pointing to the smoking car. They told Charlie goodbye, and did not look back. As Jess left, she heard the woman say she had to get as far as Rome, Georgia. Charlie lifted the hood of the Studebaker, and steam roiled out.

Jess walked behind the repair shop and waited. She leaned against the brick wall, unable to think of anything but Adam's body on the riverbank. One shoe gone. Her legs shook and she wanted the image of him to leave her mind. Everything was her fault. She should have told those troopers that it was all her fault. But the thought of the boardinghouse was stronger than the need to turn herself in. She waited almost thirty minutes before she heard the hood slam down and Charlie call to the woman that her car was ready. Jess walked to where the woman was paying for the repairs.

"I forgot to get a map," Jess said. "I need a map, and I need to make a call to my aunt. She's real bad sick."

"That phone won't work," Charlie said. "Been broke for couple a days." He brought out two old maps. "Might not show some of the new roads," he said. "Pretty old."

"Where you going, honey?" the woman asked.

"My aunt lives right outside Rome, Georgia," Jess said. "I need to take care of her." She gave the woman a fake name.

"Maybe I can help," said the woman. "I'm going twenty miles the other side of Rome."

"Your car really needs a new transmission, lady," Charlie said.

Jess opened the car door and put her satchel on the floor. "That would help a lot."

The woman turned on the ignition. They both heard a scraping sound, but ignored it. "Don't you have to go to school?" she asked Jess. "Where's your mother?"

"She's already there." Jess had a spasm of coughs and the woman reached into her glove compartment to get some Kleenex and a box of Luden's Cherry Cough Drops. "My aunt's real sick."

"Sounds like you are, too."

They rode for two hours while Jess slept, then she woke to make conversation. Riding and sleeping made Jess relax; but, when the woman asked questions about her family, Jess began to forget what she had already told her. When they reached the outskirts of Rome, Jess asked to get out.

"You want me to let you out here?" The woman's head wagged back and forth trying to see where they were. "No houses around here."

"It's just down this road," said Jess, pointing to a long dirt road. She gathered her satchel and moved out of the car. "This is fine. I know just where to go now. Thank you."

The woman left, telling her to be careful. "And take care a'that cough."

Jess walked along the road for almost a mile before entering the woods, where she found an abandoned shed. She opened the broken door to see a large rat and three squirrels scatter through a hole in the wall. A mattress lay twisted in the corner and she unfolded it, brushing off leaves and dirt. She could not stop coughing, and felt a chill deep in her bones. *I cannot be sick,* she thought. She willed the fever to leave her.

She gathered some sticks, tore pages from an old Marshall Fields catalogue that lay beside the wood stove, and lit a fire. In only a few minutes the small room grew warm. She reached into her satchel and took out a bag of oranges someone had left in the bottom of a grocery cart. Jess had whisked the oranges underneath her coat before running away. Behind her a girl had yelled, "Hey! Stop! Stop her!"

The oranges were an unexpected bonus. She imagined they were an answer to prayer, if she had been able to pray. *I used to pray,* she thought, as she shifted sideways on the mattress. *I used to be able to pray so easy.* Jess opened a can of corned beef hash and ate with a smooth flat stick. She stuffed the hole with the catalogue, then lay on the mattress, trying to ignore the stains and mildewy odor. It was the softest bed she had slept on in weeks. The air smelled of rain, but May rain felt more like summer than winter. She took a few crackers, some of Sam's letters, and drank an RC Cola. A spray of birds blew across the tiny window and landed on the shed's roof.

Sweet Jess,

I've had more time to think about you, since we're having three days of rest camp. We've got clean clothes, showers, haircuts, and, also, we've been fumigated because of fleas and lice. It feels good to be clean again. And to shave. There are times when I would not want you to see me, but never a time when I don't want to see you. Yesterday we found some time to hunt. Me and Carl Hill and Billy Keifert (all of us southern boys who grew up hunting with our dads) went bird hunting. Billy dropped a bird and when it fell, it set off a land mine. We were hunting in an old mine field and didn't even know it! We left fast, and won't ever go there again.

We get so hungry, and had planned to eat the birds we shot. Did I tell you about the South Korean service guys (choggis)? They stay in their own tent (not far from mine) and they have a little stove. I can smell food they're cooking, and one day I went over to their tent. They were cooking a big pot of rice, with fish-heads. It smelled good, but I could see little bugs in it. I motioned to them that I wanted to eat and they moved over and we all ate together, with our fingers. It was good, I tell you. I didn't care what was in it. The other guys said they would never eat that stuff. I kept telling them it was good.

Here's something else. I found a guy here (in the next camp over), somebody I went to school with named Petey Ross. We went to grammar school all the way through high school together. We weren't friends or anything, but I wanted to see him real bad. I asked my Capt. for permission to go. He said I probably shouldn't, but I kept insisting and finally, he let me visit him. Petey was in a mortar unit and we met in the Mess Hall. We talked about high school mostly. It started getting dark, and I had a hard time finding my way back. I had to say the password to get back in my camp. The password was "Hopalong Cassidy." I said "Hopalong" and the guy on guard duty said "Cassidy."

When I get home I want us to get married and live in a nice house somewhere near a fire station. I want an American flag to fly on holidays, even Christmas. I want our kids to know what America is. I don't know what's wrong with me. I guess thinking about Hopalong Cassidy makes me homesick. Seeing a friend from grammar school meant the world to me, and I think about Roy Rogers and Hopalong and I get a lump in my chest. When I think about you all I want is to hold you. Remember when we spent long mornings together? I keep remembering.

Jess remembered too. She smiled and wished she could be clean, fumigated, or eating something cooked by someone else—without the bugs. She and Sam were sharing parallel lives, only Sam had an enemy trying to kill him and Jess was just alone. She wondered about the things he had to do, and all that he was not saying, and she wondered how different he would be when she saw him again. How different she would be.

She opened the sack of oranges and chose one, digging into the peel with her thumb. An orange mist sprayed her face. She ate the sections, relishing every bite, then licked her fingers and palms where the sweet juice had dripped. She wrapped Adam's raincoat tightly around her and lay back with the taste of oranges in her mouth.

— 9 —

On the first night that Clementine moved in with Edward, Adam wandered through the house like a restless wind. He kept asking where he was and, after a few unsettling nights, Clementine let him sleep in the locked basement. "Because sometimes when Adam goes to a new place," Clementine explained, "he tends to wander off in the middle of the night. I think he's trying to get back to where he was, but doesn't know how to get there." She spoke as though this had happened before.

They set up a rollaway bed, a table and lamp, and his stuffed animals, but Jess heard him whimpering every night; then she heard Clementine open the basement door—talking to Adam or singing until he felt right. After four days Edward suggested that Adam spend the night in his own room— the guest room they had fixed up for him. So he did, and the whimpering stopped.

"He's just different. He's been that way since he was born," Clementine said. "But he always looked like a regular boy." Adam was lean and tall, with thick hair—handsome, even. "He couldn't walk until he was three," she said. "He couldn't talk right until he was six."

He still can't, Jess thought, but didn't say.

Those next few months brought a shift of roles to the house: Clementine embraced the chores that had been Jess's pleasure, Edward Booker took Adam to the zoo and to ball games, Jess spent more time with her friends. And even though Jess had not welcomed Clementine into their family, she was forced to agree with her father that the woman was a fine cook.

Clementine spent whole afternoons in the kitchen, and by six o'clock the house smelled like suppertime. Everything she made was good. She baked chocolate cakes and blackberry cobblers. She asked Jess what kind of cookies she wanted for lunch and sometimes made cupcakes, placing them on a square plate in the shape of a pyramid.

But Jess objected when Clementine moved the furniture to suit her own taste, moving the sofa and chairs to face the TV, and bringing in a rug from her own house. She took down a mirror out of the hallway. Jess remembered when her mother had bought it, and hung it there. She couldn't bear the changes, and complained to her father.

"She lives here now, Jess," her father said; but the next day the mirror had been re-hung, though other tables and chairs were rearranged. Clementine told Adam he could arrange his room the way he wanted, and one afternoon passing by the room, Jess saw Adam bending over a framed photo of his father and Clementine and Adam (at about five years old) standing beside a picnic table. His father had one arm draped around Adam's shoulder. Jess had seen Adam touch the face of his father in the photo, moving his finger over the tiny face trying to feel the cheeks, the nose.

But the one still-sacred part of Jess's life happened each Saturday when she rode her horse, Buckhead, at some nearby stables. Her father was proud of Jess's riding skills. Over the years he had travelled to see her perform in shows, bragging on the ribbons she had won; but when he began to bring Adam to the stables on Saturday, Jess felt another part of her life slipping away.

"Maybe he could learn to ride," Edward said. "Maybe you could teach him."

"It's not that easy," Jess said.

One Saturday, Jess let Adam mount Buckhead and, reluctantly, led him around the ring. Adam pulled back too hard on the reins and kicked Buckhead's sides, the way he had seen cowboys perform in the movies. When he dismounted on the wrong side, the horse spooked, kicked out his back leg, and ran to the other side of the ring.

"My Gosh!" Jess said. "Can't you do anything right!" Adam backed away. Jess approached Buckhead, calmed him and led him back. "Come here," she said to Adam, and pushed a brush into his hand. "Whenever you ride you have to brush down the horse and cool him off with a hose. "Like this." She moved Adam's arm abruptly toward the horse. Buckhead shied away again before allowing Adam to brush his back and mane. Adam brushed slowly, methodically.

Jess did not expect Adam to enjoy the chore of grooming. She hoped he would never want to come back; but, instead, he thrilled to the brush against the neck of the horse. He brushed with one hand and smoothed with the other, coming alive in the world of senses. He used gentle strokes across the horse's back and sides, belly and legs. Adam, in the grip of something remote and wild, worked with the thorough care of a stable-boy.

Jess had never seen Buckhead stand so still while being groomed. He barely breathed. A statue of a horse. Adam let water from the hose run over the horse's back and legs—like a baptism. He looked like someone in love. Nothing about this act was a chore.

Once, Buckhead turned to see who was stroking him. When Adam finished brushing the horse, he kissed the animal's nose, then started brushing again—the neck and legs and back. Buckhead had thought it was over, but when Adam began another round, he readied himself for more grooming.

"You have to stop now, Adam." Jess believed Adam could have brushed and hosed until that horse was no bigger than a thimble, or curried him into a mere speck on the barn floor. Adam could groom that horse to death. She took the bridle and led Buckhead toward the stall. "You did a good job," she told Adam. "But that's enough." Buckhead's coat gleamed like a new coin.

That evening, at home, Adam's arm kept brushing the air, as if a big horse stood before him—in the kitchen, in the hall, at the dinner table.

"What in the world are you doing?" Clementine said.

Edward told her how good he was with Buckhead.

"Well," she laughed. "You can't keep doing that all night."

Jess was brushing her hair dry after washing it. They gathered in front of the TV after dinner to watch *Candid Camera*. Before the program started, Edward announced a surprise trip they would take in August. "We're going to Myrtle Beach," he said. "I've reserved a cabin right on the ocean!" Jess and her father had not been to the beach since before her mother died. She wanted to object, but instead brushed her hair over her face so no one could see her expression.

Adam barely responded to their plans for going to the beach, though they knew how much he would love stepping into the ocean for the first time. Whenever Jess had taken him to the river behind their house, he ran in up to his knees, his waist. He couldn't swim, but didn't care. Clementine usually asked Jess to go with him. "He can't go alone," she said. "He might plunge in over his head. I have a bad feeling about that river."

For most of July Jess had taught Adam how to float, but he still couldn't swim. Sometimes she brought bright colored balloons to blow up and let Adam watch them move along the top of the water until they were out of sight. He laughed hard if they popped. She was doing her best to be helpful, but each day she looked at her father with a question on her face: *What are you doing to me?* She wanted her old life back.

"Aren't you excited about Papa B. taking us to the ocean, Adam?" Clementine asked.

Adam didn't stop moving his arms through the air toward an imaginary horse. He couldn't get out of his head the pleasure of grooming. When Jess offered to let him brush her hair, Adam used gentle strokes from the crown, lifting and smoothing every strand. He worked like that for almost an hour. He made her hair feel like water.

Adam

The first time Adam stepped into the French Broad River, he thought he could ride beneath the murmur of fish. He sank and Jess pulled him up. He held Jess tight around her neck. Her wet hair and face felt cold. She told him to let go, to try again. He knew how rivers dug a long cradle to the sea, and believed it could take him all the way to the ocean. He sank over and over, swallowing water. He coughed. He choked, but would not quit. Adam wanted to please Jess more than he wanted to become a river going to the ocean. He told strangers that she was his sister, but his mother said, Half-sister. To him, Jess seemed whole.

So Jess taught him to float, holding him firm until he could do it himself, weightless, like a leaf or stick carried by the current. Maybe he could become that water—scooting fast around bushes and trees.

After Jess let him brush the big horse, he brushed Jess's hair. His arms felt light and floaty, like he was in water. Maybe brushing was like swimming—the arms. Adam liked to watch Jess push up a window in the evening, her own white arms rising, then dropping. He liked to hear her hum a tune he had never heard before. Jess smelled like grass.

But she did not like him the way Adam liked her. Whenever he followed her to town, she yelled, Go back home, Adam— like she was talking to a dog. Sometimes, kids made fun of him, and Jess did too. In those moments Adam felt hurtled through space in the wake of their laughter.

Soon he would go on a trip to see the ocean. Papa B. said so. In the time before Jess, when Adam lived without a father, he rode with his mother so long on the train to see the Grand Canyon—early, just before sunrise. He stood on the edge of the canyon for a full long moment before a man pulled him away from the edge. It was not his father, but Adam pretended that it was. His father had been gone for only a few months, when they took that trip, and Adam kept looking for him everywhere. So when the man pulled him away from the edge, Adam could smell the man-smell and in that moment he floated inside that canyon's big air. He could see the time just before dawn, and the day folding down over the stars. Then he saw the man's face, saw that his father was not there. He saw his mother's face and knew what was true and what wasn't. He felt the coldness before daylight.

Now, Adam drifted inside the shell of this new family, and Papa B. was like a daddy. Papa B. would let him go into the ocean. All the way. Adam believed that if the ocean lived inside his body—maybe he would never be alone.

— 10 —

As time grew close for them to leave for Myrtle Beach, Jess realized that she was looking forward to the trip. She might make some friends and get away from the family. Adam had been packed for a week. He filled his suitcase with some washed stones, a plastic cup he used at mealtimes, his toothbrush, his stuffed horse, two Hershey Bars, and the photo he kept beside his bed, standing with his father.

Clementine added the rest of what he needed and they drove four hours to a beach house with three bedrooms and a small porch where they could eat breakfast. Each morning Adam went fishing with Edward, and in the afternoon they all swam in the ocean. Jess couldn't get away from them. One night they wandered to the Grand Pavilion, where bands played. Edward and Clementine rode the Ferris wheel with Adam, and Jess hung out near the bandstand looking for other teenagers. Two girls approached with Coca-Cola bottles and asked if she wanted one. Their smiles were welcoming and Betty offered Jess a sip of her own. Jess took one sip and knew it was spiked with alcohol. Jess laughed and pretended that was okay.

Betty and Marie Coggins were both older, but assumed Jess was their age, and when they asked her what grade she was in, Jess lied. Betty, a senior, was tall, with a face no one could call pretty, but she moved her body in a provocative way. Marie, younger by a year, was a short beauty with a buxom figure. She tried to imitate Betty's gestures. The sisters attended Mt. Chesnee School for Girls near Asheville. They bragged about the Christmas and Spring Formals at the school, and how great it was to room with other girls.

"My mother went to Mt. Chesnee," Jess said. "She talked about it all the time, when she was alive. My daddy promised I could go, but I think he's forgotten."

"So that woman you're with is *not* your mother?" Marie's curiosity was aroused. "Who is she?"

"Just somebody my daddy married."

"You mean she's your stepmother?" Betty asked. "What's she like?"

"Mean, I bet," Marie said, hopefully. "Do you hate her?"

"She's okay, I guess."

"What about your brother?" Betty's voice grew quiet. "I saw him today."

"What about him?" Jess knew Betty would make fun of him.

"Is he your real brother?" Marie asked. "He is *so* good-looking." They had seen Adam only from a distance—preparing his fishing gear or riding in the car with Edward.

"He's *her* son. Not my real brother."

"Does he have a girlfriend?" Betty asked.

Adam's height made him attractive. He shaved now, and his jaw had a strong, manly look. He had a sweet smile and curls falling above bushy eyebrows. Jess thought he looked like the framed photo of a younger Calder.

"How should I know?" Jess hated these questions and wanted to talk about something else, but they kept urging her to bring Adam with her tomorrow night. "I don't think so," she said.

"Why not?"

"He gets up early to fish with my dad. I don't think he wants to stay out so late."

"We'll make it worth his while," said Betty. "You could at least ask. What's his name?"

"Adam." Jess pretended she would ask him, but the next afternoon Jess saw the girls on the beach and Marie said that she had already asked him.

"What'd he say?" Betty looked eager.

"Nothing. I think he's shy. But he *might* meet us," said Marie. "Anyway, he seemed pretty excited when I said he should come."

"I don't know," Jess said. "He's kind of strange."

"I don't care," Betty said. They were irritated with Jess. "Just bring him with you. Okay? He obviously wants to."

Jess showed up alone that night. She waited until Edward and Clementine went to sleep and climbed out the window. She thought Adam was asleep too, but he was waiting to see where she went and climbed out his window to follow her to the beach. Jess was already with the girls and they kept asking 'Where's Adam?' until Betty saw him coming over the dune through the grass and waved to him. He ran across the sand at an awkward gait, and the girls were laughing. But the moment he spoke, his words came out elemental and hollow-sounding.

"I came," he said, his voice echoing in on itself.

"Damn," said Marie. "What's the matter with him?" She was speaking to Jess.

"Nothing," Jess said. "You said you wanted him to come. Here he is."

"Yeah, but what's *the matter* with him? He talks funny."

Adam looked confused. "What's the *maat-ter* with me?" He laughed too loud, the way he laughed when his feelings might be hurt.

"Look at him. He walks like an old person." Betty pointed to a gull on the beach. "Like that bird."

"Okay, okay," Jess said. "He's slow. Okay?" She turned to leave, to take Adam with her. "He can't learn like everybody else."

"No," Betty said, sounding apologetic. "Don't go. It's okay. I have some stuff stashed down the beach. Let's go." Her voice became full of mischief. "Marie has a flashlight."

"And more than just a flashlight!" Marie shouted. She gave Adam the flashlight and told him to turn it on.

"C'mon." Betty took Adam's hand, and they ran on the beach. Adam's heart pounded in his chest and his throat felt tight. He laughed loud, a real laugh this time. Jess followed to a place on the beach where a fire had been built the night before. Betty told Adam to look for sticks and brush so they could build a new fire. Jess helped him and saw how Adam loved being part of the group. They brought back an armload of twigs. Marie put paper in with the sticks and lit a fire. Betty pulled off her shoes and helped Adam take off his shoes and socks, then led him by the hand to the water where they splashed each other. He looked happier than Jess had ever seen him. Marie turned on her portable radio to hear Eddie Fisher sing "I Am Yours," then Nat King Cole's "Walkin' My Baby Back Home." Marie squatted down on her knees and swayed to the music.

When Adam came back, Marie asked him to dance and, though he couldn't, she showed him how to put his arm around her waist. She wore shorts and her shirt rose up to show her belly. Finally, she just danced alone, purring with her own vanity. Adam could not stop watching her.

Jess was observing Adam closely. She wasn't sure this was all right, but liked seeing him in such a normal setting. She was glad he came. Betty spread out a large blanket and they all sat down. She handed Coca-Colas to everyone, and cups. Then she poured whiskey into the cups. Jess didn't want to refuse, so she drank hers. Adam took a sip and poured his out. Betty laughed and gave him more.

"He might not want any," Jess said, but he sipped it trying to please Betty. The sun was down and the fire, their only light, threw sparks onto the sand. Adam shivered. He said that he felt goose-pimples on his arms and huddled closer to the fire. He kept telling them about the fish he had caught until Marie told him to *Shut up about the fish.*

"He is handsome though," Betty said, as if he weren't there.

Betty and Marie brought out marshmallows and put one on a stick for Adam to roast. Adam wanted another. Jess did the same, but since she was not used to alcohol, she grew sleepy. Just as she began to doze off she saw Betty turn up the music and sit beside Adam. She pointed to the moon. It was full. "If you could fly you could land on that moon," she said. She ran her fingers through Adam's hair and peered into the clutter of his mind.

Adam laughed nervously. That's all Jess remembered, until she woke suddenly to hear Betty scream and see Marie trying to pull him away. Betty's blouse had been pulled off her shoulders and Adam's pants were unbuttoned.

"Adam! Come here." Adam jumped back. "Come here right now!" He said *No,* as if he had heard a voice in his own head. He was pulling on his pants leg. He went to stand behind Jess.

"Damn you! What did you do to him?" Jess yelled at Betty.

"What did *I* do? Ask what *he* did, why don't you?"

"Whatever it was—you started it, not him. You led him on. Damn it! You're sick, you know that?"

"I didn't do anything," Betty was buttoning her shirt and holding her breast.

"Let me tell you something," Jess said. "You say anything about any of this and I'm telling what you and Marie have been doing out here every night. I know what you do after I leave."

"We're just drinking," Marie said.

"You're doing more than that," Jess answered. "You're making out with every man on this beach. And you tried to do that with Adam. He doesn't know any better. You should've left him alone." Adam was moving back and forth behind her. He couldn't stand still.

"You were asleep. What do you know?" Marie said.

"I know what he'll tell me. He's not stupid, you know. He might be retarded, but he's not stupid. He has the same feelings we do."

Jess helped Adam button his pants and buckle his belt. She told him to put on his shirt, and reached to straighten his hair. "C'mon. We're going back to the house." She did not say goodbye to the girls and, when Adam turned to wave, she jerked him forward.

They sneaked in through his bedroom window. Adam got into bed and Jess made him promise not to tell anyone about this night.

"I won't tell," he said. He looked worried. "Will I get in trouble? For making Betty scream?"

"Only if you tell somebody. Not if you *don't* tell. It's our secret. Just between us."

"Okay."

Jess had not felt so protective of Adam before, and she realized how sweet he was, how much he wanted to please her. "Goodnight, Adam." She leaned to fluff his pillow.

"I'm sorry," he said. Jess paused at the door. "Jess?"

"What?"

"We have a secret, so now I won't be in trouble?"

"Right." As she left the room, he was still talking, whispering to himself. Jess stood outside his door to make sure he didn't need her again.

They each had to be awakened the next morning, since they slept later than usual. "We're packing the car, Jess. Get up and have breakfast," her father called from outside.

"You and Adam could help us a little, you know." Clementine sounded irritated. "No good comes from being lazy." So vacation-time was over.

Something else was over too. Until this vacation Jess had regarded Adam with pity or irritation, as she might look at a limping dog on the street; but Adam's bright regard for her was unmistakable. He watched her peel an apple, and he longed to perform the task the same way—choosing fruit from a bowl, turning it to look for spoiled places. He laughed when she laughed; and when she laughed at him, he joined in that laughter too. His hushed sweetness became, finally, impossible to ignore.

Adam

Adam had done something wrong. When he snuck out the dark window to meet the girls, he felt glad, but the girls laughed and told him he walked like a funny bird. Then as the bird flew away, they said Nope, not that bird. That bird can fly. For many nights afterwards, Adam dreamed of heavy birds unable to lift off the ground. But he liked the girls when they said he was good-looking. They gave him something bad to drink, and when Jess fell asleep, they riffled his hair and touched his face. They kissed his mouth, and he kissed back. He felt happy, his body got warm with bubbles.

One girl unbuttoned his pants, and Adam kissed her too. He wanted to kiss everybody. He was being loved. He kissed her cheek and lips. Her name was Betty and she showed him her breasts. They were soft, but then she screamed. When Jess woke up, she was mad. She yelled at the girls and said bad words. She told Adam to fasten his pants. He didn't want to. He felt himself stopping and starting like a wild pony, until Jess put her hand on his back. She buttoned his pants and helped him tuck in his shirt. She said, We're going back now. Okay?

Okay. He did not know what had happened.

Jess led him back to the house on the beach, where they climbed in the bedroom window. She pulled back the covers on his bed and Adam wanted to fly off

48

the ground. The sheets were so white, like clouds. That night at the ocean, Jess told Adam that they had a secret. He didn't know what it was, but she said they had one and made him promise not to tell. He promised. She leaned to lift his pillow, and he pulled up the fluff of sheet to his chin. He slept in the smell of Jess leaning over him.

As Jess left the room, Adam tried to tell her that sometimes when he was awake it felt like dreaming. She paused at the door and he kept trying to tell her what was in his mind. He said sometimes he saw tiny bits of light coming out of water like shiny stones. He said that sometimes he was afraid of glass—the sound it made when breaking.

— 11 —

Jess had collected seven pebbles, counting seven weeks so far, and she real-ized it must be the middle of June. She imagined that Adam's funeral had come and gone, that people in town had attended, and that Clementine was sick with grief. She had wanted to be there, as she had been all those times when he was baptized.

The rain made the morning dark, but Jess saw an Esso Station up ahead, where she could wash herself and maybe get something to eat. She still had almost three dollars. Last night she had found a barn where she huddled and slept, but she woke coughing hard. She had not recuperated completely from her last sickness and wished someone were there to bring her soup. She took two aspirins and ate her last orange. Oranges seemed to restore her.

The man, behind the cash register, looked Jess over carefully then pointed to the wall where the restroom key hung. When she returned, he offered to share hot tea, just brewed, and gave Jess a plate of buttered toast, with a jar of strawberry jam. She made a grateful nod and leaned on the window ledge until the man gave her his chair.

"Sit down now," the man urged. "Looks like you've been sick."

Jess nodded and sipped her tea.

"Where's your car? You got a car?" He stretched his neck to look outside.

"No." She tried to chew slowly. "This's good."

He suddenly called out a name, loud, "RUBY!" so that Jess jumped and coughed even harder.

"What is it?" A woman poked her head from two curtains in a doorway that led to back rooms.

"We got somebody here might need help."

Ruby approached Jess and placed her hand on the girl's brow and cheeks. "Oh, my Lord! Come back here with me," Ruby said. "Look at you. Your clothes are wet." She turned to her husband at the cash register. "She's soak-ing, Pug." She spoke as if it might be his fault.

Jess recuperated for three days in a back room of the Esso station. Ruby called a doctor who prescribed medicine for the cough. Jess ate soup and dreamed she was home. As she began to feel better, Pug and Ruby suggested that she stay and work for them, if she wanted to.

Jess was grateful that they did not ask questions, and agreed to work for a few days, but she stayed for over a week after her recuperation. She could earn money for the last leg to Alabama. She shelved items, kept receipts from delivery men, and made change faster than either Pug or Ruby could do. She had not stolen anything from them, though, at first, she had been tempted to do so.

"I hope she stays a while," Pug said.

Jess ate every meal with Pug and Ruby around the kitchen table, the three of them talking about the day. She felt on solid ground as she entered their time of normal life and suppers. And though Jess felt the tension of their unasked questions, they did not pry. She had entered a cocoon, and hoped it would contain her for a little longer. It did, until one night Pug's brother, Bucky, arrived. "He always just shows up," Pug said. "Without warning." Jess could tell that Pug and Bucky were not congenial brothers.

Bucky was a large, rugged-looking man, who told outrageous stories about Pug's family, and made everybody laugh; but his gaze lingered too long on Jess and she did not like to be in a room alone with him. Bucky stayed the weekend. He seemed to be everywhere, and Jess wondered when he would leave.

On Saturday Jess heard Bucky talking in a low voice to Pug and Ruby. She couldn't hear everything, but she heard him say something about a girl-gone-missing. He said that this might be that girl, and that they should call the police. "You don't know what she's done," he said.

"Well, maybe," Ruby kept saying. "But we've grown kinda fond of her."

"You should think about it."

"We'll think about it," said Pug.

"Cause if you don't report her, I will." Bucky stood up as Jess walked into the room. Lunch was ready and they all began to eat together. Bucky said that he had heard about a girl who had run away from North Carolina. "Her name's Jess Booker," he said. Jess did not flinch, but ate her sandwich. She had told them her name was Mary Ellen Wood. They called her Mary.

"And there was a young man. Retarded, I think," said Bucky. "The boy was leaving to be in some institution. "

"Maybe they ran off together," said Pug.

Jess stood to pour herself a glass of milk and asked if anyone else wanted anything. She could feel their eyes staring at her back.

"Maybe," said Bucky. "Anyway the young man's dead. Found him washed up on a riverbank."

51

Jess carefully placed the glass of milk on the table, and finished eating her lunch. She would have to go now. She couldn't stay. She chewed her food and found it hard to swallow.

That night, Ruby went to Jess's room to ask if she had run away from home. "If so," she said, without waiting for an answer, "I need to know. Unless there's some good reason not to, we should get you back to where you belong."

"I can't tell you," Jess said. "You've been real good to me though."

"Well, I got to say this—Bucky's real suspicious. He wants us to call the police, Mary." She sat on the bed beside Jess. "I thought I should tell you that, just in case."

"Thank you," said Jess, her eyes wide. "Don't worry about me."

Ruby stood to leave, then turned, "I'll wake you early so you can get on your way," she told Jess. "I'll get some food ready and pack you some clothes in the old suitcase I have." She handed her an envelope. "Here's some money. You earned it."

In a few minutes she brought Pug to say goodbye. "We're gonna miss you," Pug said. "We liked having you around."

"Don't, Pug." She looked at Jess. "You do what you need to do, darlin'. You can come back anytime, you hear?"

Jess sat with her head down until the door was closed. She left early the next morning while Bucky was still asleep. She packed her clothes in an old suitcase Ruby found at Goodwill, and left with food and money. She felt as though, if she had to, she could return to the Esso Station to stay with Pug and Ruby. She could stay there forever.

As she walked she looked for barns to sleep in with fat bales of good-smelling hay. A light rain came in the afternoon and cooled her. She had not seen, or even thought of, the brown and white car with the *ike Ike* sticker; but now that she was traveling again, she grew watchful.

$$— \ 12 \ —$$

During that first summer Jess stopped avoiding Adam, but when school began again, she reverted to her earlier ways of dismissing him. If he knocked on her bedroom door, she said to go away; if he tagged along beside her and her friends, she said, "Leave me alone." At dinner she answered him with one-word responses. Adam didn't understand what had gone wrong. One morning he sneaked out the back door to follow Jess and her friends. Jess saw him lurking behind bushes.

"He acts like a crazy person," one boy said, and Jess nodded.

"He has a crush on you, Jess," a girl teased.

They saw him skulking at the edge of trees, then ducking beneath the bleachers until Jess went inside the school. Sometimes she looked out a window to see if he had gone home.

That night she told Adam not to follow her.

"I don't," he said.

"Just leave me alone! That's all I want." Her voice sounded like cursing. "Just to be left a-lone."

Edward told Adam that he could come to the downtown store with him. Edward owned two clothing stores—one in Goshen and one in Asheville. So, for almost a week, Adam rode with Edward, bringing coloring books and paper for drawing. But as his friendly manner began to disturb the customers, Edward brought him home.

Then one morning Adam snuck out of the house to follow the other kids to school. He crouched under the school's bleachers until he saw Jess disappear through the big dark doors; but as Adam stood to go back home, he stepped down hard on a nest of yellow jackets and ran in circles calling for Jess. The bees swarmed around him and landed, like a swath of cloth, on the side of his head.

Jess saw Adam from the school's window. He performed a wild dance—all elbows and arms—but he could not detach the swarm from his face. He fell to his knees, swatting and crying. More yellow jackets clung to his neck and legs. He looked as if someone invisible was knocking him around.

Several teachers came outside, and Jess ran to where Adam was trying to swim in the grass. Yellow jackets flew around them both, stinging Jess as she lifted Adam's legs and dragged him toward the parking lot. His body bounced on the ground, and he kept telling Jess that he was on fire. A teacher told someone to call an ambulance.

"It's okay," Jess said. "You'll be okay, Adam."

Adam lay on the parking lot pavement, rolling around, not standing up. He moved his tongue dryly between his lips. "Fire in my face." His face was beginning to swell. "I didn't mean to," he said, but his voice already sounded weak. He continued to call for Jess, even though she was there.

"We're taking you to the doctor, Adam." Yellow jackets stung her arms. She turned to the teacher. "Call my Dad at the store. He'll get hold of Adam's mother." She helped Adam to stand as an ambulance pulled into the school parking lot. The siren was blaring. "Look, Adam. You're gonna ride in an ambulance."

"I am?" He seemed barely conscious. One shoe was gone and he had dirt caked in his thick tangle of hair.

"I'm going with you." She motioned to let others know her intention, but everything was like a movie running in her head. She thought there were two Jess Bookers and one was acting responsibly, the other stood back unable to know what to do next. A teacher insisted on coming along, saying they should have an adult with them.

"Maybe we can get them to turn on the siren." Jess said the words without thinking. She wanted the whole scene to be a bad dream. "Would you like that, sweetie?" It was the first time she had ever called him sweetie.

Adam nodded.

"It's not your fault, Adam," the teacher told him. "You're not in trouble."

Jess stayed with Adam all day. Clementine and Edward arrived and, late in the afternoon, they brought him home. The bandages had to be changed every few hours. They applied a soothing ointment to his neck, arms, and legs to calm the burning and itching.

During the first days of Adam's recuperation, before Jess left for school, she placed a blueberry muffin on his bedside table, so he would find it when he woke—along with a fat balloon. He thought the appearance of such things was magical.

After school, she made the rounds of auto dealers, salvage shops, and garages to inquire about unusual hubcaps. She picked up three: a Plymouth Sailing Ship, a Starburst and a 1949 Desoto Center Cap. Adam recognized the Starburst, and Center Cap, but had never seen the Sailing Ship. He whooped when he saw it. He told Jess to nail the new ones on the garage next to the Cross Bars and the Baby Moon. On sunny days, the side of their garage looked like a space ship.

The fear of more bee stings kept Adam from following Jess to school anymore, but he was still restless. Clementine and Edward talked about buying him a more appropriate-size bike for Christmas.

By Thanksgiving he had looked through catalogues, choosing a Schwinn Red Phantom B-17 bicycle with chrome fenders with a headlight, white wall tires, and a cantilevered frame with pinstripe. The name *Phantom* was written in cursive on the side. Christmas morning he found the bicycle in the living room by the tree. It was red and silver and he swelled with pride at the look of it.

During the next few months Clementine and Jess noticed that Adam suddenly had friends who came by the house and rode bikes with him. John Beaner was in the seventh grade and the other two were eighth graders. Clementine was worried as she watched Adam ride away, but Edward was glad he had friends.

"Where do they go?" Edward asked.

"Just riding, I guess. Adam said something about a clubhouse."

"All boys should have a clubhouse," Edward laughed. "It'll be good for him."

"They give him candy and comic books."

"Well, let's see how it goes," Edward patted her shoulder. "He seems happy right now."

A few days later, Adam rode home and parked his bike in the garage, but didn't come in. Clementine found him sitting in the back yard looking at a magazine with naked women.

"Where did you get that?" Adam threw the magazine down and Clementine took it. "It's not mine," Adam said. "It's John Beaner's. At the clubhouse."

Clementine gave the magazine to Edward and asked if he would handle it; so Edward told Adam to take it back to the clubhouse or else throw it out. He asked Adam if he had any questions. Adam said he wanted to keep it in his room. Edward thought a minute before he said no. Then Adam asked if the women in the pictures got cold, and if they were afraid of squirrels. Edward said he didn't think so.

Clementine didn't trust the boys anymore, but Edward urged her to let him keep his friends, until a week later a policeman brought Adam home and said he had been stealing from the grocery store. He told Clementine that John Beaner was the culprit and that the boys had been sending Adam into the store to steal for them.

"What was he stealing?" Edward asked.

"Candy, mostly. Comic books. It was easy, since Adam worked there."

That night Adam told Jess that a policeman had arrested him, and that John Beaner had said "Get lost, retard." He asked about the word 'retard.' He knew what 'get lost' meant.

"You weren't arrested, Adam. That policeman just brought you home." Jess did not explain the word 'retard.' "Good riddance!" she said. "Those boys are jerks."

Adam laughed. He knew the word 'jerk.'

But after those days huddled inside the clubhouse looking at dirty magazines, Adam's desires were reawakened. He had always played with children when they came to the playground after school, but now, he rode his bike there alone and when he pushed a little girl on the swing, he pulled up her dress to see her panties. He thought no one noticed this, but mothers took their little girls away from him and told him to go home. A knock at the door one night brought everything to the surface.

Eric and Elaine Brown had drawn up a petition stating that Adam should be banned from playing with children at the playground, and the park. The petition, signed by other parents, stated that Adam was a threat to the younger girls.

"We had to do something," Eric Brown told Edward. "This was getting out of hand."

Edward apologized and reminded them that Adam had the mind of an eight-year-old.

"But the sexuality of a man," Elaine insisted. "We've got to do something about this, before something happens. I'm sorry, Clementine. We've watched Adam grow up. But now . . . this is different. I hope you understand." She took out a poster that had been drawn with a likeness of Adam. The poster was being passed around town and given to new families moving into Goshen.

"There's nothing else to do," Eric said, his voice apologetic, but firm.

When they left, Clementine looked at the poster. "Like a criminal," she said. "They have known Adam all these years. They *know* him. What are they *think*ing?"

Edward held the petition at his side as though it weighed too much to lift. "They're thinking about their little girls," he said.

"Are you on *their* side now?" Clementine had a terrible look of accusation, as if Edward did not trust Adam either.

"Clementine, don't!"

"Well, *are* you?"

"If you mean do I worry about Adam with Jess? No, I don't, but there have been times over the summer when I *did* have some concern."

Clementine did not sleep, but sat all night with the petition and poster. She kept waking Edward. "He'll have no one to play with. It breaks my heart. He'll be more and more isolated. He looked forward to playing with the children every day." But Clementine knew how strange it was to see Adam, a big strapping boy, in a sandbox or riding a merry-go-round. Over the last year he had gained some independence: riding his bike, walking to the park, playing in a neighbor's yard. Now, she had to change the part of his life that he loved the most.

The next day when Jess mentioned going to the library, Clementine asked if Adam could go with her.

"Do I have to?" she said. "I need to study."

"Just let him look at books about hubcaps. Anything to keep him away from the children."

"Hey, Adam," she called, but her voice could not hide the resentment she felt. "Want to go to the library with me?" She knew he needed to be reined in. She felt more than a little blame for his sexual urges, because of what happened with Betty and Marie.

"The library?" Adam said. "I can't read."

"You can read a few words." He could recognize Exit, Restrooms (Ladies and Men), the names of a few stores, and his favorite flavor of ice cream. Jess had taught him how to write his name. He could print A, but the D sometimes had two bumps instead of one and the M was always upside down: ABAW.

"We'll go to the drugstore afterwards," she promised. "Get ice cream. Anyway, the library has books with pictures of hubcaps. And how about the ocean? Want to see a book about the ocean?"

As they entered the library's big doors, Adam could smell the odor of books. "Smells funny," he said. Jess put her finger to her lips to indicate they had to be quiet. Jess was aware of his shuffling footsteps across the floor, how different he was from those sitting at the long tables with the green lamps. In the quiet of the large room, she saw how he lived in the familiar sting of his loneliness.

They went into the stacks to find books about the ocean, and others with photos of hubcaps. Adam whistled quietly whenever he found a hubcap he had never seen. When he finished studying his books, Jess showed him the stereopticon—a machine that could make a photo come alive in 3-D. Adam laughed loudly when he looked through the eyepiece. The librarian seemed willing to look the other way. He slipped double photos under the lens for almost thirty minutes before deciding he'd seen enough.

They walked in a drizzling rain to the drugstore. A week of steady spring storms had made the river rise. Some houses in the next town had flooded and Clementine recalled a man, four years ago, who had drowned when the swift current carried him downstream. They entered the drugstore and shook raindrops from their heads.

Billy, the boy behind the counter, called to Jess when they came in, and she walked toward him. He took Jess out most Saturday nights, but now he scooped a double dip of strawberry ice cream into a dish for Adam. Adam always chose the same flavor. He used his fingers, lifting out each strawberry to eat first, then stirred the ice cream into a soup until he could drink the last bit.

Jess ate a chocolate cone and smiled at Billy. He could not take his eyes off her. Billy made Jess laugh and talked about things Adam did not understand. He held Jess's hand on top of the counter, and when Adam saw Jess lean forward, maybe to give Billy a kiss, Adam said he wanted to go home. He wanted to go right now. He wanted to run from the small crate of his mind, and all the things he did not understand. Even before he had finished his ice cream, he bolted for the door. Jess hurried to catch him. They raced home in a downpour.

Rain pelted their faces and arms, but Adam lifted his head into it and opened his mouth. Cars honked when he rushed across the street against the light. Jess was running behind him. Grackles and crows landed and screamed from the small park in the middle of town.

Adam

His mama sometimes fussed at him for touching himself at night—if she caught him; but she did not always catch him when he dreamed of girls in pajamas and underpants, or riding a merry-go-round, their dresses flying upward above the knees. At night Adam touched himself to feel good, but the next day his mother always knew and she said loud, ADAM, like that. And he knew she knew.

He hid in his closet while she grumbled and changed the sheets on the bed. Sometimes she took his shoulders and shook him when he came out of the closet to go downstairs. She told him that he could go blind from doing that, and Adam said, What? Thinking she meant his hiding in the closet. When he remembered the sheets, he said, Oh.

Papa B. told Adam that touching himself was not a bad thing, and that lots of boys did it. He suggested that Adam touch himself in the bathroom, so his mother wouldn't have to change the sheets.

Adam did not know what came over him when he felt struck by beauty, wanting to ease the pangs with his own hand. He calmed himself on sleepless nights with his ritual of imagining a voluptuous face, or breast. When he made himself come, he thought he had experienced an exquisite thing, an unexpected pleasure.

In Adam's mind, people talked about the word Love, as though he didn't know what that word meant. He could read the word Love, and he could say it, and he thought that maybe they were the ones who didn't understand what that word meant.

When he rode bikes with John Beaner to the middle of town, Adam's chest heaved with pride beneath his thin jacket. He felt warmth settle on his shoulders and legs. He rode beside them until, at the park, the boys seemed to disappear into thin air. He rode home alone.

When that policeman came, he wasn't mad, but Mama was mad and said he could've been sent to jail, and that he was lucky. Papa B. told him not to steal and gave him money. John Beaner stopped telling him dirty jokes or calling him Buddy.

But in the drugstore, when Billy touched Jess's hand, a lonely shaft entered Adam's body. He understood something about how far his life could go—not loving, only sitting beside those who could love. When Jess smiled at Billy's touch, her eyes looked soft, and Adam pushed away from the counter-stool hurrying toward the door. Jess waved good-bye to Billy. When they got outside, Adam broke into a run. He wanted to run away, fast—to run and run. He wanted to run off the edge of the earth.

— 13 —

Jess sat down on the grassy roadside to drink water from a thermos Pug had packed for her, when a man in a yellow Packard stopped to ask if she needed a ride. He looked to be in his mid-forties, wore glasses and a slick suit.

"Yes," she said. "I'm not going far." She put her small suitcase in the back seat and kept the satchel with her as she climbed in front.

"Well, I can help you with a few miles." The car smelled of tobacco. "Where you headed?" he asked.

"Lula, Alabama," Jess said.

"That's more than a few miles. I thought you said you weren't going far." As they drove away, she could smell alcohol on his breath. He was driving too fast.

"I have kinfolks to see before that," she lied. She didn't want him to think she was alone. "That's just where I'm ending up. I thought that's what you meant."

The man was smiling, but his smile looked crooked. He wore a white shirt with a bowtie. He had age spots and his skin looked gray. "You be careful who you let give you a ride." He sounded like somebody's father. He said he had a job selling *Encyclopedia Britannica,* and expressed how worried he was about his wife, who wouldn't go out of the house anymore. "Not even to the grocery store," he said.

Jess pulled her satchel onto her knees and offered sympathy about the wife. But, as she talked, her voice stuttered. They rode for about thirty minutes before he suggested they stop somewhere, get a bite to eat. "No, I'm fine," she said.

"You're fine." The man's voice, in this moment, changed. "I wonder."

Jess looked at him.

"I'm just teasing," he said. "I thought you might be hungry."

"I guess I am," she said, changing her mind. She should get out.

"We have about twenty more miles before we'll find a place." Jess was thinking how she might get out before those twenty miles, when she felt his hand on her knee. She jumped. "You know what I re-ally think?" He pushed breath through his nose. "I think you're a girl who's running away, and I'm wondering just how wild you are." He rubbed her leg.

Jess pulled away, leaning against the door. "What're you doing?"

He had not stopped grinning, and drove the car, now, with one hand, his other hand on Jess's thigh. They swerved from one side of the road to the other. "You don't want to fall out," he said, then jerked the satchel off her lap, and threw it into the back seat. He touched between her legs. The car moved into the other lane; he pulled it back. He was grabbing her hard. He was stronger than he looked. She could smell his breath.

"Listen," Jess said, trying to seem calm. "I have some whiskey in my suitcase. Want me to show you?" She was smiling. She sounded promising.

The man turned onto the shoulder of the road to a full stop, but he did not let her get out. He continued to rub her leg. Jess stayed very still, not looking at him. His hand kept kneading her thigh. He leaned to kiss her hair, and she reached for the door handle.

"No you don't," he said. "I'll get it."

Jess couldn't breathe, but didn't want to seem hurried or frightened. "Wait, I know just where . . . " She pushed down the handle and the car door opened. Jess opened the back door, grabbed the suitcase and hooked the satchel onto her arm, running toward the trees. She ran blindly, stumbling, but not falling. The man got out, cursing. He said some word she had never heard before. He started to chase her, but a pickup truck was coming from the other direction. He yelled again. Another curse. Then Jess could hear gravel banging the undercarriage of his car as he slid onto the road and sped away. She saw him give a brief wave to the person in the truck.

As she entered the woods a soft summer rain began to fall. She thought of what could have happened and kept running. Her heart had been racing since she pulled her things from the back seat. She couldn't stop crying—still feeling the man's hand on her thigh and smelling his breath in her hair. The rain on her face felt good, but the sky had turned gray, and a dark archipelago of clouds coming toward her meant that she needed to look for shelter.

Jess wouldn't ride in a car again, except with a woman. She couldn't trust the world around her or believe in the goodness of people. She thought of Mr. Brennan and the boardinghouse. She thought how good it would be to eat a dinner prepared and hot, or get into bed with clean sheets, or have the luxury of a glass of water on the bedside table.

Adam had believed that people were basically good; but he also believed he could touch the sky, or ride the rivers, and eat the ocean like it was a cookie. She pressed her lips together. The thought of what Adam believed kept Jess going.

— 14 —

B y the time the school year ended, Edward had decided that Jess could spend her last two years of high school at Mt. Chesnee School for Girls, near Asheville. She would leave in the fall.

"Your mother wanted that for you," Edward said. Jess liked the idea of breaking away from this new configuration of family, but she would miss her father and she dreaded the thought of maybe running into Marie Coggins at Mt. Chesnee. Betty would have graduated by now.

Clementine objected to the idea. She thought Jess's departure would be too difficult for Adam. "I don't see why she has to go *this* year. Are you sending her away because of Adam?"

"This is where her mother wanted her to go to school," Edward said. "Don't make it into something big."

"But Adam is going to be even more unmanageable," she said. "He can't even play next door anymore. Nobody understands him."

Mr. MacDougal, next door, had been the most recent person to complain about Adam—even though MacDougal and Edward were friends. Their friendship had formed around a common interest in World War II Generals. They talked endlessly about Omar Bradley, "Hap" Arnold, McArthur, Eisenhower, and Patton. They could name every battle as well as the theaters of war in which these men fought. They spent many congenial hours together.

So when MacDougal came one afternoon to talk about Adam, he had waited as long as he could. He knocked on the back door and walked into the kitchen as he always did; but this time he told Edward and Clementine that Adam should not come into their yard to play with Emily anymore. "It looks strange," he said. "I mean, Adam being so big."

"What has he done?" Edward asked.

"Nothing. Not really." MacDougal did not sit down. "But I hear stories. I'm sorry about this. I just can't take a chance."

"You don't really believe . . . " Clementine began, but Edward held up one hand.

"We understand."

"I thought Emily liked Adam," Clementine said.

"She does." MacDougal shook his head. "She does." He reconsidered. "Maybe if Jess comes with him it would be all right."

"Thank you," Clementine said. "He really has no one else to be with."

"I didn't want to say anything," MacDougal said, in way of apology. "I want to do what's right."

After MacDougal left, Clementine walked back and forth in the yard in her bare feet. When she got to the end of the yard, she propped her arms on the back fence, and stared down toward the French Broad River. She did not cry. She did not feel like crying anymore.

That evening Adam poked at his dinner then went out the back door to see Emily in her sandbox. Clementine told him that if he wanted to go over there, Jess had to go with him.

"Why?"

"That's Mr. MacDougal's rule from now on."

Jess followed Adam out the back door and waved to MacDougal as they opened the gate to their yard. "Hello, Mr. MacDougal," Jess called.

Adam halted when Mr. MacDougal stood up on the porch.

"You with him?" he called.

"Yes, sir."

"Only if you're with him."

Adam stopped at the sandbox and squatted to dig a gulley of sand with his thumb. Emily wore a green checked gingham dress and was about five years old. She poured water into the gulley and they laughed. Jess sat on the corner board and looked into the woods behind the house. Through the woods she could see a single light, and a drift of mist that formed in the trees. As she dreamed of the Mt. Chesnee School and a life without Adam, the whole world seemed frail and beautiful; but her heart had grown full of tenderness for Adam, and she tried to imagine how his life would be without her in the house.

"I don't want him over here unless you're here with him," Mr. MacDougal called again across the yard. "I've talked to your parents about this."

"I know," Jess said. Tonight she would tell Adam not to come back, and tomorrow, after their final trip to the drug store, she would tell him that she was going away to school. He had not been told.

The next day Jess packed her school uniforms, but included some dresses and skirts to wear off-campus. "Do you like this?" She held up a new red sweater. Adam liked anything red. He helped her fold clothes and asked if she was going on a trip.

"I am," she said and took his hand.

"Maybe I can go with you."

They walked to town, entering the drug store with the tinkle of a bell. Adam stared at the bell when he walked in. Sometimes at home he looked for a bell, wanting bell-sounds to announce him through every door.

Some boys on the baseball team called for Adam to come sit at their booth. Jess declined, but Adam was happy to be asked. Adam had served as bat boy for their team. These same boys, last spring, had trapped Adam in the locker room—closing him in a locker until he broke the door off its hinges. Adam never told what they had done, but Jess had heard about it at school. The boys were friendly to him now, and Adam still had the job of bringing bats onto the field, and carrying them off when practice was over. He brought cold water and catcher's mitts and gloves for all the players. He came early and left late, and the Coach had praised his reliability. "Best damn bat boy we've ever had," the Coach told him. That night at supper, when Clementine asked about his day, his smile spread wide, food inside his mouth visible.

As Jess sat at the counter she told Billy that she wanted a strawberry ice cream for Adam and a chocolate cone for herself. "When're you leaving, Jess?"

"Shh-h-h." She tilted her head toward Adam.

"You're lucky, Adam. You don't have to go away to school," Billy said.

"Lucky," Adam said. He was lifting out strawberries.

As they left for home Jess told him. "You know Adam, I *am* going to leave. I'm going to school somewhere else. That's why I have those new clothes, and that big trunk."

"Can I go?" He leaned to pick up a stick and break it.

"No. I'm going to Mt. Chesnee School for Girls. It's just for girls."

"I'll be real quiet," he said. His face contorted into a frown. "Ask Papa B. can I go too."

"Would you wear a dress?"

"No," he laughed. "No!"

"Okay then."

"Is it far?" he asked.

"Not too far."

"So then you can come back home?"

"At Thanksgiving, and at Christmas."

"Okay."

"You know what I'm going to do when I'm gone?" she said.

"What?"

"I'm going to write letters to you."

"I can't read."

"Your mama will read them to you. And I'll draw pictures of where I am."

"I can read pictures."

"You can. And another thing, I'll call you on the telephone."

Anything Jess told Adam proved to be okay, even this; but on the day she left, he would not come downstairs to say goodbye. Clementine tried to coax him outside, but he wouldn't leave his room; so Jess went upstairs and whispered something through the door. The door opened. She told him goodbye and said to remember about the letters, and that he could draw a picture and send it to her. That night he stayed up late drawing a picture of a horse and himself beside the horse. He told his mother to write beneath it: *Buckhead and Adam.*

But after a few days Adam began to ask when Jess was coming home. He asked over and over, and grew inconsolable. He went next door to play with Emily, but Mr. MacDougal called Clementine to come get him.

"Don't go near Emily," Clementine kept telling Adam. "You can't do that anymore, Adam. You're too big."

"She likes me. She calls me Buddy."

"I know. But you can't go into that yard anymore, Adam."

"Buddy. I'm Buddy."

"You can't go into that yard, Buddy." Clementine tried to convince him. "Her parents say no. And when parents say no that means no."

"Maybe she comes to *my* yard."

"Adam . . . "

"Buddy!"

"Buddy, her parents say no."

"Say no."

"Yes." Clementine sighed.

"Say yes?"

"No."

Even after three weeks Adam woke at night calling for Jess. Nothing comforted him. Edward took him to the zoo and bought new hubcaps for him, and Clementine prepared his favorite meals.

"I've never seen him like this." Clementine said. "Not even when Calder left."

Then one night, a fierce thunderstorm sent wind humming around the sills, and lightning haunted Adam's room. Adam yelled out. He would not stop yelling until Clementine sat on his bed and talked his head into a good place. She could do that for him. She talked about leaves, rabbits, and streams. Little stories. Little songs. Then she told Adam to go back to sleep, tucked the sheet around his neck, and put his blue raggedy horse on top of the covers.

The next day Edward took Adam to choose a puppy from a litter at the pound. Adam chose a yellow dog, medium-sized and eager, with a long tail and wagging tongue. They named him "Hap," after one of Edward's generals.

Clementine sat on the front steps and watched Adam in the yard racing Hap, trying to teach him to fetch a stick, or roll over. Adam demonstrated what Hap should do then fell down laughing when Hap didn't do it. Edward kept saying how good it was to hear him laugh again.

Adam

When Jess was not in her room and nighttime became too lonesome to sleep, Adam felt that his world had turned suddenly crooked and everything right was struggling against itself. Why did people go away? Everything Adam feared seemed to be taller than he was, and when that crooked world came in, what was real seemed dreamy and dreams seemed real. Sometimes he dreamed of animals coming in the door, big and small: a blue horse, one elephant, and two kitties with sticky feet. Adam wanted to pick up the dream kitties. He wanted to ride that horse back into his waking life. When he woke crying, his insides felt jumpy. At those times, an odd kind of splitting took place, tearing at his mind. When Papa B. gave him Hap he had to clean up when the dog peed. But at night, Hap slept in his room. Even on rainstorm nights, Adam pulled Hap's soft body onto the bed and, together, they hid under the covers. They lay huddled with eyes closed and slept inside a loose happiness.

— 15 —

For Jess, moving closer to Alabama had turned into an ambition. She had called the boardinghouse once, but Mr. Brennan was not there. She had wanted to hear his voice. "He'll be back around suppertime," the woman told her. "Who is this?"

"I'll call back," Jess did not want to leave her name, and she did not want Mr. Brennan to call her home. Last night, she called again from a phone booth outside a diner. The phone rang four times before she heard a voice say, "William Brennan here." Jess introduced herself.

"Jess," he said. "Were you the one who called before? Miss Tutwiler said some girl called. Where are you?"

"I'm with a friend from school," Jess said, "but I'll be leaving in a few days." She told him she would travel there by train.

He sounded glad to hear from her. "I'll let Miss Tutwiler know that you'll be here. I've missed seeing you. And I've missed your mother," he added. "Can I pick you up at the depot?"

Jess said she would call again and let him know her time of arrival. The idea of a finalized plan made her feel in control of her life, such as it was. She was a long way from Goshen, North Carolina.

Jess felt tired, but it was not the kind of tired she had ever felt before. The hope she had was like a tiny light seen from a long way off, though Lula was not a long way off now. Lula seemed within reach; still, her life in the woods was a challenge. She knew how to find a place to sleep each night, but, as the tyranny of dark came on, she kept a mental list of possibilities:

1. If the police find her, would she tell them everything?
2. What if she runs out of money?
3. Is jail worse than this?
4. She could go home or she could keep on until she reached William Brennan in Alabama.

5. She could starve to death in these woods.

She still had a few dollars left from her time with Pug and Ruby, and she sometimes had the company of dogs who joined her on the road; though, at a particular moment, they usually swung from the path—going back to where people cared for them. She waved them off, but liked their presence.

A station wagon with a mother and two young girls stopped to offer her a ride. She put her stuff in the back and imagined she might be driven all the way to Lula. She hoped they might take her to the front door of the boardinghouse.

The girls sat in the back seat. They dressed paper-dolls, wrapping small tags behind the cardboard figures, so that they could wear shorts or an evening dress. The girls smelled like candy.

"Where're you going?" the mother asked Jess.

"Lula, Alabama."

"Well, I can take you part-way." She smiled and seemed to want someone to talk to. "We're going down to LaGrange. My mother's house is down there." The way the woman said it made Jess think that they might be leaving a bad situation.

"Well, that's nice."

The woman told Jess about her husband, what he did and where they lived, but not his name.

"Are we divorced?" the oldest girl said.

"We're divorced," the mother finally said, but she whispered it.

The girls talked about what they liked to do at their grandmother's house, and showed Jess more clothes for their dolls. They were well-behaved, except for one round of fighting over a blue ball gown.

"Do you have someone?" the mother asked.

"He's over in Korea," Jess said. "We plan to get married when he gets back."

When they stopped for lunch, Jess figured they had driven almost thirty miles. She saw a sign pointing to Lula, but the sign didn't say how many miles it was. Jess asked the waitress, who said Lula was about sixty miles west.

The girls ordered hot dogs and said it was their favorite food. Jess didn't order anything, so the mother shared some French fries and ordered an extra hot dog for her, apologizing that she couldn't take her to Lula.

After lunch, Jess took her suitcase and satchel from the car and thanked the woman. She sat on a bench outside the restaurant, wanting to read a letter from Sam before going on. She knew them all by heart now.

Jess,

I can't even say what your letters mean to me over here. You asked me to tell you what's happening. Last night we went to a new position. Things were quiet until about 2 o'clock in the morning, then all Hell broke loose. "A" Battery had more than half their men wounded. Just before dawn, hundreds charged about 30 of us. We ran for it. My feet felt numb from the cold and I fell down. Six bullets hit just a few yards from me. So close and so loud! I watched a good buddy die—he had a stomach wound. I have never seen anything like that. My God. I wanted to kill everybody. I couldn't do anything. My whole mind is going deaf.

We had a truck carrying the wounded and, before I knew it, it was dark and the truck was surrounded. They killed the driver. After an hour we took our position back, and I drove the truck to the hospital. I was told that I might get a purple heart, but the truth is I don't know how I'm still alive. I'm sending a picture of myself and two other guys to show you that I am <u>still here</u>. The guy be-side me, with his arm crooked around the Howitzer, is Billy Keifert. God-damn, only an hour ago, he was firing it! Billy was the best friend I ever had.

I think about the time we spent together. I don't want to forget you. I don't want you to forget me. I hope I come back.

Sam didn't even sign his name to this letter, as if he were somehow disappearing. She thought how he was no longer getting any letters from her and he must wonder why. If she wrote, she didn't know what she would tell him. She stood and began walking. She felt resigned to maybe walking the rest of the way to Lula.

APART

— 16 —

J ess arrived at the Mt. Chesnee School for Girls with her trunk of new
clothes and the hope for a very different life. Her roommates, Katy Winborn, from Tennessee, and Doris Dodson, from Alabama, became her best
friends. Marie Coggins was a senior and, though she had spoken to Jess
briefly, she seemed not to want anything to do with her.

Katy, Doris, and Jess took French class together and, for almost two
weeks, had a crush on their teacher, Mr. Fruget, who was blond, big-shoul-
dered, blue-eyed, and wore plaid madras shirts with a tie. Most of the girls
in the dorm had fallen for him and, at night, they speculated about the
women he went out with—sluts or ladies. But their obsession ended when
they learned that he was married, with two kids.

On the night their fantasy about Mr. Fruget dissolved, five girls huddled
in one room and their late night talk turned to family secrets. Katy Winborn
admitted that her father was having an affair with his secretary. "That's why
they sent me off to school," she said. Another girl spoke of her mother's
nights of drinking then passing out on the bedroom floor. "Until she went
into a hospital, and now she can't drink at all. Not even one." Jess said that
her mother had died, and her father had remarried.

"How did she die?"

"She had leukemia," Jess said. "She lived for six months and finally she
was on so much medicine she didn't know who we were anymore."

"She didn't recognize you? That's really sad."

"She went to Mt. Chesnee when she was young. That's why I'm here. She
used to tell me about it. She was valedictorian."

"My mom was too," Katy bragged.

"What *is* leukemia?" Doris asked.

"It's a cancer, but the medicine she took made her really sick. I think she
saw ghosts."

"Ghosts?" Doris said.

"My dad said it was normal. The medicine was doing it. She had to take a lot for pain."

Jess did not tell them how her father sat all night, just waiting for a moment when Daisy might recognize him. She did not say how her father kept saying, "I love you Daisy. I love you more than life itself." He wanted her to respond, because whenever he said that in their Before-life, her mother had laughed—not in derision, but just knowing that he told the truth.

And Jess did not say how she went sometimes to the river, just for the company of water, for the easy sound of currents racing somewhere else. She liked to imagine on those nights that her mother would be carried like that, floating easy into a place where she would be waiting for Jess, and for her father. The night her mother died, Jess had gone to the river to stand at the place where a line of water pushed against the ground and made kissing noises against the riverbank.

"So when my dad married Clementine Finney," Jess told the girls. "I knew it was because she never saw anything that wasn't real. He knew she would never slip away into that other-world."

The next day some of the girls whispered about Jess's dead mother, saying they thought that she had gone crazy. But Katy and Doris remained loyal to their friend. Katy warned the girls that since Jess's mother was a ghost herself now, they'd be wise not to make fun of the spirit world. Doris said that haunting had been known to happen, and that she had read about a girl whose hair had turned to broom-straw overnight because she didn't believe.

"It could happen," Doris said.

The very next day a fire truck answered a false alarm at the school, and Sam Rafferty, in full fireman's gear (large hat and various tools hanging from his belt) strode into Jess's life. Jess and Katy and Doris were between classes when the fire bell rang and, soon after, three firemen came running through the doors. One nearly knocked Jess down, and Sam Rafferty stopped to see if she was okay. He held her arm longer than necessary. The principal announced that the alarm was false and told everyone to return to class, but the young fireman lingered to see if Jess would speak to him. When she did, he made a joke about the alarm, asking if she had set it off. He teased her about setting off the alarm and Jess grew irritated.

"Don't say that," she said. "Somebody might believe you." She turned away, hurrying down the hall toward class, but she looked back at him and smiled.

When Sam Rafferty asked a teacher standing nearby who that girl was, the teacher said, "Did she do something wrong?"

"No, ma'am," he said. "Just need it for my report." The teacher gave the girl's name, but Sam waited a day and a night before calling the girls' dorm and asking for Jess Booker. When Jess came to the phone he apologized and introduced himself. Sam Rafferty. Jess remembered him and, in fact, Katy and Doris had teased Jess about the cute fireman who seemed interested in her.

"I just wanted to call and say I was sorry." He was repeating himself. "I think I must have knocked you down."

"But you didn't . . . " Jess began.

"I could make it up to you," he continued. "I'd like to take you to dinner on Friday night."

"I don't know," Jess said. She wanted to go. "Can you call me tomorrow?"

"Sure."

Jess was not allowed to go out of the dorm without permission, and didn't believe she could get permission to go out with a fireman. The dorm counselor did not check the rooms regularly, but if she did come by, Katy and Doris promised to cover for Jess. They would say that Jess was visiting another girl's room. They were all taking a chance, but could not resist the excitement.

On their first date Sam took Jess to a small restaurant in town with a porch overlooking a stream. The waiter brought a candle to the table, and they could hear music playing on the inside, but mostly they heard the water riffling below. They went to that same place the next night, and on Sunday they walked around the campus. Jess showed him where she had her classes. Sam was nineteen and had completed two years of college, but had wanted a break. He became a fireman because it had been his childhood dream, and because he didn't know what else he wanted to do. On days he was not on duty at the firehouse he read with Jess in the library. Sam did not want to leave her side.

The next week he spent four nights at the fire station, but each night he called the dorm to tell Jess goodnight. All week they thought about each other and planned the next weekend. But the next weekend they did the very same thing, as though something magical had happened and they didn't want to lose it by changing their routine. They continued to walk around the campus on Sunday afternoon until six o'clock, when Sam had to leave. Jess admitted that she wrote notes to him during classes, but didn't want to show him. He confessed that he had written letters to her. He promised to bring his letters next weekend, and to write more. She agreed to bring her notes.

Katy and Doris got nervous and told Jess they didn't know how much longer they could protect her. One night the dorm counselor noticed that

Jess was not in her room and asked where she was. They said she was talking to a friend on a different floor. Jess was back in the room by the time the counselor looked in again.

By the third weekend, Sam suggested they go to a movie, where he put his arm around her and she leaned in close to him, and neither, afterwards, could describe what the movie was about. They exchanged their notes and letters and read them solemnly sitting next to each other on a bench. The air was chilly, and Sam took off his sweater and put it around her shoulders. Jess couldn't believe how he cared for her. He looked like a man swept away by love—his eyes not quite focusing on anything in the world, except her. She knew she liked him. Neither had mentioned the word love, except in the notes and letters.

During the summer Jess had kissed Billy, and even let him touch her breasts a few times, but she had never felt like this. Sam had not kissed her yet, though she knew he wanted to. One night when Jess did not get a call from Sam before the ten o'clock phone curfew, she couldn't sleep. She sat by the window and looked out on the campus. Maybe he would come by the dorm.

"Maybe he was called to a fire somewhere," Doris said, but the idea of Sam fighting a fire made Jess worry more. She had not thought about him putting out an actual fire, even though that was the way she first met him. She mainly thought of the length of his body, his eyes, and the way his arm felt around her shoulder. She wanted him to kiss her and thought she couldn't stand it if he didn't kiss her soon.

The next night, he explained that he had fallen asleep and when he woke it was too late to call. Then he suggested that Jess come to his apartment. He would make dinner for her, and she could bring books and study there if she wanted to. "But you may not want to. I mean . . . "

Jess explained that going to someone's apartment was against school policy. But the next day she decided to go anyway. She felt a new part of herself opening.

Katy and Doris tried to talk her out of going. "You could get kicked out of school," Katy said.

"I won't cover for you on this," Doris said.

So Jess applied for a weekend pass to go home. Her friends would not risk their own status at school, and the risk would be all on Jess.

Entering Sam's apartment, Jess noticed how it smelled like Clementine's kitchen. Sam had cooked a roast. She saw how neat everything was and asked if he had cleaned up for her. He always kept it this way, he told her.

The table was set with a candle in the middle, and Sam brought out two plates. Jess wore a pink Angora sweater that contrasted with her dark hair and eyes, and Sam's face had the expression of someone who had just been stung. When Jess sat down he leaned to kiss her cheek; then he kissed her mouth. The kiss was long and slow, and neither of them pulled away. They stayed silent for a while until Sam brought food to the table and sat down.

"I thought you would never kiss me," Jess finally said.

"I didn't want to scare you away."

They ate speaking about inconsequential things until dinner was over and the dishes had been washed and put away. They both knew what would come next, but they were shy about making love: Jess, because she had never done it before; Sam, because he had.

That night Sam approached Jess with a mixture of boldness and caution. He wanted her to be sure, so he asked if she would regret making love to him. Jess thought, briefly, before saying no.

"I wanted to do this the first time I saw you," Sam told her. He rubbed his head as though he couldn't believe his life. He was sweating.

The evening moved over them in waves, and all the grief of Jess's life flew from her. They sat on the couch and Sam touched her hair and arms and legs, amazed by everything. He couldn't get over her. They moved to the bed and he undressed her, then himself. He put their clothes together on a chair. They had no light except the candle he had brought from the dining room table. They kissed and held each other for a long time before he lay on top of her.

At first Jess felt stinging and a little pain. He asked if she was all right, and touched her as though he was handling something priceless. Jess felt surprised by the fact that she was no longer a virgin. She thought she should feel guilty about what she was doing, but didn't. She felt lightheaded and couldn't stop smiling.

The next day Jess walked to classes aware of herself in a different way. Sam called her several times during the day, checking to see if she was all right, saying how much he loved her. "I'm fine," she said. "I love you too." Each time she hung up the phone she felt a desperate longing to tell her mother about Sam. "Mama," she whispered inside the phone booth on the third floor of Granger Hall. "I hope you know about Sam and me. I hope you think it's all right."

Jess did not spend another night at Sam's apartment, but she went there on weekend days. They could not get enough of each other. Over the next few weeks they discovered ways to give each other pleasure, moving into unembarrassed intimacy and abandon.

Jess watched him, his head thrown back, eyes closed, sweat standing on his brow. She heard him whisper to her, blurting out his love. Afterwards he studied her body, barely believing the sturdiness of her legs and hips, the delicate skin of her thigh. Each time he undressed her he stroked her soft belly and marveled at the firmness of her breasts. They still went out to eat, or to a movie, but in the apartment they drew a circle around themselves and felt separate from the world.

One afternoon, as they talked through a sleepy love-haze, Sam admitted to sleeping with three women in his life: two girls and a woman.

"How old?" Jess asked, more curious about the woman than about the two girls.

"About thirty," Sam said. He said he wanted Jess to know everything.

"My God!"

"Yeah. It was a mistake. She had a little boy. He was almost three, I think."

"So what happened?"

"I decided not to go back."

"Because of the little boy?"

"Because of a lot of things." He sat up, because she was sitting. They could see their shadows on the wall, two figures blending together.

"Another thing you need to know," Sam said, confessing. "Something I haven't even told my parents yet."

"About that woman?"

"No," he laughed, but grew quickly serious. "It's about something else." He looked so serious that Jess was afraid he might leave her. "I've been drafted," he said. Sam would turn twenty in a month. "I got my notice a few weeks after I met you." He kept shaking his head.

Jess felt stomach-punched. She didn't know what to say, and hoped Sam might say he was teasing. She couldn't think of who to blame for this turn of events. "No," she said. "No. You can't go."

"I know." He couldn't look at her.

"Your parents don't know yet?"

"I'll tell them tomorrow. I leave for basic training on the first of October."

"That's just three more days!" Tears filled her eyes. "So soon? It's too soon!"

"Basic Training lasts eight weeks. I can get a leave after that."

"Will they send you to Korea?" Jess looked panicked.

"They haven't told me where I'm going." Sam looked scared too, but he lifted her face and said, "You know, don't you, that when I get back I want to marry you."

"I know," she said. "But what if you change your mind?"

"I won't. Training will be over before Christmas, so I can see you then. I'll probably be shipped in January."

Jess cried, softly at first, then she began to sob. Sam held her. "It'll be all right," he said. "Probably no worse than fighting fires. I tell the department tomorrow—and my parents. Right now, you're the only one who knows. You and the United States government. I hope, when I come home, that I can finish school." He smiled, but the smile looked weak and sad. "We'll get married." The promise sounded true.

Jess missed classes the next few days to spend time with Sam. Her roommates told her teachers that she was sick. And Jess and Sam spent hours talking about Christmas and when Sam could meet Adam. Sam had talked with Adam on the phone several times, telling him that he was a fireman. Adam asked if he could wear a fire-hat, but usually he wanted to speak to Jess again. Adam would not talk to Sam for more than a few minutes.

After three days, Jess was back in class and Sam was gone. She began to write letters to him immediately, and she called home more often to check on Adam. Whenever she talked to Adam, though, he sounded different. Her father admitted that Adam was receiving treatments at the Cadwell Institution. Adam had gotten into more trouble and the doctors were trying to help him. Jess could not pry more information, but Edward promised to explain everything when she came home at Thanksgiving. He said they were counting the days.

"And when should we expect to meet this Sam Rafferty fellow?" he asked.

Adam

Whenever Jess called home, she spoke to Adam first, asking if he had gotten her letters with pictures in them. He told her how he wrapped her letters in wax paper and kept them in a cigar box in his room. She asked if he had any new hubcaps. One night she said that she had met somebody named Sam Rafferty. She told her father about him. She said that he was a fireman.

Adam knew about firemen at the fire station—how they brought big fat hoses to a burning house, sprayed water to put out fires. Afterwards the house looked dirty and wet, smoke rising in big curls, everything broken and ruined. If no one was hurt, people clapped for the firemen—heroes who wore big hats and coats and boots.

After the phone call, Adam grew sad and went to his room. His mother tried to cheer him with his favorite foods. She prepared stew, with potatoes and turnips and carrots and gravy. Adam poured gravy on his bread, made it soppy. Papa

B. told him that Jess would be home for Thanksgiving. *When's Thanksgiving?* he asked.

Sam Rafferty, the fireman, was going far away to fight in a war. To fight the Communists. *Who are the Communists? They could be anybody. Are they the ones who took Jess away?*

Jess always told him the truth. She said she would come home at Thanksgiving. She told him not to be afraid of Communists. She told him to believe in God, and he asked her who God was. Jess said nobody could see Him because he lived in the sky and looked like air.

So now, with Jess gone, Adam tried to see God in the air and sometimes he imagined he did. He wondered if Sam Rafferty might be like that—a fireman in the sky, like air, and nobody could see him. But he knew Jess could see Sam. Adam only wanted to see Jess. She was the one he believed in. Even when she was far off, he believed.

The worst thing about Jess being gone was not finding her sleepy face in the mornings. Each day, Adam woke and went to her room. He wished he could smell her hair, wet from the shower. The black threads of her hair smelled like purple flowers or woods, sometimes, in the rain. When it rained at the river, they watched a huge wall of water—from sky to ground—come down the river, like a tall ghost. They raced it home.

Adam began to start fires outside in the grass. He thought about firemen. He thought about Sam Rafferty. He took a box of matches from the kitchen drawer and lit pieces of grass to see it burn, turn from green to black. Stiff strings. He liked to touch the patch of burned ground, feel the gray ash on his fingers. He lit a match to the blades of grass and thrilled to see the fire blaze and die, though sometimes the blaze skipped out of the small circle he had drawn, and he had to crush down the flame with his shoe. Emily came to the fence to watch him burn the grass. But he would not speak to her.

When his mother asked what happened to all those patches of burned grass, Adam didn't answer, but he could not find the matches after that. Still, he returned to the patches in the yard where, for a moment, flames had burned, where he had stomped out the fire with his shoe and Emily had watched him—where he, himself, had been the one to save the world from burning.

— 17 —

When she woke Jess believed she was deep in the woods, but as the sun rose she saw three hawks circling the roof of Possum's Grill and Bowling Alley. A low hill, with a surface of white stone looked glassy, even pink in the morning light. If anything, this day seemed promising. Jess had put many miles between herself and home and noticed how she no longer felt afraid of sirens. She went toward the grill and could smell bacon. As she opened the door, a woman greeted her. "You all right?" she said. "You look white as a sheet."

The woman's name was Possum. She was not more than five feet tall with a stout body, strong arms, and a thin face. She took Jess's arm and led her to a table. "I'll make you a bite to eat. We got bacon, ham, grits. You're our first customer this morning."

"I don't have much money," Jess explained."

"Well, let Burt make you something." She pointed to a man standing at the grill. You can wash your hands at the sink there." Jess moved more slowly than she knew. Burt dropped some bacon on the hot grill and it sizzled. He made two pieces of toast and had eggs scrambled by the time Jess sat down again.

"Now you eat something." Possum sat across from her in a booth, but Jess had already started to eat, not realizing that her head was down close to the plate and that she was shoveling food into her mouth.

Possum, a plain-faced, middle-aged woman, put her hand on Jess's shoulder. "Not so fast, honey," she said. "It'll still be there." Her skin looked wrinkled and splotchy, her eyes light green with yellow flecks; Burt looked more dilapidated and saggy. He cooked whatever orders were called out to him.

Jess ate everything on her plate, drank coffee and a glass of orange juice, and ended with biscuits and jam. "Why you walking along by yourself?" Possum asked. "Somebody chasing you?"

The question made Jess recall the *ike Ike* bumper sticker, but she suppressed it. "I'm going to Lula, Alabama," Jess said proudly. She liked having a destination and saying it.

"You look like you've been scared to death."

"I'm okay."

"You coulda fooled me."

Jess took out two dollars to pay for the meal.

"Lord, I don't want your money. Let's say it's on-the-house. Right, Burt?

"Okay with me." He kept cleaning the grill.

"You got a name, honey?"

Jess told them a made-up name, and Burt, without looking up, said, "Possum takes care of most everybody. Nobody much she's not willing to help."

When Jess exited the grill, she moved back toward the woods through feather-weeds and purple love grass. She was right; this day had been promising.

— 18 —

Jess came home for Thanksgiving to find Adam sedated, not himself at all; and Jess wondered if he was still angry at her for going away. They ate dinner and talked about Sam Rafferty's visit at Christmastime. Then Jess promised Adam that he could go with her tomorrow to see Buckhead; but Clementine said she had taken Adam out there yesterday. They had given Buckhead fresh hay and water. "Adam brushed him good," she said. "Gave him some apples." Edward bragged about how Clementine and Adam went regularly to the barn. They would take care of Buckhead until Jess came home for the summer. Adam was still picking at his food, and when Jess asked what was bothering him, he said he didn't want to go back to Cadwell.

Jess had heard talk about Cadwell, North Carolina's State Institution for the Mentally Ill. People called it an "asylum." Clementine said a lady had once suggested, years ago, that she send Adam there, but she couldn't do it. In Jess's civics class they had studied institutions and the teacher described Cadwell as a place with crowded conditions, with people sleeping in hallways or cuffed to the bed so they couldn't wander off. The small staff, overwhelmed by the load given by the state, had few choices. Sometimes patients were locked in a broom closet for the night. The teacher spoke of operations that made patients easier to handle. The word "eugenics" was mentioned. Jess could not believe that Clementine, or her father, would take Adam to such a place.

"You're not going to Cadwell, Adam," Jess said.

"Just for the day," her father said. "He's getting some more tests."

"What kind of tests?" Jess asked.

"They don't like for me to look at girls." Adam coughed nervously. "They say they'll help me not to look at girls."

"What's he talking about?" Jess asked.

Her father shook his head, indicating that he would explain later. So Jess said, "I'll go too," and Adam's face brightened slightly.

83

"No, honey," her father objected. "You stay here and see your friends. We'll be back in the afternoon."

"I want to go with Adam," she said. "I'll see my friends later."

After Adam had gone to bed, Jess asked her father and Clementine for an explanation.

"The doctor said that a series of treatments might make him not so, you know, sexually inclined," her father said. "We've been dealing with more than you know, Jess. Adam has caused trouble at the park and with a few of the neighbors' children."

"What's he done?"

"They have operations they do on these people," Clementine said, "but we wanted to try the treatments first." When she spoke she looked above Jess's head, as if she could not quite bring herself to meet the girl's eyes.

"*These people?*" Jess said, with a twinge of panic.

"Jess," her father said. "Adam's been bothering little girls at the park, and the grocery store too. We have to do something."

"Like what? What did he do?"

"He tries to hug them. It's getting worse. More parents are calling to complain. The police have been called in again."

"But he hasn't hurt anybody, has he?"

"No." Edward paused. "Not yet."

The next morning they rode to Cadwell, a two-hour drive. Adam squirmed in the back seat with Jess. He kept asking, "What'll they do?"

"They'll see how you've progressed. Ask some questions. Give you some tests." Edward tried to reassure Adam. After a short while, Adam fell asleep. He seemed drugged, and Jess asked if they had given him something. Her father looked awkwardly at Clementine.

Edward had a fringe of gray hair around his ears and the back of his head, but otherwise he was bald, and he had grown fat under the roof of Clementine's cooking. He explained to Jess that the doctor had prescribed some drugs to help Adam sleep, and to lower his sex-drive.

"And they give him shock treatments," Clementine said. "It's worked very well in many of the patients. They put electrical leads on his head, and Adam wears a kind of helmet so he can't pull off the leads." Clementine's face bore a look of tired acceptance.

"It sounds horrible," Jess said.

"Now honey, this is the treatment decided on by the doctors," her father said. "They know more than we do about these things."

As they drove onto the grounds of Cadwell, winter grass and shady trees made the place look like a campus. The buildings were gray stone, and most stood around two or three stories high. She could see a variety of entrances into each building, but the patients all seemed to be using one main entrance. Some patients wandered the grounds alone; some had a nurse or attendant with them. A group of people sat beneath a tree in a circle talking,; others were in groups, but not speaking to each other. Those groups each had an attendant.

"Wake up, Adam. We're here." Jess touched his arm gently to wake him.

The entrance to the main building had five columns. Vines of English ivy made spidery patterns over the gray stone, and the columns were a dirty white. The day was bright, and the buildings cast brownish shadows across the quadrangle, where cars were parked. Two men in white coats waited at the entrance, and one lifted his arm when he saw Mr. Booker's car.

Adam, still sleepy, saw the two men and began to yell. He looked to Jess. "What?" she asked him.

Before they had come to a complete stop, Adam opened the car door and ran across the lawn, bumping into a few people, knocking one man down. He ran without knowing where to go, until finally two young attendants in white coats brought him back to the entrance. They led Adam away, his head down. One man leaned to whisper something to him.

"We can't do this," Jess said.

Neither Clementine nor her father answered. They walked to a waiting room and each sat in a separate part of the room. Jess saw three people in housecoats roaming the halls. No one seemed to know where they were going.

After three hours, Adam was brought back to them. Jess and her father had gone to wait in the car and they both looked up when Adam came out into the crisp November light. He was holding his mother's arm and limped slightly on one leg. He seemed not to recognize anyone. Adam shook hands with Edward—a single quick pumping action, without looking at him.

Clementine said that the doctors had had a good session. "This was his second time," she said, "and he might need another one." Adam didn't speak all the way home, except to make small animal sounds, grunting whispers.

Jess kept trying to make him respond. Once or twice he tried to speak, said something about "going to the moon;" but his face, rising out of the collar of his new shirt, turned again toward the window.

"What are they doing to him?" Jess cried. "You shouldn't take him there."

"You have to tell her, Clementine," Edward said.

Clementine turned around to face Jess. "The doctor said he wanted to try a series of shock treatments, but usually they have to perform an operation. They wanted to try the treatments first."

"An operation? To do what?" Jess turned to touch Adam's arm. He jumped.

Cadwell, under state law, could perform shock treatments, lobotomies, hysterectomies. They could induce comas using heavy doses of medication. The dorms often had twenty patients sleeping in one long room. Some patients were strapped to their beds. But she did not know what her father was about to tell her.

"Jess." He looked straight ahead at the road. "We're probably looking at a kind of castrating procedure. For women they remove the ovaries; for men they remove the testicles." He had said what he dreaded saying.

Jess grew quiet as she leaned back and closed her eyes. "Don't do anything until I've talked to him. Will you promise me that?"

"I'll let you talk to him, but this is our decision. The doctors have explained everything to us."

"The doctors . . . " but she stopped, deciding not to argue. She only hoped she could prevent this future shadow-life for Adam. "What were those iron rings hooked to the wall?" she said. "I saw iron rings on the wall in one of the rooms."

Her father looked at the road, without speaking, then said. "I didn't see those."

They rode awhile in silence. "Is he able to talk?" Jess finally asked. "He hasn't said a word."

"The doctor said he would be talking again by tomorrow." Clementine looked like a statue. "We have to do it," she said to no one.

That night Adam slept without waking once. Hap slept on his bed beside him. But Jess could hear Clementine crying downstairs. Jess found her in the kitchen, her head on the kitchen table. She was sobbing hard. When Clementine looked up, Jess was making cocoa for both of them. Neither said a word until Jess put two cups of steaming chocolate on the table.

"My biggest fear," said Clementine, "is that Adam might be put in jail. I wouldn't be able to help him then. He wouldn't understand what had happened."

"How will he understand *this*?" Jess said.

"Cadwell gives me a way to keep him out of jail. What other choices are there?" Her jaw was set hard, and she looked both angry and sad.

"Anything," Jess said, but she couldn't think of another choice.

Clementine sipped her cocoa, but tears streamed down her face and fell into the cup.

"Don't do this," said Jess. "We can talk to him about sex. Maybe he'll understand."

"I wouldn't know where to start," said Clementine. And it was true.

Adam

When they put the helmet down tight on his head, he said, No. He said, No, no. The doctors held him down, clamped cuffs around his ankles and wrists. He felt locked in. Cold. He twisted his hands in the cuffs, trying to pull them out, trying to take off the helmet. They kept saying they didn't want him to hurt himself. Adam could smell the doctor, how he smelled; and medicine, how it smelled; and he begged to go home. So he went home in his head. He went to be near Hap, where Hap licked his face and hands, in his head.

The fire came in through the leads placed so carefully on him. He wanted them to stop, told them to stop. He tried to move over—inside his body—tried to settle the fire, the fear of more fire, but the burning continued over and over until they were through. He thought about bees stinging, stinging. His vision blurred until his mother led him by the hand. When he could smell his mother, he knew the fire was gone. No more for a while. He saw Papa B. and Jess near the car, but he could not name what a car was, or who they were, and he could not form words in his mouth. Words were gone, but Adam was not gone.

Adam waited for words to come back, then Jess said something about Hap and he remembered Hap, but he couldn't smile or move his mouth in the way he wanted to. He wore the face of somebody else. He did not know where he was, but he knew they were driving somewhere. He rolled down the window and let air blow onto his face, into his mouth. They passed small shacks nestled in trees, and poor people living in broken-down huts. They passed old tires under porches and hubcaps in a yard, silver and shiny, the sun making them too hot to touch. Adam remembered hubcaps, but he did not remember yesterday. He sat in the car beside Jess, his window open. Air cooled his face. He tasted the wind. He hoped they were going to the ocean now. Maybe they would never leave.

As they crossed a long wooden bridge, a man leaned over the rail. Adam wondered if the man could swim. Below, he heard the chop-chop of water. The river looked wide, and Adam thought it was the ocean. Jess told him they were going home now, that they were leaving Cadwell. Adam wondered if Cadwell was a place for bad people who had to be punished.

"Voltage," he heard somebody say. Bright lights and stings of lightning. Men wore white. Everything looked white like in a cloud, like moving in space without a place to land, like spinning toward a thousand worlds. He smelled something burning, not like grass. Did somebody say, "Voltage"? Somebody said, "Lobe" and "brain." Somebody said, "Man in the moon."

What was this other world of white, this moon-landing, this lack of gravity, and love?

— 19 —

Sam planned to visit Jess a few days before Christmas. He had completed boot camp and would leave soon for Korea. Jess drove her father's car to the train station, and all the way to the house he described, in a bragging way, the hardships of Basic Training. Jess tried to prepare him for the tension in the house. Clementine now, strained by her determination to protect Adam, carried a burden finally too large for her heart. She was civil, but distant, and Edward worked hard at remaining reasonable. Jess told Sam that she was bringing him into a home that even she did not recognize.

As they pulled into the driveway, Jess could see their Christmas tree inside, with bubble lights and tinsel. Bubble lights had been her mother's favorite part of the tree, and Edward insisted they stay part of their tradition. They got out of the car and heard Clementine yell from the kitchen window, "They're here!"

Sam wore his army uniform, and Jess knew her father would be pleased to see a man in uniform. "This is Sam Rafferty," she said, without needing to introduce him. "He's *Private* Rafferty now."

Sam put out his hand, friendly and straightforward, toward Mr. Booker. Everything about his uniform looked crisp. The belt buckle glowed bright and flat at his waist, his cap held neatly under his arm.

Edward smiled at Sam, but tried to gauge the worth of this young man who had stolen his daughter's heart. He couldn't help but distrust him. "Are you going overseas soon?" he asked. He kept his arm around Jess.

"Yes, sir. Pretty soon."

Edward led them into the living room and motioned for Sam to sit down. "Do you know yet where you've been assigned?"

"No, sir, not yet."

"This is Miss Clementine," Jess said, politely, but without much affection.

Sam addressed Clementine as Mrs. Booker, before she could say that she had kept the name Finney. Sam looked surprised, so she explained that it was Adam's name. "I wanted to keep it easy for Adam."

Jess turned to Adam, who had come into the room and stood in the doorway without speaking. "And this is my Adam," she told Sam.

Adam's eyes beamed, though his complexion looked sallow and old. "I'm her Adam," he said. "I don't have a uniform."

"You want to try on my cap? I don't have my fire-hat with me."

Sam placed the Garrison cap on Adam's head and straightened it. "You look just like a soldier, Adam." Adam rushed to see himself in a mirror, and Jess noticed that, as he ran, he limped slightly on *both* feet.

"Come on and eat supper," Clementine called. "Before everything gets cold. We made Christmas dinner a few days early, so you could share it with us." She was being overly cheerful. "Save room for dessert."

The dog followed closely on Adam's heels and plopped down at his feet beneath the table. "This is Hap," Adam told Sam.

"Named after a general, I'll bet. 'Hap' Arnold?" Sam looked to Mr. Booker. Edward nodded, impressed but not wanting to be won over too quickly.

"Seems like Jess has already told you everything about us. Maybe you should tell us about yourself."

"I'm a rookie fireman in Mt. Chesnee," he said. Sam wanted to feel comfortable, but felt tension all around him. He did not know if the tension was due to his presence in the house, or if this is the tension Jess warned him about. "I finished two years of college, but stopped. I've been working for the fire department for almost a year."

"You plan to finish college?" Clementine came in with dressing and a bowl of sweet potatoes topped with marshmallows.

"I do. In fact, if I hadn't been drafted I might have gone back this fall."

"How did you and Jess meet?" Edward asked. The turkey was already on the table and Edward took the long carving knife to begin cutting.

"We met the first time when a fire alarm went off in her dorm. False alarm. One of the girls pulling a joke," he said.

"Not Jess, I hope," Clementine said.

Sam leaned down to ruffle the hair on Hap's back and rubbed his ears. "Not Jess. But I got to meet her that day. Fell in love right then, actually."

Everyone looked up at once. Even Jess was surprised— not that he loved her, but that he said it so bluntly. So soon. They had not even said the blessing yet.

"Well," Edward sliced off a leg and began to cut thin pieces of white meat.

"And we've been seeing each other ever since." He wanted them to know how he felt about Jess before he went away. He did not have time for coy politeness.

"Well, it's still early," Edward said. "You're both young."

"Yes, sir." Sam turned to Adam. "Jess told me about Adam, and about Hap here too."

"And my hubcaps?" Adam asked. "I have a lot of hubcaps. You want to see?"

"Sure."

Adam moved to get up.

"Not now, Adam. Wait till after supper," Edward said. They said the blessing and Edward served their plates with generous amounts of turkey. Adam helped himself to a large spoonful of sweet potatoes and three rolls. He kept rearranging his cap, which he wore through the whole meal. Just before he, had second helpings of turkey, he stood and sang "My Country, Tis of Thee," but he didn't know anything after "Of thee I sing."

"I'm hoping General Eisenhower can get us out of Korea pretty soon," Edward said.

"President," Clementine said. "He'll be inaugurated soon and he'll be *President* Eisenhower."

"Well, I'll probably always think of him as General. You know much about generals, Sam?"

"I've heard about General Patton, and Omar Bradley."

"Well, those are two big ones. And, of course, MacArthur. You should remember him, especially since you shake hands and walk a little like him."

"I do? Maybe that'll help me over there."

Edward laughed through his nose. "Might help you get fired! Truman lost my vote when he relieved MacArthur! Dumbest thing I ever heard!"

"Don't get started," Clementine said.

"It's not just me. The man was a war hero." He stopped himself from complaining more. "Anyway, maybe Sam here will be a war hero."

"I told him not to," Jess said.

"Not much chance of that," Sam responded. "They'll probably have me putting out fires."

Edward reached to offer Sam more dressing. Clementine rose to bring in apple pie and a coconut cake. When she left the table Jess leaned toward Sam. "Something's wrong," she whispered. "Adam's limping on both legs now."

"Pie or cake?" Clementine offered.

"I don't like coconut," Adam said. He asked for apple pie with ice cream. Sam chose cake.

"Adam?" Jess asked. "Were you limping a little while ago?"

Her father interrupted before Adam could answer. "Lots of young men around Goshen have left for Korea. Many are back now though. If Ike can just win this war. If anybody can, he can."

Jess turned again to Adam; his Garrison cap askew, but still on. He bent over his pie and ice cream. "Adam, what's the matter with your leg?" Jess reached to raise his pant leg and saw a band of purple-bruised skin around his ankle. She raised the other pant leg to see the same of bruises. "What happened to your ankles?" she said.

Clementine's eyes flicked toward Edward and they both slumped slightly. "He had a treatment at the doctor's office and they had to restrain him a little," Clementine said.

"*A little?* What did they use?"

"Jess. Let it be." Her father did not look up.

"Adam?" Jess continued interrogating.

"Jess!" Her father spoke sternly. "I'll talk to you about it after supper."

Jess stood up. "It's after supper now."

Adam stood too, thinking they might all go somewhere.

Jess turned toward Sam. "Sam, don't you want to see Adam's hubcaps?"

"Sure do." Sam got up. "Leave my cake right there. I'll finish it in a little while."

"More than a little while," Clementine said. "You don't know how many hubcaps you've got to look at." She smiled, not a real smile, and began to clear the table while Jess and her father went into his study.

Edward told Jess everything.

While Adam was visiting a family across the street, he tried to kiss their ten-year-old girl. Two policemen came to the house and explained that a restraining order had been filed. Other neighbors were filing similar complaints, so that Adam could no longer enter the neighbors' yards.

"They don't want Adam talking to their children. The children are afraid of him," he said. "So the officers issued a warning and said they couldn't keep answering complaints without some kind of action. It was an official warning."

"What were the other complaints?" Jess asked.

"When he was carrying out a mother's groceries, he picked up her little girl to put her into the car."

"He thought he was helping," Jess whined.

"And at the park he chased a girl. He lifted her up."

Jess's face closed tight.

"Not the first time. If it keeps happening, he'll go to jail. So . . . " Edward could not look at Jess. "Adam has to be moved to Cadwell. He'll have to live there. We don't have a choice now."

"For how long?" she asked.

"They didn't have an opening until May. We'll take him then."

"But, how long does he have to stay?"

"Jess, honey. Look. He could end up in jail. Don't you see?" Edward sat on the sofa and Jess sat beside him. "They can help him. He can't control himself. We have the problem of his sexuality." He spoke slowly, embarrassed at having to say it at all. "The doctors say that sexual drive in the retarded is a normal thing. They have all the normal desires, like anybody else, but they don't understand what's happening." Then he asked Jess a question that had lingered in his mind. "Has Adam ever been inappropriate with you?"

"No." She did not look at her father. At times, Adam had touched her back and shoulders with tenderness. Once when she was sleeping he came in and touched her face. She said, "What happened to Adam's legs?"

"It was during the treatment. They used metal clamps."

"You can't let this happen to him, Daddy."

"What can we do? We can't keep him locked in his room all day!"

"But that's what an institution does!"

"No. They have activities and a place to go outside, and doctors, and even classes."

"What kind of classes? Can he take his hubcaps?"

"Probably not."

"Daddy!" she wailed.

Her father walked to the window, looking out as if some answer might appear. "When Clementine looks at Adam now," he said, "she looks at him as though he is already gone." He turned back to Jess. "Somebody called the other night," he said. "Claimed they saw Adam peering into a window. I didn't even tell Clementine." He waited a long moment. "I think he was looking for you."

"I could come back home. I could leave school."

"No. I won't keep your life on hold for Adam. And I won't let *you* do it either." He walked toward her, held her. "Not an option. Your mother would never forgive me." Jess liked when he mentioned her mother as though she were still alive.

Later that evening she told Sam what her father had said. Sam suggested that Jess go with Adam when they took him to Cadwell. "You should be there with him," he said.

"I don't think I can do that."

"It'll be hard on you," Sam said, "but easier on Adam."

"I wish you were going to be here."

"You'll write and tell me everything," Sam said. "I'll write you every day. You'll get so many letters from me you'll be sick of them."

"No." She wiped her face on his shirt. "I won't."

"I'll write to Adam too," he promised.

Jess loved this man. She loved him more than she thought it was possible to love anyone. Tonight she would sneak into his room to be close to him. Sam would sleep on a rollaway bed in the room where Clementine kept her new electric Singer sewing machine. She still did sewing for people in town, but not as much since Adam had been in trouble.

Jess went to tell Adam goodnight. "Remember after the bee stings, when I used to put a muffin on this bedside table?" she said. "So you would wake up and find it?"

Adam laughed. "Papa B. still does sometimes," he said. "But Hap eats it before I wake up, and crumbs spill everywhere."

"Did you show Sam your hubcaps?"

"Yeah. He said he would bring me a new one next time he came here."

Jess helped Clementine clean up the kitchen, and Edward talked with Sam in the living room. Probably about generals. Jess had told Sam that she would come to his room when everyone was asleep. The idea made Sam nervous, but he didn't tell her not to come.

At one-thirty a.m. Jess tiptoed down the hall, stepping on boards she knew would not creak, but if she did make a creaking sound she rushed quickly over the spot. When she got to Sam's room, she pushed the door slightly, but the sound of opening made her stop so she squeezed her body the rest of the way through. Sam stood beside the bed, and they sat down, huddled together.

Sam moved to close the door.

"Don't," Jess said. "It falls open again, and makes a sound when it does. We should lie down on the floor, I think. We can be quiet." They slid to the floor, pulling a blanket and two pillows from the bed. They touched each other, barely whispering, and gave long silent kisses.

"We have to do this fast," Jess told him.

Sam touched her legs and breasts until he pulled her on top of him, then turned her over. Only their swishing and turning could be heard. "This is crazy," Sam said. "Your dad would throw me out so fast."

Jess wanted him and she urged him inside her. This memory would have to last a long time. She couldn't help but make little noises. As they lay back, happy, but not quite sated, they heard Clementine's voice in the hallway. Jess stood and pulled some cover around her.

"Adam, what are you doing up?" Clementine said.

"Nothing," Adam was standing in the hallway, near their door. "Get back in bed. Did you go to the bathroom?"

"Yes, ma'am."

"Okay then. Go back to bed."

Adam went to his room and closed the door. Jess listened for Clementine's bedroom door to close, hearing her father ask what was wrong and Clementine explaining, while Jess slipped quickly down the hall to her room. She lay awake wondering if Adam had stood at Sam's door, if he had seen them.

The next day they opened a few early Christmas presents. Sam would leave that afternoon to spend the rest of Christmas holiday with his parents. Adam gave Jess the first present—a necklace made out of metal and beads. "I made it at Cadwell," he told her.

"It's beautiful, Adam." She held it up to her neck.

"I hate Cadwell."

"Next time you go, maybe I can come back from school and go with you." Jess still wasn't sure she could do it.

"You will?"

She gave Adam the coveted Cadillac hubcap with chrome covering the spokes. It was wrapped in red tissue paper with a huge green bow. She gave Sam a photo of them both on a hillside. An old farmer had come by and she had asked him to take their picture. All day they had walked the countryside, unable to leave each other. "You can take that with you," she said.

Sam gave Jess a record album that included their song "The Glory of Love." When she opened it, they both sang together:

You've got to gi-ive a-little, take a-little,

And let your poor heart a-ache a-little,

That's the story of, that's the glory of love.

Adam

"Nothing comes easy," his mama had told Adam, as if he did not already know this lesson better than most, as if he did not wake in the night in some lonesome space with wide bands of emptiness.

When Adam saw Jess go into the room where Sam was sleeping, he put his head in the crack of the door and saw them rolling on the rug. The blanket flopped off. Jess lay naked—the way he had seen her once in the shower—and Adam's heart hammered in his head. Jess kissed Sam's mouth, and rolled on top. She made sounds like a kitty.

And Jess said, Yes. She said, Yes, like that. Then his mother came into the hallway. She said, Adam, go back to bed. Adam, what are you doing? He said,

Yes, ma'am. And the apple pie smell was everywhere, like suppertime. In his room Hap lay asleep on the floor.

After a little while, Adam heard Jess in the hall. She stopped at his door. She touched the doorknob, but did not come in. The shape of her in his mind was soft like roses, with a sound like kittens. And Adam felt mashed down, pushed into the ground under honeysuckle where he played Hide-and-Seek with Jess, getting tangled in the vines until she lifted his arm and pulled him out.

His room was dark now; everything was dark now. Light came from the bathroom and Adam cried softly, his face ran in the dark. Hap jumped onto the bed and licked him, but Adam could not forget seeing Jess lean over Sam. Nothing inside him could be quiet; but he lay in his bed, his arms and legs like a man floating in the water. He stayed that way, mashed down, until he was asleep.

— 20 —

The return to school, without Sam close-by, was lonelier than Jess had imagined. She looked for his letters each week, and though they never arrived regularly, they came in packs of three or four at a time with postmarks from odd looking places. When Katy brought her three letters from the post office, Jess took them to the corner of a study room to be alone.

Jan. 18, 1953

Sweetheart,

I'm thinking about you right now. Every part of you. You know what I mean? I wish I could come to the campus where you are and walk under the trees. But I'm so far from that! Last night air strikes made these hills shake. I'll tell you this, I understand now what my training was all about. Yesterday when we landed and waded ashore, I remembered "not to run in water, to let the waves carry you." Then, as soon as we hit ground, we ran. You never know what you're going to do under fire, but we found out real fast. Big guns fired from ships to the shore, but I didn't know we were being shot at until I saw slugs hit the sand beside me. We ran full speed to find cover under a hill of ground. Another thing from training, "don't fall on the ground when running under fire."

Planes fly over us all the time. You can see how nobody sleeps much at night. Right now is pretty quiet or else I could not be writing and thinking about you. Now I will sleep, and maybe dream too.

Jan. 1953

Sweetheart,

I'll be glad when this war is over, and I wish it was over right now. Your letters come and I read them so many times. You can't even know what they mean to me. I got two from you today. I keep them in my pocket. It makes me feel normal to read your letters. And nothing here is normal.

Yesterday we got new vests, and a good thing! We had to string barbed wire in front of the infantry positions. We were loading the wire and stakes when we heard Chinese mortars firing just over the hill. I ducked down under some old railroad cars, so did everybody else. My lieutenant (Lt. Frank Mason from Kentucky, kind of quiet, shy) said we better get out of there. We ran down the hill and under a bridge, and walked down the middle of a river about a foot deep.

When we got back to camp, somebody with a bullhorn said, Hit the deck! We all fell down flat real fast, and these lights come on, searchlights, and our guys start shooting with machine guns. Jess, that weapon is crazy. Bullets come out like from a fire-hose. But it was _our_ guys firing, so bullets went right over our heads. They chopped down those Chinks. When I looked back, I could see how close they'd been. I could've thrown a rock and hit them. They had bayonets. But after the machine guns started firing, they took off.

Seems like I've been here a long time already, but it's not even a month yet. I keep your picture and look at it every night before I sleep. I'd like to have another one of you. I like when Adam draws pictures for me. Anything. I'll write a letter to him. Tell him that.

Jess opened the next envelope with her thumb, and hoped that President Eisenhower could make the war end soon. This letter was short, different.

Jess, maybe I shouldn't say this, but two days ago I shot a guy at close range. And, even though I've shot the enemy plenty of times, it was never so close before. I saw his face when he fell. He was young, probably sixteen. He saw me too, and said something. I don't know what. When I shot him he fell right next to me. Blood was everywhere. Maybe I shouldn't say this. I lay for a while in a ditch next to him and pretended we were both dead. I could feel his uniform against my arm, and knew he probably had somebody at home waiting for him too. I hope I never have to do that again. And when we're not fighting, we're just waiting for something, food, letters, a night maneuver. I don't know. I don't know why I'm here.

Over the next weeks Jess reread Sam's letters, weaving them into her days and nights like a strong fabric. She didn't tell Katy and Doris what Sam was saying. His letters felt like a secret. But she did tell them about Adam. "He'll be sent to Cadwell in May. He has to live there!" She shook her head. "Sam thinks I should go when they take him." She got quiet before admitting, "I don't want to. I don't want Adam to think I'm the one deciding to send him there."

Katy agreed with her, but Doris sided with Sam. Doris was the kind of girl who thought it important to do the hard thing, rather than the easy thing. She had come to Mt. Chesnee two years ago and last year had won the Danforth Award for character. "What he'll remember is that you were with him. He'll know you'll come back to see him."

"You don't understand," Jess said. "After they operate on him and he has more treatments, he might not even know who I am. They do lobotomies there."

Neither girl knew what that was.

"It's when they operate and take out what makes Adam Adam. They cut out part of the brain, so he won't feel much. Just calm. Sometimes it damages other areas too, like speech or memory. After a while, Adam may not know any of us, not even Clementine."

"Why does he have to go?" Katy asked.

"Clementine can't stand the thought of Adam going to jail. She really can't stand it."

"She can stand *this* though?" Doris said.

"I guess she can stand Adam being under a doctor's care more than the thought of jail."

"Some choice," said Katy. "What will you do?"

"I'll probably do like Sam says." Jess sighed. "I don't know."

It was three weeks before Jess got another packet of letters. The girls all had mid-terms that week, but Jess was only half-prepared. She knew she wouldn't make herself study any more. She waited until the other girls were asleep and stepped onto the porch at the end of their hall.

Mar 1953

My Jess,

What I did not say in my last letter is that while I was in that a ditch I saw blood coming through my own sleeve and pants, but the medic came and fixed me up. If you get a wire saying I was wounded, just ignore it. I am telling you the truth. I was only grazed, and though there was a lot of blood, nothing was hurt. I wrote to my parents too, so they wouldn't worry, but who knows when they, or you, will get my letters.

Anyway, we moved back out of the line of fire for a few days, so I'm getting some rest. It feels good to sleep all night long, keeping both eyes closed. This afternoon I walked beside a river and found these two violets, and I'm sending them in the letter. If it's getting to be spring here, maybe it's spring there too. I'm just now beginning to see the importance of little things, but don't know how to explain what I mean. There's so much wreckage over here. These fucking people have been living like this for so long. Excuse my language, but how do they stand it? This country is so small, and with so many people. They all look alike. It's hard to tell the good ones from the bad ones.

The moon is full tonight and I am sending you two violets from a river near where I am. So that is something good.

Jess lifted the smashed, dry violets and held them to her lips. She wanted to smell something of the fragrance, but couldn't. The petals were still intact and she left them in the letter as he had sent them. Some of the purple color lingered near the center.

Dear Jess,
It must be almost April by now. Nothing much to say. It's been raining for twelve hours straight. We were flooded and the water supply was screwed up for a couple of days. We move out tomorrow. There are so many times when I'm out in the field and I want to talk to you, like tonight after everything is set up and in position. Nothing to do but lie here and think about why the man behind me and in front of me gets killed, and I don't. I spend more time thinking about saving the guys around me than I do killing the enemy. If we don't watch out for each other we'll get our shit blown away. Excuse the language, but that's the way we say it over here.

If it weren't for the other guys around me, I don't know what I'd do. My God, all we do is just wait for another day to start and finish, and keep following orders. It helps to think you are listening to me. I just wrote to my Mom and Dad, but I don't tell them what I tell you.

Another one, short, scrawled, written quickly:

I was about 12 yds behind the red panel that shows the end of friendly territory. All of a sudden a mortar came in. It hit my Captain and killed the radio operator. The Capt. started walking towards me, holding his chest and I was lying on my stomach looking up at him. He almost fell on top of me. He went to the hospital. He is all right, I think. Then another mortar hit and it lifted me about a foot off the ground. I got a piece in my arm, but I'm okay. I don't know what kept me from being killed. Maybe I was so close to the explosion that stuff just blew over my head. I don't know. But that radio operator (I didn't know him very well) told me to write his wife if anything happened to him. He has a boy, 5, and a girl, 2. When I think about writing that letter I get nervous. I don't know what to say. If you hear that I've been wounded, don't worry. The medic fixed me up and I'm fine now. I hope I come back home soon. I hope for a lot of things.

Silent lightning flared up like a huge sheet in different parts of the sky. *Sam. Sam.* Jess heard her breath soar out of the silence, and imagined that he could hear her call his name half-way across the world.

As time grew close for Adam's trip to Cadwell, Jess knew she would go with him. She wondered if Clementine had thought about the fact that he might die there, or worse: he might live a dead life. With so much on her mind, her grades were suffering. Finally, she called her father.

"We can't do it," she said when he picked up the phone.

"Jess. The doctors have assured us . . . "

"I don't believe them."

"It's Clementine's call, Jess. She's Adam's mother. She gets to decide."

Jess did not argue with that reasoning. "How is he? Can I speak to him?"

Adam came to the phone and told Jess about Hap and the tricks he knew, and the booby trap he had made with a bucket, pancake batter, marbles, and grape jelly. "I put it over the door so it would fall on somebody, but Papa B. found it."

When Edward got back on the phone, he asked Jess about Sam. Jess told him a few things, and her father made sympathetic sounds through the phone.

When they hung up, nothing had changed.

— 21 —

It was the end of April and the middle of the night when Jess arrived home. They would leave for Cadwell on Wednesday and she had a day or two to be with Adam. When she opened the door, the house was dark. Everyone was asleep. She went to Adam's room and woke him.

"Hey," he said, sleepy-faced.

"I just got home," said Jess. "It's late, almost two a.m."

"Is it tomorrow?"

"Well, yes. I guess it is.

Adam looked at the clock. Over the last year he had learned to tell time but with the series of shock treatments he had forgotten some things. "It's tomorrow," he said. "Are you home for good?"

"Not for good," she said.

"Do I still have to go to Cadwell? Don't make me. I won't be bad anymore."

"You're not bad, Adam."

"I'm bad for touching. Police man came." Adam stared hopelessly at Jess, his hand rising up, then stopping in mid-air.

"Listen," she said. "Let's go downstairs and get a snack."

Adam threw back the covers. He wore pajama pants, but no top. His shoulders looked broad but he had lost weight and Jess could see his ribs. He slipped on some socks and Jess told him to put on his robe.

They went downstairs quietly, not speaking until they reached the kitchen.

"I don't want to go to Cadwell tomorrow."

"You're not going tomorrow."

"Is it tomorrow now?"

"You're not going today or tomorrow," she said. "Not until Wednesday. What do you want to eat?"

"Milk-toast." Clementine usually made milk-toast, sprinkled with brown sugar and cinnamon, when Adam was sick. It comforted him, and Jess believed he needed that now. He might not get it again.

They both ate milk-toast and drank the rest of the sugary milk from the bowl. When Adam put down the bowl he reached to touch Jess on the lips, but suddenly halted. Jess's heart cracked at the thought that Adam could never touch a woman. His normal desires, without direction, were stifled completely. She felt pity for all the tenderness he felt, but could not show.

"It's okay," she said. "We're friends." So Adam ran his fingers over her lips and cheek, then touched her hair and shoulders, as he might stroke a puppy.

"I like you, Adam," Jess said. But Adam didn't speak. Jess rose to turn on the radio over the stove. "You want to dance?" She found a slow song. "Remember when I taught you dance steps, and took you to my school dance? You liked that, didn't you?"

Adam nodded and stood to take the correct position—the way Jess had taught him. He stood like a manikin as Jess placed her hand on his shoulder, then lifted his other hand into the air. Adam laughed as they glided around the kitchen. Neither spoke, as music softened the room. He leaned to smell her hair. When another song came on, Adam wanted to dance again. He looked excited now and, as Jess moved in close to him, she could feel him grow hard against her. When he did, Adam caught his breath and made a sound. He was breathing hard. He didn't know what to do with himself.

"Adam?" Jess shifted under the pressure of his hand at the small of her back, their arms still in the air. Maybe this had been exactly the wrong thing to do, Jess thought, but in a few days it wouldn't matter. After the operation, it wouldn't matter. "Adam?" she said again.

Adam jerked away from her. He murmured words too indistinct to hear, talking to himself rapidly. He had a look of terrible guilt. "I won't," he said. "I won't make you mad."

He turned and scuttled away down the hall into his own room. It was not enough to say that she knew how he felt; she didn't know, but she hoped that she might have offered more pleasure than alarm.

"Adam! Come back! I'm not mad."

Adam came to the doorway and leaned against the jamb, and Jess walked over and kissed him lightly on the lips. Her hope was that Adam would feel some release in his bones and that the voices in his head could find a gentle gratitude. She hoped she had given him something, anything; she hoped she had not, instead, unleashed more dark loneliness.

"Now you know what kissing is," Jess said, smiling. "But you can't go kissing anybody else. Hear?" Then she added. "Adam, you're a good kisser."

He smiled and turned to go back to bed.

The next morning at breakfast Jess told Clementine that she had gotten in at two a.m. and she and Adam had come downstairs and made milk-toast. Clementine smiled.

"I'm a good kisser," Adam said, but Jess shook her head hard.

"What did he say?" Clementine turned to face them both. At that moment Edward came in and welcomed Jess with a big hug of his own. "Did Clementine tell you that Calder was coming? He's going with us to Cadwell." Edward seemed relieved that Calder (instead of himself) would be the one to sign Adam into the hospital. Adam smiled at the thought of seeing his father.

"He won't be here until the day we go," said Clementine. "He wanted to stay for several days, but I didn't want that. I wanted us to have these last few days together." What Clementine did not say was how she was afraid that Calder might make the whole thing more difficult. He had already objected to sending Adam away.

Over the last days Clementine's old thoughts were returning: how it would have been better for Adam if he had never been born, how the world offered nothing but hard choices for him. A few weeks ago she mentioned her thoughts to Edward, saying she wished Adam could suddenly get sick and die, then she could care for him until his death. "I wish he could die here under my care." She put her hands to her face.

"Clementine!" Edward couldn't believe his ears. "A life is a life. You mean it would be better for *you?*"

Clementine was sorry she had said anything. "You think Adam really wants to live the life he'll be living?"

"I think they'll take care of him. Doctors and nurses will care for him every day." Edward didn't know what else to say.

Clementine shook her head furiously. "Still." Edward left the room. He could not listen.

The family spent the next couple of days together; but, to Jess, the time felt like a death watch. On the day before they went to Cadwell, Clementine packed a large bag for Adam and sobbed behind closed doors. No one wanted to stay in the house. Edward went into town to settle things at the store and go by the bank. Clementine bought groceries for Adam's favorite meal of Salisbury steak and gravy and biscuits. That evening they would go to a movie, one with cowboys that Adam had chosen.

So, in the afternoon, with no one in the house, Jess and Adam walked the path to the river. Adam wanted to tell the river goodbye, but kept repeating how he didn't want to go away. He walked ahead of Jess and held his shoulders back as if they were braced. There was a force in him, but a force that was held caged. His eyes over the last couple of months kept a blank look, as though forgetting had already set in. His gait was awkward over the bumpy path. Still, he walked fast.

The day had turned sunny, but the air held a chill that, in a few weeks, would be gone. They walked past a weeping willow where Adam reached for a limb and swung forward landing flatfooted. His jacket was new and red, and had a brown corduroy collar that he liked.

Once, he turned and looked at Jess, and it seemed as though he might laugh. Then he ran forward yelling, "Last one to the river is a rotten egg."

— 22 —

For a whole day an upcountry river had rolled along beside her, and Jess wanted it to follow her all the way to the boardinghouse. In the late afternoon she saw the mouth of a rickety barn. She slept there all night in the smell of new hay, and woke to a dog barking. Jess sat up to see if it was close-by.

She washed her face and brushed her teeth in a stream at the foot of the hill, then checked to see how much money she had. Not much. The dog still barked, though his barking had grown hoarse and frantic. She thought he might be hurt, so she stepped through the trees to look. The dog, a mixed breed—something between a hound and a German shepherd—was tied to a dog house with a long chain.

A man walked across the yard toward the dog house. He carried a base-ball bat and stumbled as though he were drunk. He yelled at the dog, and Jess moved behind a tree to watch. The dog was about a hundred yards away, and could not stop barking until the man raised his bat and swung hard, missing the dog, at first. It circled the dog house, shorting the chain. It cowered with the approach of the man. The man had him trapped, so the dog began to growl and tried to bite the man's leg. This time the man did not miss, but missed the dog's head, hitting it somewhere around the mid-section. The dog cried out with a woman-sound, a high-pitched yelp that told Jess his ribs had probably been broken, maybe more. Then the barking stopped, but not the man, who reached back again and brought the bat down hard onto the dog's head this time, ending the suffering.

What struck Jess was the dull sound of the blow and the blood that sprayed so variously with the force of the bat, and the man's face that held a look of calm determination. He wore a blue chambray shirt with trousers too short and a cap that shaded his eyes, but not his expression. His hat had come off with that last blow, and he picked it up. He was not over forty, with shoulders broad as a lumberjack's. The house, this man's house—a creepy structure, dark inside, though the porch light was on—loomed behind him. He stumbled towards it. The dog's head, Jess could see it, was not recognizable, though his lower body convulsed for a few moments before it lay still.

Before the man opened the screen door, he turned and, in one terrible moment, looked straight into the woods. At first, Jess imagined that she had blended in with the trees, then she slid down slowly to move out of sight. She did not believe he had seen her, but his eyes seemed to pick her out. She knew he could use that bat on her, do the same thing to her, without a hint of reservation. He entered the dark house and closed the door.

Jess hurried toward the road and stumbled as if she, too, were drunk. The sun was almost up, and a Negro woman stood in her doorway waving Jess over.

"What are you doing in this part of town?" she said. "You shouldn't be here." Jess moved straight toward her voice. When she got close, the woman grabbed her arm to bring her inside. "You hear that dog? You see what happen? You better get out of here. Where're you going, anyway?" Then she turned her head toward a man in a back room. "He finally did it, Eli," she told the man. "Murphy finally killed that dog. Come help me get it. We'll bury that creature. Least we can do." She turned to Jess. "You see it?"

Eli listened while Jess described what she had seen. "I'm not going over there, Gracie," Eli said. "You crazy, if you go. He could do the same thing to us."

"Well, I'm going," said Gracie. "At least, you can get me that little wagon out back."

Jess followed Gracie and said she would help.

"I can do it myself." But Gracie did not refuse the help. "Knew it would happen someday." They pulled the empty wagon toward the man's house. "Murphy's a mean drunk. Known him for years. He used to be good to his dog, but he went to jail twicet, and come out mean. Like he is now." Jess followed Gracie, a big woman with legs like stumps. They walked straight into the man's yard and saw the dog short-chained and dead. Blood covered his head and eyes, and his mouth had frozen into a strange grin.

"I been bringing this creature food ev'ry night. He bark 'cause he hungry, that's all." She leaned to unhook the chain and began to lift the dog's hind legs. The dog had urinated on himself and Gracie wanted to spare this girl that, at least. "You get the head, what's left of it. We can take him away. He's done now with all his suffering." She spoke as though she knew something about suffering herself.

Jess lifted the bloody head and front legs. Blood soaked her pants and shirt, but she couldn't help that. The dog's middle drooped, and Gracie put one hand under its stomach, then shifted the body into the wagon. Gracie's arms seemed to be all muscle. When they pulled the wagon out of the yard, Jess saw the man standing at the window watching them. He stood very still. The sun was coming up over the hill.

"Don't look at him," Gracie said. "No telling what could set him off." They left, and buried the dog behind the grill.

"Now we gonna wash up," Gracie said. "Then you gotta go. I swear, you not big as a kitten."

"Yes, ma'am."

Jess entered the bathroom and found it sparkling clean—not new, but clean. She removed her bloody clothes and washed her face with a bar of soap, rubbing it with paper towels. Somebody knocked on the door.

"Just a minute," Jess said.

"I brought you a rag and towel you can wash with," the woman said. "And some other clothes I think can fit you. Just thow those ones away."

Jess unlocked the door and the woman stuck her brown hand around the doorsill, giving her the rag, towel, and clothes. The dog's blood lay smeared on Jess's arms and legs. She scrubbed hard, then washed out the rag, seeing red, gritty water move down the drain. She washed herself until the rank smell of dog had drained away, and she began to smell like the soap itself— slightly disinfectant and barely sweet. She saw a bottle of Jergens lotion on a table where toilet paper and extra soap were stacked. She lotioned herself all over, until her skin began to feel smooth again.

She even leaned into the sink and washed her hair, soaping and rinsing until her hair began to squeak like baby birds. She took a brush out of her bag and brushed until the water was out. She tried to wipe the floor with paper towels, but hesitated to use all of them. One of the clean shirts had a ragged ribbon around the hem, and Jess tore it off, choosing the ribbon to tie her hair into a ponytail. She felt fresh when she exited the bathroom, but the image of the man hitting the dog kept playing in her mind.

Gracie had already cleaned up and wore a dark dress and apron. "Just set down here," she said. Gracie was not young but not old, her skin slightly lighter than coffee, her hair short and oiled. Eli was black as coal. His eyes, arms, and face were all one color of black. "Where you goin'?

"Lula, Alabama."

"You almost there. Too far to walk, though. You got any money?" Then she turned to Eli. "Eli, give this girl enough for the bus ride. She won't need to be walking all that way."

The man looked up from where he was sitting in what Jess knew must be his favorite chair. "How much you want?"

The sun no longer burned red over the yard where the man called Murphy had killed his dog. The dog lay covered with soft dirt, positioned in a shallow grave. Jess saw that Gracie was not afraid of Murphy, even as they lived next to each other; and she marveled how this man with an impulse toward such cruelty lived in such close proximity to Gracie's kind efforts toward consolation. The thought disturbed her.

When Jess left she looked like a different person—her face shining, her hair wet, but growing long again. She smelled like a mixture of Jergens and lye soap. "Don't come back around here," was the last thing Gracie said before she went back inside.

Eli called to her. "Bus depot's in the middle of town. Right next to the fire station."

Fire station. Jess's heart leapt at the thought of a fire department, of maybe running into a fireman named Sam Rafferty. And though she knew he would not be here, that he was far from home, in another country, in another world, she looked for his face anyway.

As she passed the firehouse, three men came out. One whistled at Jess and she waved. They could not guess how much her life had changed in the last two-and-a-half months. She thought about riding the bus, the ease of just sliding smoothly along the highway, sitting in a comfortable seat and not lugging her suitcase and satchel.

— 23 —

The bus driver told Jess that he was going all the way to Gadsden, Alabama, but that Lula was one stop before Gadsden. He had only eight passengers, but would pick up others on the way. She climbed on and walked midway back, sitting huddled against a window.

Jess thought again of the muddy brown and white car with the *ike Ike* sticker, and felt clear of it now. She hoped she would never see it again. Everything about that car seemed like trouble. And she had not forgotten the appearance of those two men coming up so fast in the woods—the older man's fat nose, the boy's furtive glance, their sudden exit as though they had never really gone. And the slick salesman in the car, her quick escape. Pug and Ruby's Esso Station and Possum's generous breakfast. But, even more vivid in her mind's eye, was the brutal way the bat came down on that dog, and Murphy watching as Jess and Gracie rolled the dog away in the bloody wagon.

She clutched her satchel tightly on her lap and settled into the comfortable seat. No one sat near her, but someone had a transistor radio and she could hear Patti Page singing "The Tennessee Waltz." She rode awhile with her forehead against the cool window. It was toward the end of July, and the weather had turned hot and lush. Plumes of cattails and stalks of bee-blossom grew beside the road. Wide fields bloomed full with cotton plants. Jess felt new life forming all around her.

A newspaper lay on the seat beside her and Jess examined it for casualties or deaths from the war. She looked for the name *Sam Rafferty,* and was relieved not to find it. She could barely think of the war without thinking of Sam lying hurt somewhere in a ditch. She read an article that described the UN's proposal; the article said the war could end soon.

She took out the pack of Sam's letters. She knew whole paragraphs by heart, and liked the idea of reading fragments of them as she rode along.

Anything could have happened during these past months, but reading his words kept her hopeful.

My whole mind is going deaf. . . . I don't want to forget you. I don't want you to forget me. I hope I come back.

What do you think of this war?

. . . that radio operator . . . a boy, 5, girl, 2 . . . told me to write his wife . . . When I think about writing that letter . . .

. . . the truth is I don't know how I'm still alive.

Last night . . . all Hell broke loose . . . We ran for it. My feet felt numb from the cold . . .

Six bullets hit just a few yards from me . . . I watched a good buddy die . . . stomach wound. . . . I wanted to kill everybody.

. . . I wish I could come to the campus where you are and walk around under the trees . . . I am so far from that.

A few new people boarded the bus. The radio person had turned the music down, but Jess could still hear it, a slow song with violins. She looked again through the newspaper, reading that some American soldiers had come back home in June. Then she saw, under a list of missing persons, her *own* full name next to a school photo. Jess stared at the photo for a long moment. She looked nothing like that now. Her heart stuck large in her throat and the memory of leaving Adam at the river that day filled her head. All her decisions, since then, seemed to be made from a different mind.

But Adam, now, would not suffer shock treatments or drugs or locked doors. He would not have the operation. He would not leave home. He died in a river going to the ocean, and Jess, in her private self, felt relief. She tucked the newspaper in her satchel as the drift of ground moved beneath her.

Maybe she would call her father. Let whatever happens happen. She remembered on television shows where the person robbing a bank was caught, or a gangster on-the-run was found. "The jig is up," the cops would say. Jess felt that now. She didn't know what a jig actually was, but it seemed to be just about up.

After a while she fell asleep to the gentle rocking of the bus and the tinny-sounding radio playing Tony Bennett's "Rags to Riches." When she woke, the bus had stopped.

She was here.

REPRIEVE

— 24 —

Jess approached the town square in Lula, and saw, first, a diner—Honey's Last Stop. The air smelled of wild onion and honeysuckle. She wore a dark blue skirt that ruffled around her knees and a white blouse that pulled slightly across her breasts. Her hair was growing long again, curling around her neck and shoulders

Honey's diner was a neat place with booths and tables nicely spaced. Behind the counter was an overweight sixty-year-old man who looked as though he might have grandchildren and could be patient with anyone. Jess asked if she could use the phone.

"You looking for a motor court?" The man wore a tag on his shirt that said Leonard Reese.

"I'll be staying at the boardinghouse. Mr. Brennan said he would come get me," Jess said. "And I'm looking for work." She had seen the Help Wanted sign in the window.

"That boardinghouse is just down the street. You could walk there," Leonard Reese told her. "You had any experience waiting tables?"

"A little," Jess said. "I'm a fast learner though."

Leonard wiped down the counter in front of him. "If you know Mr. Brennan, I'm willing to try you out, I guess. See how you do. We could sure use the help." He leaned on the counter. "When can you start?"

She told him she could come in the next day.

"That's fine." A couple paid their bill. Leonard pushed four keys on the cash register and gave them change. "See you later, Lenny," the man said.

Jess walked to the back of the diner toward a sign that said Restroom. She washed her face and hands, straightened her skirt, and brushed the dust off her shoes. When she came back, she sat in a booth and observed how the waitress took her order: how she wrote everything down and then called out the order to a cook behind the swinging doors.

The waitress, Maggie, brought Jess a ham and tomato sandwich with two pickles on the plate. "You the new girl coming to work here?"

"I think so."

"That's good. We get worked to death around noon and again at six o'clock. This's the best eating-place in town." Maggie was short, and older than Jess by about twenty years. She wore a white uniform with a light blue apron and a white hat propped on top of her head. "So, when you starting work?"

"Tomorrow."

Jess ate her sandwich. For once, she was not very hungry. Maggie brought a large glass of iced tea. "We got good chocolate cake." She patted her round belly and smiled.

"Not today. I'd better go to the boardinghouse. Mr. Reese said I could walk there."

"Lenny. Call him Lenny. Everybody does. Even me, and he's my daddy." Maggie slipped into the booth with Jess. "Miss Tutwiler runs that boardinghouse—just two blocks away. You can't miss it."

"I've been there before," Jess said. "My mother knew Mr. Brennan, and we visited when I was little."

Maggie stood when three men came in. She waved and scooped up four menus. "Henry coming today?" she asked the men. "He'll be here directly," said one.

Jess went to the cash register to pay Leonard Reese for her meal, but he said she could eat here for free now that she was hired. "Want you here tomorrow by nine. I can get you ready for the lunch crowd. I pay seventy-five cents an hour."

Jess left two dimes on the table for Maggie and started walking.

The sign on the lawn said Tut's Boardinghouse, and its turrets and intersecting roof looked exactly as Jess had remembered. She knocked on the screen door and could see the dark, high-ceilinged hallway. Miss Tutwiler, a short woman with deep green eyes, greeted her. She wore a scooped-neck dress and had a handkerchief tucked in her bosom. "Lenny called and told me you'd be coming. He said you're working for him, and that you were a friend of Will Brennan's." She looked cautiously at Jess, but invited her in. "Did he know you were arriving today?"

"No, ma'am," Jess said. "He offered to pick me up at the train, but I didn't know exactly when I would be here, so . . ."

"We have two rooms open. You can choose which one you want. Where're you from?" She wanted some kind of explanation.

"Mr. Brennan and my mother were childhood friends. I came here when I was ten, but you probably don't remember me."

"I do remember a woman and a little girl. I guess that was you then."

Jess entered a corner room with two windows that looked out over the back of the house. Woods came up within a hundred yards of the back porch.

"Now, where'd you say you were from?" Miss Tutwiler's eyes squinted to inspect Jess more closely. Jess lifted her suitcase onto the bed and felt the sting of this woman's scrutiny. She kept her back to Miss Tutwiler.

"I am so tired," she said. Jess stood almost five feet eight inches tall. The small of her back had a curved posture that made her appear proud. She carried herself erect, even when tired.

Miss Tutwiler took the hint and closed the door behind her.

All Jess wanted to do was soak in a tub for a long time, wash her hair, and sleep for a few hours. She walked down the hall to the oversized bathroom, filled the big claw-foot tub, and lowered herself into warm water that closed up around her arms and neck and breasts. Jess couldn't believe the dirt and dust that collected in the water. She washed her hair vigorously, soaped herself again, luxuriating, and almost fell asleep in the tub.

After drying off, she slipped on her underwear and borrowed a robe from the back of the door. She heard voices downstairs. In her room Jess lined up her toothbrush and toothpaste, hairbrush, and comb on the counter just above the private sink. She combed her hair, shaking it dry. Her body glowed from the bath, and light had come back into her eyes. Her brows, dark and naturally arched, made her forehead translucent.

She unpacked her suitcase: three shirts, two skirts, a dress, a pair of jeans, a pair of shoes, the pair of old boots she had found (but would throw out now), two coats, socks, and some new underwear, stolen and still unopened.

She placed Sam's letters in a drawer beside her bed, and what came to mind was the first time Sam had removed his fireman's hat. Her cheeks had filled with heat. She felt dazzled by his light brown hair, his blue eyes, his face, serious, important. He had filled the dormitory hall with his presence; but Jess felt struck hardest by his laugh. She had made him laugh and, when he did, his whole face changed. She had thought every eye was fixed on him. And, later, when she returned to the classroom, her math teacher called her to the blackboard to work a difficult algebra problem. She solved it without even trying hard; and she thought, *this is love.*

Jess felt foolish remembering that younger self, which was only last fall, and she wondered about Sam's face now, if the war had changed it. She wondered, too, if she might be ready to call her father and even imagined dialing the number, but knew she could not bear to hear his sad voice through the phone. Then she lay down and slept the sleep of someone who believed that maybe everything was going to be all right.

— 25 —

Around six o'clock someone knocked on her door. Jess startled awake. The house smelled of chicken stew, and Jess could hear the voice of Edward R. Murrow on the television downstairs saying something about the war.

A man's voice said, "Jess? It's me, Will Brennan. Miss Tutwiler sent me to knock on your door. See if you want to have dinner with us. I'm glad you're here. And hey," he said, "an armistice was signed today. The war is over. Did you hear?"

Jess slipped into some jeans and a t-shirt. "It's over?" she yelled. Sam would be sent home. She opened the door. "It's really over?"

"Sure is. It was on the news just a few minutes ago." Mr. Brennan looked older than she remembered, but he had an amiable face and he walked her downstairs to the dining room, where six people already waited at a big table. "Eisenhower threatened nuclear power. That's what pushed them into the armistice."

"China had to stop and think, at least. When China came in, we *had* to make a big threat." Miss Tutwiler touched Mr. Brennan's arm and smiled. He held her chair and sat beside her. They looked like a couple. Two little boys sat on the other side of Miss Tutwiler and she told them to put their napkins in their laps.

Shooter, who was eight, wore a baseball cap that said Birmingham Barons, which he kept turning around on his head. He wanted someone to notice. Ray, almost six, wore a Mickey Mouse shirt. He had a cold and kept wiping his nose on his shirtsleeve. Miss Tutwiler told him to use a tissue, but he didn't.

"Tell us where you got your baseball cap, Shooter," Mr. Brennan said.

"Rickwood Field," Shooter said, leaving the cap sitting backwards. "We went to Birmingham and saw them play there."

"Yeah," said Ray. "I got one too." His mouth was full of potatoes.

A young man named Frank O'Malley, who appeared to be not much older than Jess, sat beside Albert Chapin, a professor with a moustache and glasses. The professor talked about the POWs. "That was a real sticking point, you know." He spoke as though he were teaching them something.

"Frank works at the newspaper," Will Brennan told Jess. "Think you might get to write something about this armistice, Frank?"

"Not likely." Frank looked more interested in Jess than the end of the war. He could not take his eyes off her. She was the only one even close to his age in the house. "That's a good color on you," he told her.

"What?"

"Red. It's a good color on you." Frank blushed and went back to the subject of war. "Seems strange to end a war without unconditional surrender."

Rosemary Owensby sat beside the professor. She wore a pink satin dress and had a pack of Viceroy Cigarettes tucked in her belt. She stood and leaned across the table to greet Jess, "I wondered if it would ever come," she said, one arm held out straight in front of her, as though she had been in charge of ending the war and wanted to be gracious about it.

The table could easily accommodate four more people, and Jess wondered if some of the boarders were absent. She thought of Sam and suddenly, her eyes filled with tears.

"Somebody you know coming home?" Miss Tutwiler asked her.

"Yes, ma'am. I know somebody over there."

Frank took note.

A Negro woman brought in steaming bowls of vegetables and a huge platter of chicken stew, with two bottles of ketchup to be passed around the table. The honey-colored woman was tiny, probably a little over a hundred pounds, but no one looking at her would think she was anything but capable.

"Zella's been with us for five years," Miss Tutwiler said. "Best cook in this county."

Zella smiled, a smile that said she had heard this before.

"Zella Davis," Will said, introducing Jess to her, "this is Jess Booker. I knew her mother when we were kids. She'll be staying with us for a while."

Zella nodded to Jess and put the platter down in front of Miss Tutwiler.

"And she already has a job at Honey's. Waitressing," said Miss Tutwiler. She turned to Will and asked the question Jess had been curious about for years. "Was Jess's mother your girlfriend, Will?"

"I wish that had been true," Will said, without apparent embarrassment. "No. Day never saw me that way. Then when she met Edward Booker, she never looked at anybody else."

"Day?" Jess looked at him curiously.

"Everybody called her Day in high school."

Her mother had a name she didn't know. "Day," she said under her breath.

"When's your daddy coming back, Shooter?" Zella asked. She turned to Miss Tutwiler. "Mr. Long's not coming to supper again tonight?"

Shooter turned his cap back around and pulled the bill down over his eyes.

"He's still looking for a job," Miss Tutwiler said stiffly, but she glanced at Will to change the subject.

"Mr. Brennan . . . " Jess began.

"Everybody calls me Will." He served himself some stew. Jess wanted to ask about the name "Day," but didn't know what to ask.

Shooter laughed. "He has a middle name though. Cor-*ne*-lius."

"You weren't supposed to tell anybody that."

"*Noblesse Oblige.*" Prof. Chapin taught Latin at the high school, and never let anyone forget it.

"My name's Ray," said the other little boy, who seemed left out.

"That's a fine name for a little boy," the professor said.

"I'm not little anymore," Ray said. "I used to be."

"You and Shooter are big enough to pull in that bluegill today," Will announced. You did a good job of it." Will and these boys were friends, anyone could see.

"Where're you from, Jess?" Rosemary had inherited money that never seemed to diminish. She held her fork in an awkward pose, leaning slightly forward, feigning interest. "Didn't your mother used to visit here with you, awhile back?"

"Yes, but she died a few years ago," Jess said. "Leukemia. My dad and his new wife took a trip, so I came to visit a friend in Gadsden." Her words sounded practiced. "I'm from North Carolina."

"I remember when you were born," said Will. He turned to the boys. "She was born in a river. You ever heard of that?"

"Gah!" Shooter said.

"And I even remember it," Jess mused. "I mean, being underwater, everything murky, then breaking up through the water. I remember it like that."

"Murky," Ray said.

"That's amazing." Frank sat up straighter in his chair, and paid attention to everything she had to say. He had been sneaking glances throughout supper.

Rosemary, who defined herself as a kind of social director of Lula, interrupted the talk, "Would anybody like to hear about my plans for the Christmas-in-July party next Tuesday?" The annual summer Christmas party was always held the last day in July, and had been going on for many years, long before Rosemary arrived at the boardinghouse.

"What's that?" Jess asked.

"Oh, it started with my father when he was running this place," Miss Tutwiler said. "He did it one year. Seemed kind of silly, but it's been going now for twenty-five years. People liked it. I can't imagine July anymore without it."

The invitations were sent out weeks ago. Christmas lights and decorations waited in the garage, and ingredients for cakes lay in the pantry. Rosemary had taken over the preparation for the last five years, and though everyone around the table liked the party, they dreaded her military style of planning.

"I need to assign a few tasks." She held her fork in the air, ready to make a pitch. The satin on her sleeve fell into the stew gravy.

"Not now," said Miss Tutwiler, who could barely tolerate Rosemary.

"I was thinking that if we . . ." She knew they would help, but their help usually came at the last minute. She tried to ignore the gravy dripping from her sleeve.

Zella piled dirty dishes noisily onto a side cart. "Peach pie?" she offered. "Who wants peach pie?"

They all did.

— 26 —

Two days later the boardinghouse buzzed with talk of Sonny Long and when he might (or might not) come back. He had been gone for almost three weeks. He had left to look for work, but packed all his belongings in the car and had not called home. The boys asked about him every day and cried at night.

"He took all his stuff," Ray wailed.

"He's looking for a job a long way off," Will explained.

"But why didn't he take us with him?"

Jess heard Ray's wailing, and came in just as Will was saying, "Your daddy's just down the road somewhere. No need to take you boys with him."

Frank explained to Jess that Sonny Long had left to look for work before, but he had always kept in close touch. This time he hadn't called or given any indication of his plans. "Miss Tutwiler worries he might not come back at all. The boys' mother left a year ago. Nobody's heard from her."

"So what would happen?"

"They'd go to the orphanage near Birmingham, I guess. I mean, we don't want that. But Miss Tutwiler says she could get in trouble if she doesn't report it. She might lose the boardinghouse. She's threatened to call Social Welfare." Frank shook his head and smiled. "Will Brennan says 'over his dead body.'"

The first thing Jess noticed, and liked, about Frank was the deep tone of his voice. Everything he said sounded true, like a radio announcer. He wasn't handsome, but had a rugged look, slightly mischievous, and he always seemed to know where she was in the house.

"Could they stay here?" Jess asked.

"I think so." Frank had the look of someone who wanted to ask a question, but was making himself wait. "We all watch out for them anyway. They'll go back to school in September."

He was nervous whenever he spoke to Jess. Finally he asked. "Who did you know in Korea? I mean, do you have a brother in the service?"

"No," she said. "Not a brother."

The next day Miss Tutwiler bought two goldfish in a bowl with pebbles and plants. She did not allow pets in the house: "No cats, no birds, no anything" she had said. But she made an exception for fish.

"I thought you boys might like it," she said. "Let's keep them here in the hallway so, when your daddy comes back, he'll see them." Shooter pressed his nose against the glass, and Ray stuck his hand in the water to scare them. "You can name them anything you want." They named one Goldie and the other one Truck.

Each night the boys looked out the window, hoping to see their father drive up. In the morning they looked again to see if his car was there. When Miss Tutwiler told Will that she had called Social Services, he was furious.

"Damn, woman." Will paced the length of the room. "That was a foolish thing to do."

"But we could get into legal trouble for this, Will. We can't be responsible."

"Sonny Long will come back, I'm sure of it. Anyway, I'm not letting some agency take the boys away."

"I'm not with you on this, Will." Miss Tutwiler was almost whispering now. "I can't lose everything."

Later that day a policeman and a lady from the local Social Service Agency came to ask about the two boys who had been abandoned by Sonny Long. Will and the professor stood together, walling off the lady and the policeman from the rest of the house. Zella stood with Shooter and Ray in the kitchen doorway. Jess hid at the top of the stairs listening. She was still not comfortable around policemen.

Frank saw Jess in the hall and stood with her, listening to Will and the professor talk to the social worker. They leaned on the stair railing, their arms barely touching.

"Sonny Long went to look for work," Will told the lady. "He'll be back. It's taking longer than expected. Miss Tutwiler shouldn't have called you. She just misunderstood."

"We hate to have wasted your time." The professor sounded authoritative. "I imagine Mr. Long would be angry if he returned to find his boys taken by Social Services. He might decide to sue. Anyway, he called just the other night."

"He did?" Shooter said. "Nobody told me. Why didn't anybody tell me?"

"Is my daddy coming home?" Ray said.

"We can take care of them," Will's voice sounded firm, in charge. "Heck, we've *been* taking care of them. The professor here has already taught them some Latin. Say something, Shooter." He motioned for Shooter and Ray to come out from the kitchen.

"Anon," Ray said.

"E Pluribus Unum, and Anon," Shooter said.

"See?"

"Vini, vedi, vici!" Shooter looked proud.

The Social Services lady turned to Miss Tutwiler. "If Mr. Long is coming back, we can't call it abandonment. But," she said, "I'll be checking in again real soon." She and the policeman turned to leave.

"Quanta?"

"Shut up, Shooter," Will whispered. "Let it be."

"But you *told* me." Shooter thought for a moment. "Vere furis." He smiled at his own proficiency, and the professor nodded.

"What does *that* mean?" Will asked.

"It means, *You must be mad.*"

"Well, I'm *not* vere furis," Will said.

That night Jess helped put the boys to bed. Shooter told Ray that, since the lady and the policeman didn't take them away, it meant that their daddy was coming back. Shooter already knew how to comfort Ray.

"So is he coming back tomorrow?" Ray asked.

"Probably not tomorrow," Shooter said.

Jess turned back their covers and brought them each a glass of water. She showed them a photo of Buckhead, anything; but the boys stayed at the window watching for their father's car, until tiredness closed their eyes and they stumbled into their separate beds.

— 27 —

Pauline Tutwiler had a pretty, round face and a full figure. Her hair was white and framed her face like cotton, but she carried herself as if she were young, swinging her low hips like a girl. She was in her mid-fifties, ten years younger than Will. Her eyes were a deep turquoise color, changing hue with the colors she wore. And though she was mostly a cheerful woman, she kept alive, her suspicions about people. She had repeatedly voiced to Will her suspicions about Jess, and though he told her not to worry, she did so again at breakfast. "She's running away from something. I'm just telling you to keep an eye on her."

"I'm taking care of things," Will said. "You need to trust somebody." He spoke with a mixture of affection and frustration. "Like *me*, for instance."

"Don't start, Will. I'm not in the mood to be courted today."

"Well, let me know when that day is," he said, crossly. "If it ever comes. No wonder you aren't married. You don't let anybody come within twelve feet of you."

"Don't start. I mean it."

"You got it, Pauline." He left the kitchen mumbling. "Where's Shooter?" he said. "I'm seeing if he wants to go fishing today."

"It's Sunday." Zella Davis had given everyone a lesson at breakfast about keeping Sundays holy. She had definite ideas about how Sundays should be spent. Zella attended the One-Way-Up Baptist Church. The marquee in front of the church had a finger pointing up to heaven and the word ONE was capitalized.

"Am I gonna get another lecture?" Will said.

"Not from me. Honey, if you'd heard my first lecture we wouldn't be having this conversation."

"Is there a moral to this?"

"I can give you one, you want it."

"How did I know that?"

"We're talking breadcrumbs here." Zella drummed her fingers on the kitchen table. "You may be hopeless."

"You just want me to go to church." Will laughed. "Tell me, any white people in your church?"

"Not if we can help it." Zella smiled in spite of herself.

Will went out the side door calling for Shooter. Jess came into the kitchen and poured some coffee. She stood with Miss Tutwiler at the back door and watched Will and Shooter walk together across the yard. Will Brennan was a good-natured man, even his irritation felt good-natured. He was tall, with thick grey hair, grey eyes, and a deep, measured voice, that sounded like Gregory Peck.

Miss Tutwiler's eyes grew soft as she watched Will walk away, and she confessed to Jess that she had almost married at the age of nineteen. When the boy had proposed he assumed that she would leave Lula, leave her father, and move away with him. "I couldn't leave," she said. "I didn't marry him, but I didn't know I wouldn't have another chance."

Pauline Tutwiler had managed the boardinghouse with her father since she was fifteen. He had owned the place for twenty-five years. Her father had taught her how to hire and fire people, judge a tenant, keep food in the pantry, and get a handyman for the inevitable repairs. Pauline learned her job so well that when her father grew sick, she ran the house and looked after him until he died. "By then," she told Jess, "it was too late for marrying."

Will and Shooter had moved out of sight now and Miss Tutwiler said she was leaving for the store, did Jess want to come with her. Jess declined but decided that this was the moment to ask permission to start a garden. Zella had wanted a garden for years, and suggested that Jess ask—just to see if "the old bat could be persuaded."

"A garden?" Miss Tutwiler looked suspicious. "Flowers or vegetables?"

"Both, maybe. Zella and I want both."

"Did Zella put you up to this?"

"No, ma'am. I wanted it the first time I looked in the backyard. She just agreed with me."

Miss Tutwiler said she would think about it.

"Yeah," Zella told Jess later. "She always be *thinking* 'bout something."

By the next Tuesday everyone had been assigned a specific task in preparation for the Christmas-in-July celebration. Everything about it seemed wrong to Jess, but the whole house was entering Rosemary's project with excitement. Zella and Miss Tutwiler were cooking meats and sweets. The professor, Will, and Frank were decorating the outside of the house: lights were strung in the bushes, with wires going across the porch and into plugs in the front rooms.

"This place is going to catch fire," Miss Tutwiler warned, but Frank and the professor helped Rosemary string the lights, then carried the nine-foot tree into the living room, making sure it was straight. Shooter and Ray helped wrap presents to place beneath the tree. Zella made cookies shaped like wreaths and Christmas stars to arrange on silver platters. A life-sized cloth Santa Claus was placed in a rocker on the front porch, though his head kept falling over as though he were asleep or dead. Rosemary taped his neck to the back of the chair, so that, now, he looked startled, rather than asleep.

A fake holly wreath hung on the front door, and smaller ones had been attached to the windows. Candles were placed around the rooms, and a bowl of rum punch sat on the long dining room table, along with platters of turkey and cranberry sauce, Zella's homemade rolls the size of baseballs, cornbread dressing, green beans cooked all day with ham hocks, corn pudding, and a large bowl of ambrosia. Four seven-layer cakes and six pies were showcased on a side table. The deep blue and purple hydrangea bushes were in full bloom around the house.

Neighbors brought champagne and bottles of wine. They had loved these Christmas parties when old Mr. Tutwiler was alive and, now, even those who never knew the man, expected to be invited. Rosemary took credit for everything, but no one seemed to care.

By seven o'clock people began to arrive and the house smelled of mulled cider, cherry pie, and roast turkey. Pauline's face bloomed from being in the heat of the kitchen, and she had already had too much of the spiked cider. Will also got drunk that night, though he proved to be as friendly drunk as he was sober.

He followed Miss Tutwiler into the kitchen and as she opened the door to the pantry, he went in behind her. They stood awkwardly together in the small room. Everything smelled of spices.

"Tut," Will said, tipping slightly forward.

She caught him. "Don't you fall down, Will. You're gonna fall down."

He did fall, but took her by the shoulders and she lifted her face. Her breath smelled sweet with rum, and he kissed her on the mouth. "Your eyes are like the sky," he mumbled. To her own surprise, she kissed him back. He pulled away, took a breath, then leaned in again.

"Whoa," she said. "William, you're drunk."

"I'm not that drunk, Tut. I'm remembering this." He leaned low and kissed her again on the neck.

She let him. She let him lean against her. They heard someone come into the kitchen, then leave.

"Let's get out of here," she whispered. "Now you straighten up."

"I'm straightened fine," he said, with a slurry, mischievous voice.

"Stop that now." She laughed a little. She might be falling for this man, but didn't want to.

"You are a good-looking woman. You know that?" He stepped back and she opened the door. "You like me, don't you?" he whispered hoarsely into her ear. "I know you like me, Tut."

"Yes," she said. "Yes." She was still smiling when they both entered the parlor with trays of fresh pastry shells filled with berries and whipped cream. Fans were strategically placed to give a breeze in all directions.

A hundred people had come and gone by ten o'clock, and Zella was worried they might run out of food. Rosemary (who liked to quote Bible verses because the professor admired her ability to recall them) quoted a verse about the feeding of the five thousand, then turned to Zella and said, "Let not your heart be troubled." Zella turned away disgusted and returned to the kitchen.

"No one else will show up this late," Miss Tutwiler said.

Ten people were gathered around the piano singing "God Rest Ye Merry Gentlemen." Will stood close to Miss Tut, leaning on her slightly. She had her arm around his waist. Prof. Chapin played the piano, his hands moving smoothly over the keys. He paused only briefly to wipe his neck and face with a handkerchief. Rosemary stood beside him, grazing his shoulder with her breast as she turned the pages of music. She was smoking a cigarette and from time to time threw her head back and blew blue smoke toward the ceiling.

That night Jess felt the possibilities of love about to blossom in the house. The air was full of secrets. Frank had followed her around most of the evening. If she lifted a platter, he helped her carry it and when she was singing around the piano, he was close beside her. His hair looked thick and brushed back into a thin ducktail. He wore a dark suit and tie, and looked different in his grownup clothes.

"Maybe you want to dance?" he finally asked her.

"I've been wanting to."

"So you'll risk it?"

"I guess."

Frank reached around her and placed his hand on the small of her back. She placed her hand lightly on his shoulder. Jess had bought a full-skirted, red taffeta dress for the party, and her hair lay loose. Frank held her close and breathed into her ear. She liked the closeness. Frank smelled like soap and lime juice.

"I can't get over you," Frank said, his voice a little shaky.

"What do you mean?"

"You take my breath away, Jess. You know that?"

"You are pretty interesting yourself," she said.

"So you would go out with me? To a movie or something?"

"If I'm not doing anything. I mean, I work most nights." She planned to tell him about Sam, but not right now.

"Well just sometime then, when you're not working."

"Maybe," she said.

They had stopped dancing and Frank touched her arm in an awkward way. "You surprise me," he said. "You're not like other girls." He couldn't say why.

"I'm not what you think," she told him.

"How do you know what I'm thinking?"

"Whatever it is, I'm not that."

Frank pulled back and looked at her a long moment. "Miss Tut thinks you're running away from something."

The music started now. A slow dance. They turned toward each other, both wanting to dance again.

"She's been saying that?"

"Maybe you should talk to her," Frank said. "Set her mind at rest. I can't advise you though."

"But you are advising me, aren't you?" They were dancing close, then Jess pulled back.

Frank looked around. "It got dark in here. Did somebody turn down the lights?

"When we started dancing they did."

"More romantic." He smiled, then said, "I really do like you."

Neither noticed that the music had stopped.

Cleanup of the Christmas celebration took about two days. The lights had to be taken down and decorations packed in boxes, the tired Santa returned to the attic, and the food—what was left—was served for supper the next night. The rest they gave to Zella.

Over the next week Miss Tutwiler was more affectionate toward Will. She made lunch for him and brought it to the porch. Jess heard them laughing together in the late afternoon. Rosemary was calling Albert Chapin by his first name. Frank whistled in his room and Jess found herself watching for him, glad to see him in the evening when he came home from the newspaper.

Clearly, Christmas had come early and left some happiness in its wake.

— 28 —

Social Services had called Miss Tutwiler to say they would arrive late Wednesday morning to check on the boys again, so Will suggested that Jess take them out of the house. Wednesday was her day off. They would tell Social Services that Sonny Long had called and that he had been sending money. Prof. Chapin forged a letter from Sonny to each boy.

On Tuesday night Jess told Shooter that she wanted to show them something down by the stream, and she would take them there tomorrow. "We're going on a treasure hunt," she said. "Tomorrow."

"When tomorrow?" Ray asked.

"Right after breakfast."

The next morning Jess's bedroom door yawned wide open. Shooter and Ray, their fragile boy-bodies in a room yellow with sunlight, made her heart leap.

"Is it tomorrow yet?" Ray asked. A stray orange cat, that Frank had been feeding on the sly, had slipped into the house and found its way upstairs, scooting around the boys and jumping onto Jess's bed. The cat didn't have a tail.

"She likes you," said Shooter. "But Miss Tut won't like it in the house."

"What's the matter with its tail?" Ray asked.

"Something chopped it off when it was little," Shooter explained. "She looks okay though, don't you think? I like it better that way." Ray rubbed the cat all the way down its back and into the air, as though it *did* have a tail.

Breakfast was unusually quiet. Everyone but the boys knew that Social Services would arrive soon. "We're going to look for buried money today," Jess announced. "I'm taking the boys on a treasure hunt. We'll be gone until after lunch."

"Buried money?" Rosemary felt overly involved in the boys' upbringing. "The root of all evil."

"That's, 'The *love* of money is the root of all evil,'" Zella Davis told her. "Not money *by itself.*"

Rosemary no longer wore her satin dresses, but instead, wore lightweight cotton skirts and blouses, or sometimes pants. Prof. Chapin was noticing her. He had given her rides to town. Her hair hung loose around her face and she smiled more often, but she still spouted her verses.

"Lunch gonna be at straight-up twelve noon," Zella said.

"We won't be back for lunch," Jess told her. "We'll take something with us."

"I'll make some sandwiches and give y'all some soda, maybe potato chips for a snack." Zella wanted to make it easy for them.

Jess, Shooter, and Ray walked toward the stream with a wheelbarrow. When Ray got tired, he climbed in to ride. A few times Shooter let him ride piggyback. Jess led them to a place where the soil was rich. They had brought shovels and a bucket. They were to put the soil into the wheelbarrow. "I'll take this back for a garden," she said. "But any money you find you can keep."

After a few minutes, Ray found a nickel. Shooter found a dime. They dug harder finding three pennies at one time. Jess could not remember how many coins she had buried, but hoped she'd scattered enough to fill the morning.

At eleven-thirty they washed their hands in the stream-water and sat on a log to eat lunch, the three of them lined up like different-sized bumps.

"So, how much did you find?" Jess asked.

Ray had ninety-two cents, but Shooter found four quarters, five dimes, and a nickel. Ray whined, so Shooter gave him a quarter and two dimes from his own stack. They wanted to dig for more, but Jess led them downstream to where a large pile of sticks had dammed the water.

"Beavers," she said, and pointed to a beaver poking up its head.

"Hey!" said Shooter.

"Stay real still. We don't want to scare them."

Ray sat on the ground and Shooter moved to stand behind a tree and watch them go under and rise back up.

"They're baptizing themselves," Jess said.

"What's baptized?" Ray asked.

"It's when the preacher sprinkles water on your head at church, or sometimes they dunk you all the way under the water," Jess told him.

"Whoa!"

"Then anything bad you've done is just let go," Jess said. "I used to know a guy who loved being baptized."

Ray looked thoughtful. "Did he do a lot of bad stuff?"

"No. He just liked the feel of water on his head, and he liked going under. He liked so many things." She liked telling them about Adam. "He liked hubcaps and horses and dancing. He could hum a made-up tune, and he always wanted to go to sleep at night listening to the sound of grownups talking in another room. But he did *not* like a sharp voice or bad dreams, and he did *not* like to have the door to his room closed."

Shooter cupped some water in his hands and dumped it onto Ray's head. "There," he said. "Now, you're baptized."

Ray's hair dripped with water and drops rolled down his face. He beamed.

"Now, you don't have to be scared anymore," said Shooter. "I mean, when it thunders and lightnings." Both boys watched the beavers' slick brown bodies moving in and out of the water. They studied the animals until Shooter tugged at Jess to say that Ray was asleep. He had slumped over onto his side.

Jess lifted Ray and put him, like a rag doll, onto her shoulder. She motioned for Shooter to follow and push the wheelbarrow back home. It was heavy, and a short way from the house, he wanted to quit. Jess said to park it on the side of the path. "I'll pick it up later."

When they got home, all they talked about was the found money, saying they wanted to go back tomorrow—to find more.

"See what you've done?" said Rosemary. "You've tapped into their greed. You kids are too young to feel greedy."

"I'm not greedy," said Shooter. "I just don't see why we can't get more. Boy! I could buy me a model airplane."

"We saw some beafers," said Ray. "They built a dam out of sticks." He wondered if he would get into trouble for saying "dam."

"They are smart creatures," said Will. "I bet beavers don't need to dig for money all the time."

"They might have a whole chest of money down under that dam," said Shooter. "No telling how much they got."

"You have certainly started something, Jess," said Miss Tutwiler. "Now what're you gonna do?"

"Sometimes when you dig for treasure," Jess told the boys, "what you find first is all there is. I mean, there *could* be more, a little more, but I don't think you're going to find a lot of money, Shooter."

Rosemary had more Bible verses on the tip of her tongue, and couldn't help but spit them out. "Sufficient unto the day is the evil thereof."

"Does that mean I'm bad?" Shooter asked.

"No, it means the world is bad," Will explained.

"I want to buy a beafer," Ray said.

"Go to the ant, thou sluggard." Rosemary was on a roll. "Consider her ways and be wise."

"Are ants smart?" Shooter asked.

"Some are. Not many though," said the professor.

"Shooter baptized me today," Ray said.

"Get thee behind me . . . " Miss Tutwiler chanted, but no one was listening anymore.

Social Services had believed the story about Sonny Long, because of the forged letters, and because Rosemary, and even Zella, had joined in the lie. "Maybe you should tell Mr. Long to call *us*," the lady had said. "Good idea," said the professor. "We'll suggest that next time we talk to him." Will suspected that all that lying had brought about Rosemary's flurry of verses.

The next day the boys returned to the stream and brought a bucket instead of a wheelbarrow. Jess couldn't go, but they promised to bring back some pennies for her, if they found any.

The professor saw them leave. "Apostates," he said, but he looked happy for them, and hoped they would find enough to satisfy their appetite for wealth. He knew that Jess had buried only about three dollars' worth of change; but the professor and Will had buried some coins for today's excursion.

A little later the boys returned with more coins. One had eight dimes and two quarters, the other had found five nickels, three dimes, and a quarter. They reported their findings at supper and Ray offered Jess two nickels. Everyone smiled at the treasure.

"We're going to be *rich*," said Shooter.

"This has *got* to stop," Miss Tutwiler said. "I'm putting an end to it right now."

Will told them that he didn't think they'd find any more. He said he thought the well was probably dry now.

"What well?" Shooter said.

Prof. Chapin held up one hand and asked the boys to let him look at the coins, especially the quarters. When they showed what they had found, he appeared surprised. "You know, boys. These aren't quarters. They're ancient coins," he said. "Rare. You're very lucky to have found them. I imagine that you've dug up all the real money now, because this is money used a long time ago. You've got something nobody else has: a coin used by the Roman soldiers. A Roman coin."

Their eyes grew large.

"Imagine that," Miss Tutwiler said. "A coin all the way from Rome, Italy." She winked at the professor. "Probably brought by the explorers to this very place."

"Let's go look up these coins," said the professor. He scooted back from the table and motioned for the boys to come with him. "You each have one, right?"

"Yeah," Shooter said. "Are they worth a lot of money?"

"Even better—they're worth a lot of history."

"Wow," Ray said, without knowing what that meant. The boys followed the professor to his room, which looked more like a library. In the hallway they passed the fishbowl on the hall table. Ray sprinkled some fish food into the water and watched the flakes drift down. Both goldfish darted quickly toward the food.

Jess followed the others to the porch. The world looked fragile, about to rain.

"You'll bring coffee out to us, won't you, Zella?" Miss Tutwiler called.

"Yes'm."

"A merry heart doeth good like a medicine," Rosemary said absently.

They sat and waited for Zella's coffee. They could see her in the kitchen talking to herself, her hand knifing the air like a thin black fish.

Jess felt charged by the sweet night air and a strong desire for home. This place was good for her, like a tonic. A sharp pain opened her heart and gave her a flicker of belief that hope could rise out of nothing. She longed to be lifted out of this weave of uncertainty, to be lowered again into the fabric of familiar days.

— 29 —

The next day at Honey's, a man came in and sat down in a booth. Jess went to take his order and could see how his clothes were all wrong. He wore a coat and tie and muddy shoes. The tie looked stained. Outside the window Jess could see the brown and white car with a dent in the door. It seemed that there had never been a time when that car was not following her.

The diner was suddenly empty and Jess turned around, wondering where everyone had gone. The man held a menu and looked at her, without speaking. Jess asked for his order. His hair was gray, and the wide-brimmed hat that usually covered his eyes lay pushed back on his head. When he still did not speak, Jess said, "Why are you following . . . ?"

He interrupted her, his voice low and quiet. "Jess," he said. "I *saw* you, I saw you at the river."

He knew her name. He looked straight at her and, though he did not look angry, his words sounded harsh. "I want you to know," he said. "I *saw* what you did. And Adam."

Jess ran to get Lenny and Maggie, but when she got back the man had gone. She saw the car pulling away, and the *ike Ike* sticker. Two customers, a man and a woman, had come in. They sat at a table on the other side of the room and asked for menus.

"Where did he go?" Jess asked the couple. "That man sitting in the booth over there. He was right there." They had seen a man rush out, but could not say more about him.

Jess wiped her palms on her apron. She felt the dark pressure of threat, and began to tremble. He had been at the river.

Lenny was worried and suggested that Jess find someone to walk her home, and that she get someone every night to be with her, so Jess called Frank, who was more than happy to oblige.

That night Frank asked what had happened and Jess explained that she had seen the car before, but she did not want to explain where she had been when she saw it. "Maybe it wasn't the car, maybe it was just the man who looked familiar," she said. "Frank, let's change the subject. Okay?"

"Sure." They walked a short way before Frank asked what he really wanted to know: who she knew in Korea. He had the habit of brushing his nose with his thumb and often performed this gesture when he was nervous. He did it now.

"The guy you know in the Service," he said. "How well do you know him?"

"Pretty well," she said. "I dated him for a while."

"Oh."

As they climbed the steps to the boardinghouse, Jess could not remove from her mind the image of the man in the booth who had looked straight at her; she couldn't stop hearing his low voice saying, "I *saw* you." That phrase rolled through her mind for days, until the phrase, itself, became a mantra.

Though Christmas-in-July had been over for three weeks, Rosemary continued to brag about its success. The hot month of August had begun and Frank still lingered around Jess. He kept his promise to walk her home each evening from work.

Usually Frank played poker with his buddies on Sundays. They played at a pool hall on Broad Street. He might win twenty or more dollars, and he liked to brag about pots he'd stolen with only a pair of threes, or about a miraculous draw to a full house. But, tonight, he cancelled poker to take Jess to a movie. When he arrived at the diner, he was driving his truck. Jess had put the last of the cups upside down on a paper towel, and was cleaning the grounds out of the coffee pot.

"Let's go to a movie before going back home," he said lightly.

"I don't think so," she said. Jess didn't like to admit that she was still rattled by the man in the diner last week. Everywhere she went she looked for him. She felt he was always watching her. "I'm pretty tired."

"You can do better than that." Frank laughed. "You can come up with a better excuse, can't you?" He smiled—a long smile.

"What's the movie?" she asked.

"Some Western. Has cowboys."

"I like cowboy shows," she said. Adam had dragged her to so many cowboy movies that she had grown to like them. She knew she shouldn't encourage Frank, but she enjoyed his company. One movie wouldn't do any harm.

They drove to the Riviera Theatre in Frank's truck with big tires and a screech in the brakes. He bought tickets, popcorn, and two Grapettes. They sat in the third row.

On the drive home Frank told Jess about the day he arrived at the boardinghouse. "First off, Miss Tut told me to go get a haircut. First thing she said. Then she gave me that ad from the paper. You know, 'Reporter needed. Training level. Local and regional coverage.' She kept saying 'You could do that,' until I believed her. She called somebody at the paper to set up an interview. I got the job." He smiled. "She helped me even though I kept stealing things from her. Vases, ash trays, little stuff."

"You steal things? Why?"

"Who knows?" Frank laughed. "I take them to a pawn shop in Gadsden, then Miss Tut drives over there and brings them back. Sometimes, she makes me go get them. But," he added, "I haven't stolen anything since *you* came."

"So I'm a good influence. That what you're telling me?"

"Yeah. And maybe I could be a good influence on you."

"Maybe you already are."

"Jess, what's the worst thing you've ever done?" Frank asked.

"Why? You think I've done something bad? Why not ask what I've done good?"

"Okay. Tell me the good first."

"Maybe they're both the same thing," she said. "What if the worst thing someone has ever done is also the best?"

"You're a puzzle, you know that? You dodge questions better than anybody I've ever seen."

"Maybe you ask too many of 'em—ever think about that?"

"Have you got something to hide?" he asked. "Because I sure do. I'll tell you. If it hadn't been for Miss Tut, I might be off somewhere hiding in a ditch."

"She pull you out of a ditch?" Jess chuckled.

"Might as well. I snuck into the boardinghouse late one night. Climbed through the kitchen window and stole a radio and some silver. She caught me, but she didn't call the police. Instead she gave me something to eat, and said that stealing silver was stupid, because this silver had her daddy's initials on it. She gave me a room and told everybody that I was the son of a friend of hers, and that I was looking for a job."

"You broke in? Had you done that kind of thing before?"

Frank let his hand rest on Jess's shoulder where he rubbed circles with his finger. "After about a week Tut sent me to the newspaper. She knew I'd had three years of college. She told me I'd better give it all I had, and then with my first check I'd pay for room and board. I was a copy boy for a year, then they let me write a few things, and I caught on pretty fast."

Jess did not respond, and Frank misinterpreted. "You hate me now? I shouldn't have told you about the breaking-and-entering thing."

"I don't hate you. I like you, Frank, but . . . you know, I can't stop think-ing about that man at the diner. He scared me."

"Sure. I understand. I do. Listen, I can walk you home every night. I'll be there whenever you get off."

"Thank you." Frank was trying so hard that Jess felt she should tell him about Sam, even though the memory of Sam had begun to fade since she had been at the boardinghouse. "Frank, you asked me about the man I know in the service? Well, his name is Sam Rafferty. He's a private in the army."

"A boyfriend, then?"

"He wants to marry me when he gets back."

"He might be back already," Frank said. He tried not to show emotion. "So what are you doing here?" He had moved his hands into his lap.

Then Jess told him about her mother's death, her father who owned two clothing stores, and a dog named Hap. She did not mention Adam, but felt Frank's curiosity pressing on her.

"I'm glad that damn war is finally over," he said.

"Frank?" Jess asked. "Why weren't you drafted? I've been wondering about that."

"I don't know why you'd be wondering about that," he said. "It's a rude question, actually. You think I didn't want to go? Is that it?"

"I'm sorry. I just asked," said Jess.

"Yeah, you ask stuff, but you don't tell me a damn thing." He turned the key to start the truck, cranking the motor twice before it started. "Anyway," he said, "maybe you should find somebody else to walk back with you every night." They drove toward the boardinghouse without speaking. But Jess was not thinking about Frank. She was thinking about the possible return of the man in the booth. She could not shake the image of the brown-and-white car from her mind.

— 30 —

Frank and Jess pulled the truck up to the boardinghouse and saw Miss Tutwiler sitting on the porch swing. Frank went inside, still irritated by their conversation. Jess sat on the swing. Miss Tutwiler pushed them back and forth with one foot before speaking. "You haven't seen that man again at the diner, have you? The stranger in the car?"

Jess shook her head. "I'd seen the car before that day," Jess explained. "It had that *I Like Ike* sticker on the back. But part of it had come off and it said *ike Ike.*"

Miss Tutwiler cleared her throat. "Anybody else see the man?"

"Not really," Jess said. "But it was the same sticker. That's what convinced me."

"Lots of those around," Miss Tutwiler said. "Had a sticker just like it on my own car. Said *I li e.* Cheap glue." Then she said, "I'm glad Frank's bringing you home, though. He's been here a few years now and I haven't thrown him out yet. Others have wanted me to. Sometimes he steals things. Just little things. I usually get them back."

"He told me about that." Jess said. Late evening shadows grew long, and dogs slunk along the edge of the road. Dark would not come until after nine o'clock.

"Just something off the hall table," she said. "I've told him to stop. He won't. Or maybe he can't, like that disease some people have." She shifted on the swing. "Will thinks I favor him too much."

"I wouldn't want him stealing from me," Jess said.

"He's been better about it since he started working for the newspaper. Did you read the article he wrote in this morning's paper? Pretty good."

Frank usually wrote pieces about small happenings around town: how kudzu was creeping over the fences by the school, or the problem of stray dogs in the town square. This morning, though, he had reported on the death of a man who had been living (nobody knew how long) in a nearby barn.

"At first," Miss Tutwiler said, "I thought it might be the same man you saw, but then this one had been dead a few days already."

"I didn't read it," said Jess, "but I heard about the police finding a man under the bridge a few days ago."

"The man's name was Ezra," Miss Tutwiler told Jess. "He was a veteran of WWII—shell shocked and wandering around these parts for years. A missing person, but nobody knew where he was from." She repositioned herself on the swing. "But Frank told me he was working on something even better now. A big story. He wouldn't say what."

Jess thought Frank might have heard something about *her*, how she was a missing person. She should try to dispel any suspicions he might have. Maybe everybody knew more than Jess imagined.

Shooter and Will came out of the house to join them. "You talking about Frank's article this morning?" Will said. "Ezra jumping off that bridge?"

"Why'd he do that?" Shooter asked.

"I don't know," Will said. "Sad, I guess,"

"I would never do that," Shooter asserted. "Would you?"

"I don't think so. I never had that inclination. Guess that's why I've lived so damn long."

"I'm eight," Shooter said, proudly. "How old are you?"

"Sixty-eight."

Shooter grew quiet, thinking. "You said 'damn.' You're not supposed to say 'damn.'"

"Sorry."

A mild breeze had come up. Will settled onto the swing between Miss Tut and Jess. He pulled Shooter onto his lap.

"There's not room for all of us on this thing," Miss Tut said. Will ignored her.

"When we going fishing again?" Shooter asked.

"Soon. But we have to find a new place."

"I know a place where nobody goes," Shooter said.

"I bet you do."

"And I have a boat!"

"Where'd you get a boat?" Miss Tutwiler asked.

"I found it. It had some leaks, so I patched it up. Went to the hardware store, got some strapping tape and waterproof glue. It still leaks a little, but if we don't stay out too long we'll be all right. Can you swim?" He was looking at Will.

"Yes," Will said.

They, all four, rocked gently in the swing. Miss Tutwiler leaned her head back. "Last time it got this hot I like to died," she said, absently.

"Where are the others?" Jess asked.

"The professor's in the kitchen with Rosemary," Will said. "She made chocolate milkshakes for the boys, and she's teaching Ray some Bible verses."

"Rosemary and her verses," said Miss Tutwiler. "Did she put Ray to bed, Shooter?"

Shooter laid his head on Will's shoulder and closed his eyes. He had not cried about his father for almost four days, but he looked on the verge of tears now. They listened to the roar of tree frogs and crickets.

The orange cat with no tail rubbed against Miss Tutwiler's legs. "I hope nobody thinks we're keeping this mangy kitty," she said. "I have said again and again, no pets." She stood up and shooed the cat off the porch. "Look at it. Somebody cut that poor cat's tail off." She held out a hand for Shooter. She would put him to bed.

Jess moved to go in too, but Will touched her arm to make her stay. Jess knew he wanted to say something personal, but didn't know what it would be.

"Life can turn a different direction in the space of a moment," Will said, looking out across the yard. "What's there one day can be gone the next. I know about that from my own years in the war." He looked at her now. The swing was still. "I know how you can be one person one day and different the next, and after that you're different for the rest of your life. At least, I was."

Jess made a sound low in her throat. The whole yard, steeped in the logy heat of summer, wore a circle of sadness.

"I need to tell you something," Will said, with the tone of a confession. "I've called your father. I told him you were here."

Jess looked stunned. "He knows where I am?"

"As soon as you got here. I called him so he wouldn't worry, Jess. Forgive me. I don't know what's going on, and he didn't tell me. But I asked him to let you stay here, and I said you would call him soon. Just don't wait too long."

"I was going to call him." She sounded defensive.

Will nodded without judgment. He leaned forward to get up from the swing. "That might be a good idea."

Jess followed Will into the boardinghouse. The day, not yet dark, had ended. A rotten scrap of loose screen hung from the door. The house was quiet, usual for a Sunday—a heavy Sunday lonesomeness hung over all their lives.

— 31 —

Calder Finney had rushed out of the diner when he saw how scared Jess was, how she had called for help. She accused him of following her, and he guessed he had; but not the way she thought. She had thought that he meant to do her harm. He never meant that. But he had been following her.

On that day in late April, Calder arrived in Goshen and drove first to Edward Booker's house on Dogwood Avenue. He parked across the street, hoping to see Adam, talk to him alone for a little while before going to Cadwell. There were no cars in the driveway. He sat for a moment before he saw Adam run out the front door with a young girl. He presumed the girl was Jess. Jess followed Adam into the woods. Adam seemed excited, though he wasn't smiling. They went towards the river.

Calder got out of the car and followed them through the trees. From a distance he could see they were talking. Adam cried a little, waded into the river, then took off his jacket. Jess spoke to him softly. Calder believed this would be a good moment to interrupt, but as he approached, he saw them embrace. Jess kissed Adam, then gave a little wave as if she were telling him goodbye.

So Calder paused and saw Adam enter the river. Jess called to him a few times—just his name, or saying she was still there, then she went back to the house. Calder returned to his car, and waited.

When Jess left the house a few minutes later, she went back toward the woods with a satchel and some food. Calder believed she was taking these things to Adam. Maybe she would meet him downriver. Maybe she was helping him to escape the trip to Cadwell. He hoped so. If she did that, he would help her.

A month ago, after Clementine told him she would send Adam to Cadwell, he visited the institution, and immediately tried to persuade Clementine not to send him there. "Don't do it," he had pleaded. "He can't live there."

"You don't know." Clementine railed at him. "You haven't been here all these years."

Calder could tell she was crying on the phone. "But Clementine, I've seen what they do."

"Those doctors can help Adam." Her voice turned high-pitched. "They said they could help him. And maybe he can come home afterwards. But . . ." she stopped. "They have to take him for a while."

"Clementine?" he said. "Are you going to let them operate on him?"

"They might. Yes."

"Oh, Clementine."

"You'd rather he be in jail? With no one to take care of him? The doctors will take care of him."

Calder made a sound in his throat. He had no right to make a big decision like this, unless he could take Adam himself. But Calder had remarried and knew his new wife would not be willing to bear the responsibility of Adam; and he knew that he could not work and care for Adam on a daily basis by himself. Clementine had done a remarkable job with him, and Edward Booker, a patient, loving man, was footing much of the bill for Cadwell. Still, Calder wanted to take Adam away. Maybe Jess was helping him do just that. So he tried to find Jess and Adam by going downriver, trying to see where they would meet.

The next day he called Clementine, because she would be expecting him to come by the house. She sounded hysterical as she told Calder that both Jess and Adam had been gone all night.

"Jess took him away. She didn't want him to go there," Clementine said.

"We'll find them. Let me talk with Edward."

"Hello," Edward said.

"Have you reported them missing?" Calder asked.

"Yes. The police are searching for them. They're hiding somewhere. We're checking the houses of Jess's friends."

"Should I come?"

"No. No. We'll call you when we find them. We'll have to reschedule the trip to Cadwell." He cleared his throat. "I'm afraid this will just make it harder, though."

Calder heard Clementine yell something in the background.

"We'll call you when we find them."

Calder followed Jess, guessing she would try to get a ride and that she would go south. He saw her first on highway 53 going toward Rome. She was outside a grocery store, but he didn't know if it was Jess. She looked different, her hair shorter, something. He looked to see if Adam was with her, but did not see him anywhere. He saw Jess again in a shopping center, as she stole a bag of oranges from a cart. But, still, no Adam. He wanted to offer his help, but was waiting to see Adam. He wanted to be sure. After a couple of weeks Calder could no longer find Jess and went back home. He told his wife about Adam and Jess. He said he might go looking for them again. Then the day came when Clementine called to say that Adam had drowned in the river, and Calder had to rethink everything.

"They found his body near Sudderth Creek. A man named Bobby Coe found him." She sounded as if she had memorized the information. He pictured her face set in stone. "The service will be held in the Methodist Church next Wednesday."

At the funeral the church was full of townspeople, men from the garages, school kids and parents, and others Clementine did not know. Calder insisted on paying for everything himself, especially the gravestone. He followed Clementine's instructions of engraving Adam's name, his nickname "Hubcap," and the date of birth and death.

At the cemetery Calder and his new wife stood beside Clementine and Edward as they lowered Adam's body into the ground. The crowd sang a hymn, their voices rising up through the trees. Calder sobbed as he remembered Adam riding his bike, playing ball—all the things that made Adam seem normal, though Calder's real sadness came in the realization that he had never known Adam as the son he actually was, but only the way Calder had wanted to see him.

"I was always afraid of that river," Clementine said, as they left the graveside. "I always thought something bad could happen there."

Over the next month Calder renewed his search for Jess. He asked at gas stations and stores, and had almost given up when he saw her walking on a back road near Georgia 20, which went toward Alabama. He followed her ragged trail toward Lula. When he asked at Honey's Last Stop, someone said she worked there. He waited, then confronted her; but she was so frightened of him he decided to leave. He hadn't planned what he would say to her, but had said the wrong thing.

When Calder called Clementine, Edward told him that she had moved out two weeks after the funeral. "She's living in town. In an apartment," he said. "She's made a formal accusation against Jess."

"Do you know where Jess is?" Calder knew that Edward would be waiting to hear if Jess had been washed up on the riverbank, like Adam. He would tell Edward where she was. He was surprised at Edward's answer.

"Yes. She's with an old friend in Lula, Alabama."

— 32 —

Will Brennan liked to carry a shoehorn in his pocket, but had to remove it when he sat at the dinner table. Tonight, as he placed the shoehorn on the floor beside him, Ray picked it up to inspect its shiny curve. Will said that Ray could keep it for a couple of days while he was out of town. "I'm leaving tomorrow to see my son in Virginia." Ray rubbed his thumb in the curve of the shoehorn and asked, if he blew it, would it sound like a horn?

Shooter didn't want Will to go. "What if Ray gets scared at night?" Shooter said.

"I don't get scared." Ray hit Shooter's arm, and Shooter dropped a roll into his soup. He said a bad word.

"You shouldn't say things like that." Miss Tutwiler looked at both Shooter and Frank. "You've been hanging around Frank, I'll bet." She started to say more when Shooter spoke up.

"Mr. Will says bad words, sometimes."

"No, I don't," Will said defensively. "Where did you get a notion like that?"

"You did too. Remember?" Shooter pointed accusingly. "You were telling me about that war you were in."

Will remembered, he remembered exactly where they were.

He had taken Shooter to dig for worms. They put them in a tobacco can for fishing, and Shooter said he wanted to be a soldier someday. It was early in the morning, and they had brought some apples to eat. Will had his coffee in a black thermos.

Shooter kept talking about the war in Korea and how he wanted to go, to wear a uniform, and to carry a gun. Finally he held up a worm three inches long, and whooed. He said, "I could kill me some people."

Hearing those words come from Shooter unlocked something in Will. Without thought or plan, he began to speak. He shook his head hard. "Son, you don't want that. Not unless you like the idea a being out in some field thick with mud, and deer flies landing on you like fucking birds, eating you up. Welts come up on your neck and arms, itching and stinging." He took a deep breath and looked straight at Shooter. He was teaching this boy about war. "Then the man beside you, who's your good buddy, he gets hit. The incoming falling so fast and you didn't hear anything, it was so loud, everything so loud."

He was looking far off now. "Son-of-a-bitch coming at you, and you might see his face, and you might not even *want* to shoot him, but you got to. See? And then, afterwards, you gonna always see his face hit, exploding like some kinda god-damn balloon, and him falling and his blood all around." Will leaned back, his eyes bright as marbles. "And you can't help wondering about his life."

Shooter did not say a word.

"But after that first one, you don't think on it anymore. You kill men like swatting flies. And that friend of yours, he just fell and you can't believe it, 'cause, when you look, his arm's not on his body, but off in some bush ten yards away. And your buddy's saying your name. Then he's dead, and you carry him out over your neck like an animal. And you been shot too, but you can't think about it."

Shooter hadn't moved, just listened and waited. "And besides that, you're in another country and nobody says anything you can understand, but their voices say *Hate,* say *Kill.* Then you think about that day the rest of your life. Nightmares too. You won't ever be the same." He took another long breath and let it out slow. "That's all I'm gonna say now. Give me some of that coffee."

Shooter handed the thermos to Will and unscrewed the top for him. "Did you really do that?" he asked.

Will poured coffee, black, into the cup-top. "Yes."

"Was he your friend?"

Will drank a long gulp. "Hell, we were all friends."

The rest of that morning Will seemed to have gone somewhere else in his head, his face ringed with sadness. He had said more about the war to Shooter in those moments than he had said to anyone in years.

But, now, Will turned to Shooter and Ray at the table. "Miss Tut's right about that kind of bad talk, and though I admit to sometimes falling backwards, she's taught me that it's wrong." Zella came in and mentioned dessert, which was lemon pie.

In this way the matter was closed.

After supper Jess helped Zella wash the dishes; Frank, in a hopeful mood, came in behind Jess and offered to dry. Miss Tutwiler and Will cleared dishes from the table and collected the napkins. They were openly affectionate now.

Zella was going out tonight, but complained about how much it cost to go anywhere. "Barely have enough to go out anymore." She had been plugging for a raise, and Miss Tutwiler knew that, eventually, she would have to give in. Then Zella said, "One person I knew growing up gave away *all* they's money."

"All of it?" Will asked.

"Well most, anyhow. They had to move to a little old place, hardly nothing compared to living in a big two-story house. They learned to live real spare."

"Now that is *good* folks," said Miss Tutwiler.

"Or stupid," said Frank.

"He owned a restaurant in town," said Zella.

"Did he keep the restaurant?" asked Frank.

"Nope. Give it away too."

"That sounds crazy to me." Frank dropped the plate he was drying, but caught it.

"Uh-uh, they just got the Spirit," explained Zella. "Spirit said, 'Sell what you have and give to the poor.' Wife never was too happy about it, but she didn't leave him. They still living down there. Old now. Live on Sweetmilk Creek." She paused wiping the counter, then placed the rag neatly over the faucet. She shrugged. "Seem happy whenever I see them."

"Maybe people don't need as much money as they think," Miss Tutwiler said. "People always asking for more money, seems to me." Jess looked up. She had heard the women arguing over Zella's raise, and enjoyed seeing Zella work her way toward the final closing.

"They need enough to live on, though," Zella said. "What I'm talking about is a gen-er-ous spirit." She paused. "People can always go somewhere else to work, I guess."

"Well, I wouldn't want that," Miss Tutwiler relented, and Jess knew the raise was solid.

Will stood to go upstairs.

"Where're you going, Will?" Miss Tutwiler asked.

"To bed. Unless you got a better offer."

"I might," she said, and motioned for him to follow her onto the porch where she had a bucket of ice cold beer.

Will had three grown children who constantly asked him to come live with them. Miss Tut was afraid that one day he might leave the boarding-house. She wanted him to stay.

He leaned to lift a beer, and give one to Miss Tut. "Well," he said. "I thought you were going to propose."

She patted a place for him to sit beside her on the swing. She wiped her neck and forehead with a handkerchief and slipped the white lace cloth between her breasts. She looked like a woman who had decided something, as though the Tut and Anti-Tut faced each other, deciding whether or not to love Will.

"So, are you proposing?" Will said again. "Soon as I say I'm leaving for a few of days, you want to marry me."

"You wear me out," she said. "You just keep on 'til you wear me down."

"I'll take what I can." He took a long sip of beer. "I'm tired of chasing after women."

"I thought you just chased after me. I thought I was the only one."

"Well, that's what I'm tired of."

"Don't get tired, Will. Christmas is coming." She smiled to let him know she remembered their time in the pantry.

"I might be dead by then," he said.

She lifted another beer and gave it to him. Jess loved hearing their banter and could see them falling in love through these pointed remarks.

"You gonna wash up before you kiss me goodnight?" Miss Tutwiler asked.

"Do I offend you, Tut?"

"Not so much," she smiled. "I like a man to smell like the earth."

Jess came out with Frank following her. "Are we interrupting anything?" Jess asked.

"Yes," Will said.

When Jess sat in the rocker, the orange cat jumped onto her lap.

Zella came out to say she was leaving for the night. "What do you suppose happen to that cat's tail?"

Miss Tutwiler turned to inspect the kitty.

"She's still pretty though," Frank urged. "Look how clean she keeps herself. Didn't you ever have a cat when you were a girl, Miss Tut?"

"I did, as a matter of fact." Miss Tutwiler's face broke into a smile.

"What was its name?" Frank asked.

"Mimsy."

"What a coincidence! *This* one's named Mimsy." The cat walked up to Miss Tut and, as she leaned to pet it, the cat curved its neck and back into her hand, coming around again for another pass.

"She is a sweet kitty, isn't she? C'mere," she said. C'mere, Mimsy." Her voice grew high and soft, like a girl's.

"Hope she won't eat the goldfish," Zella said, and waved goodbye raising one hand. "I saw her looking in that fishbowl."

Jess lowered herself into this odd family of people and wished for something that was gone. Her dance with the world had changed into this stumbling rhythm, and she felt a profound need to apologize. But at that very moment Frank leaned over and whispered, "I'm sorry. I said too much the other night. None of my business." She could feel his breath by her ear. "I'm sorry," he said again.

Jess could name the moments in her life that had made her who she was. This was one of them. An apology, not her own—one that was coming in from the side—made her feel stripped down to her most secret self. Her face flinched slightly, like a bird's wing had brushed her cheek, and she felt struck by the human need for apology, and forgiveness. She would call her father.

"That's okay, Frank," she whispered.

No one was aware of the clouds that had rolled in, of the distant thunder, or the impending rain.

— 33 —

When Will had been gone two days, Jess took some quarters and went downstairs to the hall telephone booth, where long distance calls could be made. She closed the door and slipped in the coins, giving the operator her home phone number. If Clementine answered, she planned to hang up, but when she heard her father, she began to cry.

"Jess? Jess?" He was yelling.

"I know," she said. "Daddy, I'm calling to say I'm all right. I wanted to hear your voice. I'm sorry. I'm so sorry."

He urged her to come home, come home now.

"I know Mr. Brennan called you," she said.

"I was grateful for that. But I want you to come back. I can help. I'll do anything, if you just let me."

"I will," she said. She liked hearing him, but he sounded different, his voice urgent.

"Jess, you know Adam drowned the same day you left. I imagine you knew that. We didn't find him for almost five days."

"I know," she whispered.

"His body washed up near Sudderth Creek." When Jess didn't respond, he said, "Why did you leave, sweetie? Why did you run off? I've been so worried."

"I didn't know what else to do. I was afraid," she said.

"But are you all right? Nobody hurt you, did they? I kept thinking about you, wondering where you were."

"I slept in the woods. Sometimes people were good to me and gave me food or a place to sleep. I'm all right. One couple gave me a place to stay for a while. They let me have a job." She added, "I've got a job now."

"I have to ask you some things," her father said. He was trying to prepare her.

"No, don't. I can't. Not now."

"I want to come get you. Listen . . . " He didn't want her to hang up before he could say this. "Clementine moved out of the house, Jess. I told her to leave. She made a formal accusation against you. She blames you for Adam's death." He waited a moment, then said, "Come home, sweetheart."

"You don't blame me then?"

"Oh honey. I don't blame you for anything." She could hear him sigh through the phone. "I want to help."

Jess leaned over inside the phone booth, sobbing.

"Jess!" he said. His voice sounded old and he had to catch his breath. "I've found a good lawyer, but he has to have some answers. We all do." He was talking fast as though he expected her to end the call.

"I'm sorry," she said, again. "I'm sorry about Adam too." She felt sadder now than before; maybe her father did too. Maybe this call had made things worse.

"Sam will be coming home soon," he told her.

"So will I," Jess said. It sounded like a promise.

Jess went back to her room and could see a hard rain blowing on the windows. Wind rattled limbs and pushed trees into a frenzy. As she was getting back into bed, she heard whimpering from the boys' room. The sound was similar to the noise made by Adam in the basement when he first moved into their house.

As Ray's whimpering turned into bawling, Jess opened their door. Shooter had his hands on Ray's shoulders, protective.

"Ray's scared," Shooter said, his eyes wide.

A streak of lightning followed by thunder made Ray bolt into Jess's arms. The lights went out in the hallway. Jess tried the lamp beside the bed, but the click brought nothing.

"What happened?" Shooter's voice was a whisper.

"Rainstorms do that sometimes," Jess sat on the bed and held Ray. "I mean, take out the electricity."

"I know." Shooter stood close to the bed, close to Ray. "I keep telling him, but he's still scared."

"I am," Ray confessed.

"C'mon," Jess said, quickly. "Let me show you something." She grabbed a blanket from the end of Ray's bed and wrapped it around her shoulders. The boys pulled the ends of the blanket around themselves. This felt like a game that might make everything okay. Jess took each boy's hand as they went to the stairs that led to the attic. If someone had seen them in the hallway, the wide dark specter would have looked like a huge bat.

"Where're we going?" Ray urged.

"You're gonna love this," she told them. She reached into the drawer of a hall table. "Here, Shooter, hold this flashlight. Make sure it works."

Shooter clicked it on and off a few times. Each time the light flicked on, the boys looked relieved. The lightning had subsided, but rain fell hard, and thunder rumbled in the distance.

"This house has a tin roof," Jess told them. "And sometimes I just go upstairs to listen when it rains. Sounds like a big drum." She opened the attic door, and they could hear the rain thrumming hard on the roof. A short deluge.

"Sounds like a big drum," Shooter said. But Ray had never heard such a sound before and believed he might never hear it again. He stood still and let the drumming move into his chest and head. For an instant they all had an expression of rare surprise. No one spoke until the rain let up.

"Turn on the flashlight, Shooter." They could see the way to the middle of the attic, where they sat, all three of them in Ray's blanket, and listened until their breathing calmed. Jess's love of the rain-sound was contagious. "Don't you like it?" she asked. "Even a little rain sounds good up here."

"You don't get scared?" Ray snuggled close.

"Nothing up here but old boxes and a chair."

Shooter shone the flashlight into the corner. Something was in the chair, and he jumped.

"It's just our July Santa," Jess laughed. "I brought it up here for Miss Tut."

"I don't like when Mr. Will is gone," Shooter said.

"He'll be back tomorrow," Jess said.

"My daddy left," Ray said.

"I'm sure he'll come back too," Jess said.

"When?"

Thunder barely rumbled now. The rain was letting up.

"Want to turn off the flashlight for a minute?"

"Naw," Shooter said. They sat, and in a minute Shooter clicked off the light. The air in the attic turned black, but the outside appeared gray, and the rain grew softer and softer, plinking drops from the trees. They listened and relaxed against Jess. The boys smelled like Adam.

Adam. Adam. Your shadow is here in this dust of the attic, in the sleep-hair of these boys. Come back. Your arms full of silver hubcaps, or carrying Hap some place he doesn't want to go. If you were here, I might do something different. I don't know what.

"I think Ray's asleep," Shooter said. He held the flashlight to the boy's face, flicking it on.

"Hey." Ray squirmed. "Quit it!"

"Let's go back down now," Jess said. "Let's not tell anybody about what we did. It'll be our secret."

"We won't," Shooter said.

"Secret," Ray said.

The next day Will arrived at lunch and commented on last night's storm. "Woke me up—all that noise."

"It did? " Jess reached for a piece of toast.

Will turned to the boys. "Thought you boys might have been scared."

Both boys looked quickly at Jess, but Jess pretended not to hear. She realized that they usually went to Will when they were afraid, but last night, in his absence, they had come with her.

"So you weren't scared?" Will asked.

"Not me," Shooter said.

"Not me too," Ray said.

Will nodded, perhaps believing that he had taught them something about courage.

The next night Ray spiked a fever of 104 degrees. Jess saw him in the hall, sweating. He kept saying, "I don't feel good." His body was burning up. She alerted the others. After an hour he had grown lethargic.

"My God, we've got to get this fever down." Rosemary called the doctor who urged them to put Ray into a tub of cold water, and said he promised to come immediately. The doctor told them to keep the body cool or else the fever could damage the boy's brain.

Miss Tutwiler ran a tub of water while Jess and the professor took off Ray's pajamas. Jess held him and the professor pulled off his underwear. They carried his small-boned body to the tub. Shooter kept asking, "What's the matter with Ray?"

Jess and Frank tried to calm Shooter by taking him back to his room, but they could hear the commotion in the bathroom. Will and Miss Tut brought ice cubes to make the water as cold as possible, so when the professor lowered the limp body into the icy water, Ray screamed and Shooter yelled for them to *Stop it!*

"I can't do this, Miss Tut," Prof. Chapin said.

"We have to. We have to do this." She held the boy in the water. Will spoke to him gently, until Ray stopped yelling and began to cry softly.

By the time the doctor arrived the fever had dropped two degrees. The doctor stayed until the fever lowered sufficiently. He gave Ray an aspirin and said to watch closely in case the fever returned.

The professor and Rosemary took first watch over Ray. The next watch would be Jess and Frank, then Will and Miss Tut. They would divide up the night. Jess decided to stay the night with Shooter, but she kept waking to check on Ray. Possible brain damage. She kept imagining if Ray could turn into someone like Adam. That night, Jess promised God that if Ray got well, she would go home to her father and to whatever else came with that return.

Ray's fever spiked once more around four a.m., but when they lowered him into the tub, the water wasn't as cold, and they were able to keep him soothed. Rosemary gave him ginger ale, and Will promised to take him to the Birmingham Zoo when he got better. They spent a long time talking about animals they might see.

Around five a.m. Frank came to Ray's room, but the professor would not relinquish his station. Frank warned them. "If something happens to Ray, and Social Services finds out that we lied about Sonny Long, we'll be liable. All of us." He said this as though no one else had thought of it. But Jess had thought of it. She felt a piling up of all the things for which she could be condemned.

"The fever has already broken," the professor said. "Ray will be fine." Behind his glasses, his eyes blinked slowly. It was early morning when Jess went back to her room, and she realized that a fever of her own had broken.

Ray was sleeping soundly. Prof. Chapin was in his room, or else he was with Rosemary in her room. They had been seen together in town, holding hands, but their trysts in the boardinghouse had been full of stealth. Lately, Rosemary wore no make-up, her face more calm and natural. She sometimes wore jeans and a pink cotton shirt, with a vintage straw hat. She looked lovely, and for the first time, she seemed to feel lovely. She had stopped quoting so many Bible verses. The professor smiled all the time.

Zella and Miss Tut had gone to buy groceries, Shooter was sleeping late, and Will sat on the porch smoking a long cigar. Mimsy sat in his lap, licking herself. In the hall the fishbowl had only one fish, but no one commented.

— 34 —

Early on Saturday morning, Zella Davis, looking eccentric and happy in her garden-pants and man's shirt, had started planting her vegetables. She obviously was not interested in preparing everyone's breakfast, so when Will came in asking "You got any coffee?" Zella opened the refrigerator door and stood back, looking in.

"*Might* have some," she said.

"Can I get some?"

"Don't matter to me." Zella still stood in front of the open refrigerator. The morning's soft blue light came into the kitchen, where Will was sitting.

"Got any biscuits left from yesterday?" he asked.

"You can look good as me."

"You're in a *mood* today, aren't you?" Will said. He lifted the lid of the bread box and took out a cold biscuit.

"Always in *some* kinda mood."

Will poured coffee into a mug and poured another mug for Zella. "Come on. Sit down here with me."

"I ain't got time."

"You got time."

Zella sat across the table from Will and spooned three heaps of sugar into her mug. They sat in silence for several minutes, sipping. Jess came in and sat at the table with them.

"I been planting since early morning," Zella said. "Not in a mood to get breakfast for nobody today."

"Then don't," said Will. "I'll make a batch of scrambled eggs and toast. If anybody's hungry they can help themselves."

"And too, this's the anniversary of when my daddy died. We buried him 1945. I dreamed about him last night. More than a dream. Seems like he come to my room, talked to me, made *me* talk to *him*.

"You mean like a ghost?" Jess said.

"I don't know. He can show up in dreams, or sometimes just a spirit-thing in my room. Scare me to death first time I seen it."

Jess was leaning toward Zella. She knew about spirits too.

"That man never did get the hang of being dead." Zella shook her head hard. "I swear, I wish he'd just go on to where he's going. Leave me be."

"You want to go lie down awhile?" Jess asked. "Maybe you're coming down with something."

"I be all right. This coffee'll help some. Anyway, we got lot more work to do in the garden before we can quit. You ain't even started yet on your flowers."

"I will," Jess said.

Zella finished her coffee and leaned back in her chair. "What you got there, Mr. Will?"

"Something I want to show somebody." He hesitated. "Don't know what to think about it."

"Lemme see," Zella reached out.

"It's something in the *Birmingham Herald*. Yesterday's paper," he said.

"What's it say?" Jess asked. She thought it might be about the man found dead. "Is it about Ezra?"

"I knew that man," Zella said. "He used to come around the house where we lived on Ninth Street and not that many white men come around there. We'd find empty lighter fluid cans everywhere. Somebody saw him drinking it once. I felt kinda sorry for him." She opened her palms into the air, like a preacher. "But I don't hold with suicide. That is strictly against the Law of God."

Jess kept her eyes on Will as he flicked the paper, straightening it out, then folding it. "Well, this is in the personals," he said. "Somebody wanted by the police, says here." Will made a point of not looking at Jess. He bit thoughtfully into his biscuit. "Here's a photo. Look."

It was the old school photo of Jess.

"Let me see." Zella took the paper. "Looka here, Jess. This looks like *you*." She laughed. "'Cept she younger." She looked from Jess back again to the photo, then to Will. "Did you think it was Jess, Mr. Will?"

Jess peered over Zella's shoulder. She felt trembly and wondered if her face looked distorted. Will still did not look at her.

"Wonder what she did," Zella said. "Probly some man looking for his wife who run away. She mighta had good reason." Zella turned to the front page. "Now here is a *real* jailbird if I ever seen one!" She pointed to a photo of a man with a number under his chin, arrested for assault and battery. "He is a *bona fide* outlaw."

Will let the subject of the photo drop, but Jess felt cold. She wanted to read the personal ad, all of it, and watched where Will laid it down.

Shooter and Ray ran fast into the kitchen, chasing each other, yelling that one or the other, was "It." Zella struck one long arm at the boys. "Go on outta here. You kids go on now." She swatted at them again, and missed.

"Let's get to work," said Jess. "I've got begonias to plant."

"I can't eat begonias." Zella went to the sink, took a wet dishrag, and shook it out. "I'm finishing up those tomato stakes and I got to plant my okra."

"Too late for okra," Will said.

"You just watch."

Will listened to the women for a while as they discussed specific plantings—their words like little songs sung by fishes. Zella touched Will's shoulder on her way out.

"C'mon, honey," she said to Jess, and Jess followed her into the backyard. They worked for almost an hour before Zella brought up the photo in the paper. "That girl look a lot like you, you know that?"

Jess admitted that she did.

"So if it *was* you I don't want to know about it. Keep me ignorant. You know what they say about ignorance?"

"'Ignorance is bliss?'" Jess said.

"Yeah." Zella Davis laughed, a chuckle. "But if that be true, I oughta be happier than I am."

She propped another stake into the ground and pushed it down hard with the flat of her hand. Jess dug a circle of holes for begonias and began to lower them in, one by one. A nice wind blew high in the trees.

"That's gonna look real good, honey," Zella told her. She could see that Jess did not want to talk.

"I'm going to need some more fertilizer," Jess said. Her voice sounded as if she might cry.

"Let me see can I get you some." Zella went across the yard into the shed, and stayed until Jess had gathered herself back into a state of calm. A drone of flies hovered over the door of the shed. Zella came out with a bag of fertilizer. "This'll be enough," she said, and dropped it onto the broken sidewalk.

In the house the phone was ringing. Maybe a wrong number—just a thin mistake in a thin blue day. The phone was still ringing, but the two women sat on the ground with the delirious songs of birds around them, and, higher, the sound of geese.

— 35 —

Frank O'Malley had been the one to answer the phone that day. His editor wanted to know about the article he was writing, and asked if it was finished. It wasn't. He told his editor that he needed to verify his facts.

Frank had been writing for the paper for almost a year, but, until he wrote the Ezra article, no one paid much attention. He couldn't help but imagine how the story about Jess might be a big exclusive, but didn't know if he could write it. For two nights he had worked until four a.m., and today fell asleep on the porch.

Jess found Frank the next morning. He looked dead on the porch step. She squatted down to look at him closer. His arms were thrown above his head as though someone had said "Stick 'em up." His t-shirt lay hiked up above his jeans and the dark hair beneath his navel curved in a line going down into his pants. His shorts were showing, at least the elastic, just below the place where the jeans pulled away from his hips. His breath came slow and soft.

He sat up quickly and frightened Jess. She jumped. "I thought you were asleep."

He looked at her sideways. "I couldn't be drafted because I have a bad heart. I'm embarrassed about not going like everybody else." He had the look of a man who had more hope than the moment deserved.

Jess turned away from his face, knowing the direction this could go. "No, that's okay. I shouldn't have asked you."

His voice got soft now, like he was cursing. "You're so beautiful. How'd you get so beautiful?" He edged closer to her. He smelled like sleep.

Jess was still squatting, and stood up fast. She pursed her mouth.

"Okay, Okay," he said quickly. "But let me ask you something about that photo in the *Birmingham Herald*. I know it's you. The police were looking for a young man named Adam, who was about to be sent away because he ran after little girls. I know Adam was your stepbrother and that he drowned in a river. He was nineteen and retarded. So . . . " he hesitated.

Jess nodded, but heard those words: *I saw you.* She pictured the brown and white car shouldering her whole burden.

"What happened?" he asked. "What made you run away?" Frank's tone had turned hard and business-like.

Jess made a small sound in her throat. "He didn't try to hurt me, if that's what you're thinking." She kept shaking her head. Frank leaned to put a hand around her shoulder. She found it hard to breathe. "They were going to send him to an institution, Cadwell, where they do awful things."

"I know Cadwell and about places like it," Frank told her. "They're mostly in the South. Do you know those practices are against the law in other states?"

"Against the law?"

"Most of the South still practices eugenics." Frank stood up. "That's what it's called."

"How do you know about this?"

"I looked into it. I did some research on those places. I'm not getting this for the paper," Frank said, but he didn't sound certain. Jess experienced a chill in her body.

"Don't ask me anymore." She kept shaking her head. "I've said too much."

"Listen, I just . . . " Frank fell backwards, stepping off the porch and into soft mud. "I want to help you."

Later that day Edward Booker telephoned the boardinghouse. Will answered and called Jess to the downstairs booth.

"Jess." His voice sounded good. "Sam is home. He called here looking for you. I told him everything."

"Is he okay?"

"His leg was hurt, and he had punctured a lung. But he's okay now. He's already walking."

She had thought so often about Sam coming home, seeing him again;,but, since she arrived at the boardinghouse, Sam had receded in her mind. Her father's words made him real again. She imagined his face close up, his hands—big as plates.

"Tell him to come get me," she said. She felt a new center forming in herself. "Will you tell him that?"

"Yes. Yes. I'll tell him."

"What exactly did you say to him, Daddy? About me?"

"That Adam drowned and that you ran away. That Clementine had blamed you for Adam's death."

"I'll quit my job tomorrow," she said. Her voice was steady. "I'll start packing."

"I can't wait to see you." She could hear her father's voice rising with hope, then trying to gain repose. "And you're really okay?"

"I'm fine," she said.

Before her father hung up the phone she heard him heave a sigh. She imagined him collapsing in his chair, relieved.

The first person she told was Frank. She took him out into the backyard and told him that Sam was back home and that he was coming to get her. "Sometime in the next few days," she said.

Frank nodded. "I meant it when I said I wanted to help."

"I know," she said. Her mind was clear. The war was over and Sam was home.

A jet flying high made them both look up. They watched white smoke trail down the sky, falling like a ribbon dissolving, loosening, becoming invisible again.

Honey's Last Stop was about to close, and Jess and Maggie had only three customers left. It was Jess's last day at work. Frank would arrive soon to walk her back to the boardinghouse. Jess had not seen the brown and white car in weeks. She was wiping down the counter when Maggie said that somebody in the last booth had asked for coffee, so Jess walked over with a fresh pot. She wore a shiny white uniform, and a small hat that sat on the back of her head.

Jess held the pot over the table ready to pour, until she saw that the man looking up at her was Sam. She studied his face and hair as if she had never seen him before. "Sam?"

He stood and held her. "I drove all night to get here," he said. "Jess."

She put her face in his shoulder and felt that she was looking down from a high place. She leaned back, making sure she was seeing and holding the right man.

"Why did you leave like that, Jess?" Sam shook her shoulders, as though he were angry, then held her close again. "What's going on?" She didn't answer, but felt the slap of his words. She breathed in the smell of him before he suddenly held her at arm's length.

"Tell me. Nobody's heard from you since April?" He shook his head. "I got back home and learned that the police were searching for you." He still had his hands on her shoulders. "Damn, Jess." Sam looked like a man begging for his life.

She stepped away from him. "Please, Sam."

He sat back down carefully. "Adam's dead. They think you did something to him." His voice grew loud.

Maggie walked toward them, but Jess waved her away and sat in the booth across from Sam.

"Listen," she said.

"Did Adam hurt you, Jess?" Sam asked. "I need to know what he did." Everyone was suspicious of Adam, who was always the least likely suspect.

"No. No."

"But he was getting all those treatments. Maybe he got messed up. I keep thinking that he . . . " Sam couldn't bring himself to say what he was thinking.

"No. Nothing like that."

"Then what?"

"I can't talk about it here." She reached for him across the table. He leaned toward her. "I worried about you too. My dad said you got hurt. Your leg?"

"I'm okay. I'm not even using crutches anymore." A slice of darkness crossed his face, a film over his eyes. She asked if he wanted to tell her about it.

"No." Sam looked pale, thinner than the person she remembered. His body looked angular, bent, and used. They were both different from what they had been.

"How did you know where I worked?" she asked.

He looked at her curiously. "A young man at the boardinghouse said you'd be at the diner. Frank something."

They heard Maggie cashing out the last two customers. Jess leaned forward to whisper, "I know Clementine blames me."

"Yeah. Because you ran away, and because you never wanted him to go to Cadwell."

"Maybe I *am* guilty."

"Not unless you held his head underwater," Sam said. "Did you hold Adam underwater and drown him?"

Jess looked out the window of the diner. "No."

"I know you didn't do that, Jess." Sam had an older face. "Jess, why did you stop writing to me?" he asked.

She moved to get up, motioning to Maggie that they were leaving. "After April," she said, "I was just trying to get by."

"I know how that is." Sam stood, then said, "Who's that Frank guy? He sure got interested when I said I was looking for you."

"He's a reporter for the *Gazette*. He lives at the boardinghouse."

"He got a crush on you?"

"I guess he might." Jess took Sam's hand.

"Well," he said. "Can't blame him for that."

Sam and Jess went toward the door. Maggie stood ready to lock up. Jess introduced Sam to Maggie, and they left. Everyone else was gone. Outside the diner Sam held Jess close and kissed her face. "I missed you so much." She leaned into the warm smell of his neck, and couldn't believe the strength of his arms around her.

"Don't be mad at me," she said. She put her arm around his waist. They walked slowly to the boardinghouse. No one was on the porch; but Jess could hear Will and Miss Tut talking in the kitchen. Sam opened the screen door, but before it slammed he lifted Jess into the air, "I went crazy without you." He kissed her so hard she cried out; but did not pull back.

Miss Tut heard them and came into the hallway. Jess introduced him to Miss Tut and Will, and they asked if Sam needed a room. Neither Jess nor Sam answered.

"Probably not," Will said.

Miss Tut looked surprised. "Well you don't think that . . .

"Stop it, Tut. Let them be. This young man's been in a war. He's older than all of us." Will waved Jess and Sam away. "Go on, he said. I'll take care of this." As they went upstairs Jess heard Will speak harshly to Miss Tut. "Leave it alone. They need to be together tonight. My God, Tut!"

"I bet you won't call her daddy about this," she said. "You gonna tell him about this too?" Will didn't answer, but by then Sam was opening the door to Jess's room. Before it was closed, Jess saw Frank's door cracked slightly, and she knew he had seen them.

That night they made love uncertainly, awkwardly, but with an urgent need to know each other again. As they lay together in the dark, Sam rolled over to look at her. "I guess you know Clementine moved out of the house. Your dad made her leave when she formally accused you."

"What does that mean exactly?"

"It means you'll have a trial when you get back."

"What did my dad tell you?"

"He told me Adam had drowned in the river and that you had run away." Sam waited. "That's all he said." A car turned its headlights toward the house and lit up their room; the shadows whisked across the wall and ceiling before fading away. Jess ran her hands over the sheet and lay silent.

"The day before Adam was going to Cadwell, he wanted to go to the river," she said. "He'd been begging us not to send him away. He wanted to tell the river goodbye. I told him the water was too cold, but he wanted to go. I'd seen him do that before—wade in a few feet then come out to go home." She started to tear up. She could not tell him everything. "But he didn't come out."

"Tell the lawyer that," Sam said. "When you get back home, just say that."

Jess didn't tell him more. She didn't feel close enough to say all that she needed to say. She wondered if he felt distant from her too. They lay for a long time before she waved her hand lightly over his leg and the long scar on his thigh. "How did you get hurt?"

"That seems like another world now," he said quickly. "I still have bad dreams though. Real bad." He waited, allowing the light strokes of her hand to soothe his body.

"Will you tell me what happened? How you got hurt?"

A breeze blew the curtains back from the window and fell across them like a sweet breath. "I don't know. We'd been fighting for almost four months. We'd been out a couple of nights, but we hadn't seen anything to make us scared until our squad leader gave orders to go about a quarter-mile to where the enemy was waiting." He stopped. "You want to hear this?" Jess said she did.

"It'd been raining for about four days straight. We were supposed to have cleats on our shoes so we wouldn't slip in the mud, but I didn't have any. I slid down into a gulley and landed in barbed wire. Everybody said, 'Don't move,' because sometimes the wire was booby-trapped. Carl Hill came down and picked the wire off me. Took forever, seems like."

"So it wasn't booby trapped?"

"Not that time. Anyway, when I got out, the squad leader said to get in a V formation but we didn't know the Chinese had formed a semi-circle around us. They opened fire and all hell broke loose. God, Jess. They had a heavy machine gun." Sam stopped as though he were seeing it again. "They just chopped us up." He lifted his arms out from the covers and sighed.

"The squad leader kept yelling orders, telling us to retreat. But I'm at the far end of the V flank. I thought for sure I was going to die." He looked at Jess. "The others pulled out, and it was just me and two other guys. Then a Chinese soldier rushed toward me. He threw a grenade. I squeezed off some rounds and he fell. I rolled to get out of the way of the grenade. But it went off."

Jess had her hands over her mouth.

"It blew me and Carl Hill away from each other, caught me on the right leg." He pointed to his leg. "Killed Carl, though. I hid under a bush when two Chinks came looking around. They went right past me. They were so close. Then, the squad leader came in and picked me up. I could hardly believe it. He put me over his shoulder and worked his way down the hill. He went real slow. It was nighttime, and bushes were thick around us. While I was being carried down, I caught a bullet in the arm. We finally got back. There were lots of new guys standing around that I'd never seen before. They'd sent some reinforcements and there was some integration going on at the time, but we hadn't seen any colored guys in the outfit before that. They gave me to a colored guy from Mississippi, and he helped me all the way back to the outpost. Probably saved my life."

"They had doctors there?" Jess asked.

"I woke up in a hospital, and remember being under an x-ray machine. I felt my dog tags and told the doctors 'I'm still alive. Don't put these in my mouth.' You know, if you're dead they just put dog tags in your mouth and jam up your jaw."

Jess listened without moving.

"So, they operated on me. I had that bullet in my arm and shrapnel in my stomach and in one lung. They kept worrying that I might get pneumonia. My leg was pretty torn up. I stayed for about a week before they sent me to Yongdungpo.

"Then some high-up medical Colonel said he was going to ZI me. I'm wondering what is this 'ZI'? and he said, 'Zone of Interior. We're sending you home.' The war was almost over by then. All I could think about when he said I was going home was that I would get to see you. Then I came home and nobody knew where you were. I swear, Jess, that was worse than being shot at."

Jess had been crying. She wanted to comfort Sam, to soothe his mind; but she suddenly felt as if they lived in different worlds. "You think we'll ever feel normal again?"

"Just being here with you feels pretty good," he said.

They slept fitfully the rest of the night. They were different people now, both of them, sleeping with a stranger. But the next morning they looked rested when they went downstairs to breakfast and explained to everyone that they were leaving.

— 36 —

"Why're you taking her away from us?" Zella asked when Sam was introduced to everyone at breakfast.

"It's time for me to go home," Jess said. "Past time, really." She looked at Will. "From that day you saw my photo in the paper, I knew I had to leave."

"I don't want Jess to go away," Shooter whined. "Everybody always goes away."

"What will happen when you go back?" Miss Tutwiler asked.

"They'll have a trial," Sam said. "Her stepbrother drowned in the river and . . . "

"They're not blaming Jess for that, are they?" Rosemary asked.

"They might be. Her dad hired a lawyer."

Ray hit Shooter, then cried.

"Eat your eggs," Zella told him.

"I don't want any eggs," Ray pouted. "I hate eggs."

"No you don't," Miss Tut said.

"You eat like I tell you to," Zella said to the boy.

Will put his hand on Sam's shoulder. "You got to understand, son, Jess brought some light into this place." The professor turned to smile at Rosemary, who looked lovely in some old blue-jeans and a t-shirt, her hair pulled back into a casual bun of curls. "Even Miss Tut started to like me," said Will.

Frank bent over his plate and grumbled under his breath, then turned abruptly peering into the woods like it was a dream forest.

"You'll get over it, Frank," Will said. "Won't be the first thing you have to get over."

Jess looked carefully at everyone around the table, taking a mental picture in her mind of all of them, and then each one in a separate frame. She had become who she would always be, here, with them, strangers honed into an odd configuration of a family, but a family nonetheless. She would miss them terribly. Will stood at the window looking out at the street. A long silence fell over them as everyone thought about saying goodbye.

They helped Jess carry her suitcase to Sam's car. Ray cried and Shooter walked away toward the stream. Jess called to Shooter, but he refused to turn around. She called again and he stopped, frozen in stubborn grief. She promised she would come back to see him.

Moths on the windshield dusted the glass with mica. Sam turned on the ignition. The car was old and the motor roared a few combustions before catching. Shooter turned to wave one hand. The professor held Ray, who had his head buried in the professor's shoulder. Jess was sure that they would take the boys somewhere fun today, distract them with ice cream, tuck them in bed with new promises.

As Sam drove off, Jess could see the grass in front of the house disappear in the side mirror, and felt the morning drag behind her. She heard the church bell toll the hour and knew that her life had come down to a decision, for good or bad. They would drive all day, spend the night in a hotel (where they agreed to sign in as a married couple), then drive part of the next day.

The road in August became a blazing strip of heat and a car in the distance looked like a liquid shape that took hard form as it got closer, then turned liquid again. They rode almost an hour without talking. Sam's eyes held a sadness, and just below the surface, anger. Something thick lay between Jess and Sam.

"You want to talk about anything?" she finally asked.

"Not now," he said.

Jess looked at the woods where she had spent so many nights. They passed houses with clothes-lines: dresses, towels, shirts, and pants she might have stolen, if she had still been running. She reached to touch Sam's leg, an expression of closeness, but he jumped, his arm rising, as if to protect himself from harm. This was the second time he had jumped when she touched him.

Sam lifted a pack of cigarettes from his shirt pocket and tapped it against the heel of his hand. "Take the wheel a minute, would you?" He lit the cigarette turning and cupping the match in his hand. Jess watched the smoke curl around his head. When did Sam start smoking? He held the smoke in his mouth, and let it out. She was fascinated.

By the time they were in the north Georgia mountains the western sky had reddened and a yellow moon came up through shards of clouds. Sam blew the horn three times and Jess jumped. He looked happy now. He blew it three more times and laughed, then three more. He yelled her name out the window, celebrating the fact that they were together. The sound echoed and rattled out over the valley, then faded into the trees and creeks.

That night Jess slept with Sam beside her; but at midnight she moved carefully from their bed to step out under the stars—the Pleiades, Cassiopeia, Orion rising up elegant, circling this world and other ones. Jess felt that she, herself, had been set in motion, like the planets spinning through space. Her new center of gravity was sending her back home, where there were things she would never tell anyone. She had wanted to give Adam something, anything. But looking back, she wondered if maybe everything she had done was a mistake. The world, it seemed, had its shoes on the wrong feet.

Jess was standing outside the motel room still watching the stars, when Sam called to her from their room. "Jess? Where are you? Come here," he said. "I miss you." Cars on the highway rolled by, a train somewhere kept announcing itself, and Jess felt suddenly large, as if she could wear those stars for a hat, or step out into the wild dark air singing.

WHAT REMAINS

— 37 —

The last time Jess saw her father he had seemed younger, more energetic. He was waiting on the front steps, but he rose quickly when he saw Sam's car, and hurried toward it. He appeared stooped, his face thinner, his sparse hair whiter. Seeing him come towards her with his arms wide open, Jess felt she had been away longer than four months.

"Jess," he said. "Oh, Jess." He couldn't stop saying her name. He thanked Sam, but barely looked at him. Hap greeted her eagerly, with his paws on her waist. Jess still carried her father's satchel, the one she had taken the day she left home. Edward touched it, as though he had never seen anything more beautiful. "I don't know where to begin," he said. As he stood back to look at her face, she held him tighter. She didn't want to let go.

Sam picked up the old suitcase given to her by Ruby and Pug. "We can throw this out," he said, inspecting its shabbiness.

"No." Jess took the suitcase from him. "I'm keeping that—to remember the people who gave it to me." As she entered the house, she felt the absence of Adam. The hallway seemed darker, the air smelled of concrete and dust. Her father followed her inside. Jess held the door open for both men. All three of them were thinking of the days that lay ahead.

Sam took his own suitcase to the bedroom off the kitchen. He had moved again into himself, a private mood. Jess assumed she would need to get used to these mood changes and blamed them on the war.

"We'll meet with the lawyer in the morning. The arraignment is tomorrow afternoon," Edward told Jess.

In the kitchen her father brought out makings for sandwiches, and placed a bowl of potato chips on the table. A large store-bought sponge cake sat on the counter. The place was different without the smell of Clementine's cooking, and though Jess was glad she was not around, the house seemed lonesome for her father.

"Who is the lawyer?" Jess asked.

"James Strickland. A good defense attorney. I began looking for him right after you left. I wanted you to have the best."

"I imagined the police would be here to pick me up," she said. "I guess I might have to go to jail." It was a question.

"That's what I hope to prevent, Sweetie." Her father looked uncomfortable. "And your lawyer got the judge to give me custody of you until tomorrow. But tomorrow . . . " His voice trailed off. On the phone Edward had so many questions that Jess would not allow him to ask; but now that she was here, Edward didn't ask anything.

"Do you want to know what happened?" Jess said.

"I don't know," he said. "It's all I've thought about for months." He opened the refrigerator and took out a pitcher of milk. "I *did* want to know. But seeing you, I mean, you can't take the blame for this, Jess. I won't have you do that. None of this was your fault." He poured three glasses of milk and set them on the table. "Let me just be glad you're home."

"Will I have a trial?" Jess wanted to know everything. Nothing inside her was running away now.

"First, we'll have the arraignment," he told her. "Strickland will see you tomorrow." They made sandwiches and ate slowly. Jess took in the feeling of being home again, but the atmosphere of the house had changed. Cobwebs hovered in the corners, and the doorknob on the kitchen door was gone.

"Jess, I don't blame you. Just don't tell me anything right now. Strickland wants to talk to you first." He coughed. "Part of the evidence against you was when you said that Adam would be better off dead than in Cadwell. Did you say that?"

Jess nodded. "But I didn't mean that I would hurt him."

"Well, I don't want you to lie, exactly. I just don't want you to go to jail. Do you hear what I'm saying?" He leaned in toward her. "I couldn't bear it. I blame myself more than I blame you."

It had not occurred to Jess to lie to the lawyer.

Edward finally asked how Jess had survived alone all those months and she told him about Ruby and Pug, the hard days of living in the woods, getting sick, and stealing the oranges. She told him about people at Tut's Boardinghouse and the man who had followed her in a muddy brown and white car. Edward listened intently, but his face looked slightly misshapen. He didn't comment.

Sam appeared around the door jamb to say that he was going to bed. Jess knew that tonight, here in her house, they would sleep apart. She cut a piece of cake, and dropped some on the floor for Hap.

How's Buckhead?" Jess asked, expecting the worst.

"He's good," her father said. "He's fine."

That night Jess slept in Adam's room, where his smell still lingered: the odor of stale cinnamon and tree roots—not always pleasant. Hap curled up on the rug beside Adam's bed, and headlights of cars roamed over the bedroom walls. Adam had liked the patterns made by the passing lights: shafts that brushed across the wall, making the room bright as day—but only for a moment. He imagined driving those cars.

Once, Edward had taken Adam on back country roads to let him drive, teaching him to shift gears, to go in reverse, which he found hysterically funny. When Adam mentioned it to Jess, he said "Don't tell." He said it twice.

Jess felt the two strains of her life coming together. Some nights in the woods Jess had felt a small dark place within her. She lay very still until she was sure that the dark place inside would not join the black of the air, and swallow her whole. When she felt safe, she would doze off, falling into a hollow place inside her chest; other nights she wondered if she had died and awakened inside a coffin built too large for her body—a coffin with trees and sky. She took the edge of the sheet between her forefinger and thumb, pressing down, not letting go; and she cried out, as Adam used to do when he woke in the middle of the night.

Clementine said Adam had always done that, even as a baby. Jess imagined that Adam was calling for a life he couldn't have. She hoped he had not suffered too much in the river. She hoped he had finally found the harmony that lived in his tall body.

On that day three months ago she was pushed by a question of mercy; now she had to focus on the matter of truth. Everything centered around an accident of birth, her own quick decision, and the absence of choices. She grabbed the sheet with both hands, and realized that she had been holding her breath. All of these thoughts had come in so unexpectedly from such a slight provocation—as Adam's old words. *Don't tell. Don't tell.*

Jess woke the next day to geese calls and Hap barking at whatever lurked in the yard. Her appointment with Mr. Strickland was at eleven o'clock, and the arraignment was scheduled for the afternoon. Her father was still asleep. She stood at the window and felt bound to whatever would come next. The pungent air of fall was just beginning. Sam called to her from downstairs. Jess dressed quickly and found him waiting at the table drinking coffee. "Your voice sounded like something was wrong," she said.

He shook his head. "That's an understatement, don't you think?" He spoke with a chill in his voice, and she didn't know how to react. She made some toast and sat at the table with him.

"What do you think the lawyer will say today?" he asked.

"I don't know," she said. "I feel guilty, but I don't feel guilty of manslaughter."

"I know about manslaughter," Sam said.

"You ever heard of Scots Law?" Jess asked. She did not say that Frank had explained the law one night when he was trying to get information out of her. "It says a person can be proven 'not guilty,' but the verdict doesn't 'presume innocence.'"

"What do you mean?" Sam said. "Being 'not guilty' and being 'innocent' are two completely different ideas."

"Some things aren't reasonable like that," she said. "Let me ask you something, Sam. If I were proven guilty, would you still love me?"

"Don't you think I wonder the same thing?" he said. "If you would love me?"

"But I do. I do love you." She didn't know if that was true. "How can you say that?"

Sam's hands fidgeted nervously. "I'm going to tell you something," he said, but then he waited so long that Jess thought he had decided not to say it. "Remember that guy I wrote you about? Billy Keifert? Well, we stood by each other through some bad stuff. We were friends. I won't ever have such a good friend, but in the end . . . " He hesitated.

"In the end . . . what?"

"It was on the day we moved into Soyang Valley, and Billy's feet were hurting. He could hardly walk." Sam seized her arm. "Everywhere the mud was deep, like glue. You'd see tanks stuck, with mud to the top of the tracks. At first, we got just light shelling, then some mortars started coming in. Made us real jumpy." He stopped and Jess sat very still.

"That's when Billy got hurt," he said quietly. "He was hit by a mortar. He was hurt bad, I mean, real bad. Should have been killed, Jess. I was about a hundred feet away, but when I got to him I saw his stomach split wide open. I tried to stop the bleeding with my shirt. Took it off and stuffed it into the wound. He was saying he couldn't stand it." Sam looked like a blind man seeing things in his mind. "I could see his insides, everything just right there. And he was screaming so loud, Jess. I'd never heard a sound like that. Then he started begging me to kill him. To shoot him. 'Just let me die,' he kept saying. He kept saying, 'Please, please.' I told him the medic would come. He lay like that, I don't know how long. I've never seen so much blood."

"Where was the medic?" Jess asked.

"We had a lot wounded that day. When the medic finally got there, I had so much blood on me he thought I was the one hurt." Sam paused, "I should have been. It should have been me."

"Sam . . . "

"I thought about shooting him—maybe in the head. He was begging me to end it, begging me, Jess. I couldn't do it. He finally died. Keifert. Fuck! Fuck it all! After that if anybody tried to touch me, even once, I thought I'd kill 'em. Even the doctors trying to help me. I couldn't stand to be touched. Sometimes even now. I don't know what that is."

He didn't speak for a full minute. Everything was tainted by the memory of blood and buddies. He could not reconcile the Sam he used to be with the man who ran blindly into a skirmish ready to drive a bayonet into the heart of a man his age with a different face, a different language. He had not known he could do the things he did and he had not asked himself what the war would cost him. "I'm just not the person you loved, Jess. I'm different now."

Jess thought about being without either guilt or innocence, and what their actions had cost them. "Oh, Sam. I'm so sorry." She waited. "Maybe your feelings for me have changed." She waited again. "Have they?" She tried to push down the resentment rising inside her. She needed him today, but he couldn't help her.

"My feelings for everything have changed, Jess." He could not stop shaking his head. "If things had just been different."

Jess stood up. "We have about a thousand *ifs* right now, Sam." Jess was the one who sounded angry now. She clenched her hands together, then unclenched them. She could feel the unevenness of the wood floor beneath her feet.

Jess left Sam sitting at the table. "I have to get ready to meet Strickland," she said. "My dad will drive me in."

— 38 —

James Strickland's office felt like a court. Edward and Jess answered questions, but finally Mr. Strickland stood up and walked around his desk. He asked Edward if he could speak privately with Jess. Edward could wait outside.

"Today," he told Jess, "you'll be informed of charges made by Clementine Finney and you'll be asked to enter a plea of 'guilty' or 'not guilty.' I assume you want to plead 'not guilty'?" He was walking the room.

Jess nodded.

"The state could charge you with negligence or involuntary manslaughter. Then the court determines whether or not to set bail or release you on your own recognizance." He shook his head. "The fact that you ran away will go against you, I'm afraid. But even if you are sent to jail, I believe I can get bail set after a couple of days. Do you understand?" A car honked irritably and made them both jump.

Jess's whole body turned rigid. "I ran away because I thought I'd be in trouble for letting Adam go into the water."

"Could you have stopped him?" he asked her.

Jess looked at Strickland for a moment. "No," she said. "Nobody could." She almost believed this was true. "He would have done *anything* not to go to Cadwell."

Strickland sat down next to Jess. "Next time you're asked that question," he said, "don't hesitate before you say no." He leaned back. A shock of hair fell onto his forehead. "Let me tell you though, Jess, I believe we'll be all right. I don't see how they can find you guilty of anything other than just talking to Adam. The best they have is Adam's limited mental ability—and whether or not he was cognizant of the consequences when he went into the river. He couldn't swim, right?"

"That's right."

"Let's take it one step at a time," he told her, and patted the arm of her chair. "As I said, I think this will be a hard case to prove." Strickland lifted his briefcase from the desk to indicate that they were leaving his office to go to the arraignment.

In the town square a September sky threatened rain. The flag was being lowered, and two dogs were barking in the street.

At the arraignment Jess pleaded not guilty, but the judge set bail higher than they expected. She was considered a flight risk so, for the time being, Jess had to go to jail. The policewoman cuffed her and Edward reached to touch her shoulder. As she was led from the courtroom, his hand slid down her arm and Jess thought he was going to ask her something, or try to come with her. Then she thought she heard him call her name—as he might have called her in from the yard years ago.

She was driven to the jail where she walked, dazed and stumbling, down a narrow corridor. Her hands were cuffed in front of her. She was led through two locked doors that shuddered closed behind her. A few of the cells were open and some prisoners stood in the corridor. They passed a heavy-set woman carrying a vile-smelling bucket. Another woman, in a cell with the door open, was bent over in a peculiar stance. Jess felt as though she might faint, but walked stolidly forward.

"You kill a husband, girlie?"

"Somebody fuck you without your consent?" Another one laughed. "You take him out?"

The policewoman ordered them to leave her alone, and they sauntered away, back to their own cells. Jess had been running from this day for nearly four months, but nothing in those months had prepared her for the Buncombe County Jail. The policewoman opened the cell door, and unlocked the cuffs before she gently pressed Jess's back, urging her in. The door closed and Jess sat on the hard metal cot. She heard someone whistling a familiar tune. Everything around her appeared lightless and fluid. The angles of the cell began to spin, and she could feel the substance of her own breath against her cheek. Her body shook in spasms.

Women in other cells yelled at her, cursed. Their words floated through Jess's mind like dust motes. The mattress ticking was soiled and sour, and she felt a chill coming through the walls, even though the day was warm. She pulled her jacket around her. The cell had nothing but the cot and a chair with one broken leg. She could smell the odor of urine and sweat and the lingering scent of the policewoman. Two roaches huddled in the corner beneath a stained toilet bowl that was bolted to the cement. Water leaked from the edges of pipes, and a small high window allowed her to see that the afternoon light had softened into a purple gauze, almost dark.

Strickland spent two days convincing Judge Horn that Jess would not be a flight risk; then he made a motion for a bench trial. He liked this judge.

By the fourth day bail was posted and Jess was allowed to leave. She heard the doors again closing behind her, then she saw her father and Sam standing beside the car. She walked toward them stiffly, like someone walking on ice.

Edward drove Jess home, but neither Sam nor her father asked her any questions—as though the decision not to ask had been discussed. At home they found that people from church had brought over fried chicken, a few casseroles, banana pudding—the way they did for a funeral. Edward filled their plates with food and Sam pointed to a stack of letters on the hall table, all from Lula, Alabama. Jess opened them and, as they ate, she read each one out loud. The first, from Zella, was scrawled on yellow tablet paper.

August 30

My Sweet Jess,

Sometimes things go wrong. I know about that. Sometimes they twist around out a shape. I can't hardly believe you did something to get you jail-time. You always been so sweet in my eyes. Us working together so close in the garden those days back. I always knew they was something wrong though, behind those eyes a yours.

But now nothing I can think of could put you in jail with people who spent they whole lives stealing and murdering. I don't think it be true. That you did a bad thing. And that Judge need to listen real close to what you say.

Miss Tut, Mr. Will, and me, and Miss Rosemary and the Professor are thinking about you. Frank probably thinks about you the most. Shooter and Ray miss you much as we do. They say they going to write you in prison. That's what they call it. To them you some kind a hero.

To me too.

Love,

Zella Davis

August 29, 1953

Quos amor verus tenuit, tenebit. Seneca

To Miss Jess Booker,

We all think of you often and wish that you were here in this house with us. Shooter talks about you, and Ray stands at the fence watching the road. He

*thinks you're coming back any day now. He keeps asking where prison is, and if
it's like a cave.*

*We know what kind of girl you are, Jess. You are young and you will have
a chance to live out the life that you should be living, the life you deserve. The
young man who came to get you seems trustworthy, a man of dignity, and you,
dear girl, are a graceful piece of this world to all who live here in the boardinghouse.*

Yours,

Albert Chapin (Those whom true love has held, it will go on holding.)

"He never stops with the Latin," Jess laughed, and folded the letter, tucking
it back into the envelope. "He's always teaching." She took a sip of iced tea.

Aug. 30, 1953

Jess, my dear,

*We speak of you often. You were a light brought into this big old house, for ev-
eryone. Even Frank stopped lifting objects from the hall table to sell at the pawn
shop.*

*Not one of us believes that you have done a terrible thing, and whenever you
want to come back and tell us you can do so. Or you can come back and tell us
nothing. The main invitation here is that you must come back to Lula and visit
us. You always have a room.*

*Rosemary has been near to hysterical about your leaving, since she thinks you
were the one who brought her together with Prof. Chapin (I still can't call him
Albert). She thinks just your being here in the house brought a kind of love potion
for everybody. She says to say how much she misses you, and that she will write
when she gets herself together.*

*Mr. Long came back. He found a job as a Fuller Brush salesman. The boys
are happy and not afraid when he leaves to make house calls.*

This house is lonesome without you.

My love,

Pauline Tutwiler

PS There will be a wedding in December. Will and I hope you will be here.

"The next one's from Mr. Brennan," Jess said. Edward stood to pour more
tea into their glasses and sat down to listen to the next one. He seemed uncomfortable at the mention of William Brennan's name.

Aug. 30, 1953

Jess,

How much we miss your presence here! I don't believe you will finally be found guilty of anything. If that judge there in North Carolina knows anything about the person you are, I believe you'll be fine. All of us here feel a love for you and want to help any way we can.

Miss Tut has agreed to marry me in December, and she and Rosemary are planning a wedding, which I now dread! Please come back for the wedding, you and your young man.

Frank wrote an article about how you were the missing girl, and that you had gone back to Goshen. He said nothing accusatory, but stated a few facts. He checked out the article with both me and Albert before turning it in. Now, he's working on an article about kleptomania!

Shooter said to tell you he bought four candy bars with his treasure money, and Ray bought five comic books. We miss you, and Miss Tut is refusing to rent out your room. She says, Keep it like it is. We all know a good heart when we see one.

Much love,

Will

"I miss him the most," Jess said. "He told me they used to call my mother Day. Her nickname in high school." Edward nodded. He knew that nickname, but looked sad at the mention of Will's knowledge of it. "You were right about Mr. Brennan, Daddy," Jess said. "He *did* have a crush on Mama, but said he never had a chance because of how much she loved *you.*"

Edward smiled, as though he had always known this.

"These next two are from the boys." Jess noticed that she did not have a letter from Frank.

Saturday

Jess,

My Daddy came back, but we miss you and look for you everywhere. Miss Zella says maybe you come back sometime, then I stop crying. Miss Zella is writing this for me just like I say, so I say this: If you come back I will let you have one of Shooter's candy bars that he gave to me, and if you come back we can play ball in the front yard like we did that day you fell down and we laugh so hard I peed my pants. Do you remember?

Are you in prison? What is that like? I wish I were there too, and Shooter, so we could throw the ball in prison like we did in the yard.

I have to go.

Love,

Ray

Saturday

Jess,

Did you know my Daddy is home? I knew he would come back. I have a birthday next week, and he's giving me a party, but it won't be fun without you, but I'll have it anyway. Maybe you could send me something for my birthday. I will be eight. I like baseball caps and I like to build model airplanes with Mr. Will, and I like just money too. If you want to send me a present you can. Ray and me talk about when you were here, and sometimes we laugh, but really we don't feel happy about you being gone, and we wish you were coming back real soon. Miss Tut says maybe you will come for the wedding, but that's a long way off. I will be in second grade and my teacher is Mrs. Bevell, but we call her Mrs. Devil because she is so mean. I don't like her already.

Please write to me and to Ray so we can act like we still know you, and maybe you will come back here sometime. You could sing me to sleep like you did that one time. We like the man name of Sam.

Love,
Shooter
P.S. You can just send my present to this address.

Though the letters were just words on paper, each separate voice crackled with the memory of reprieve that came at the boardinghouse. Edward lifted Jess's plate, along with his own, and took it to the sink. Sam had eaten with deliberate slowness, as though every bite was a difficult task. He offered to make some coffee, said he was used to drinking ten cups a day, strong as crude oil.

It was early evening. After they had washed the dishes and put away leftovers, Jess and Sam sat on the front porch steps. Edward stood on the other side of the screen door, and watched geese in a ragged V stretch over the trees, then went back into the house.

"I had a dream last night." Sam lit a cigarette and blew smoke from his nostrils.

"A bad one?" Jess didn't know what to expect from him anymore. He was sitting next to her, but not close.

"They usually are bad, but this one . . . I don't know. Maybe it was just true."

Jess shifted, afraid to ask. "What do you mean? About us?"

Sam didn't answer, and the not answering said everything.

"You don't know who I am anymore, Jess." He cleared his throat.

"I think I do. So what was the dream?"

"I only remember pieces of it. I was in a field, corn field, I think, and I

179

knew you were there, but couldn't find you. Some searchlights were sweeping over the field. I had to duck down. I began to shoot, I don't know at what, but in the dream I was sure. I was afraid I would shoot you, somewhere in the cornstalks. The shots woke people up and they came out to see what was happening. They popped off porches and out of their beds. No one was afraid of the gunfire." He shook his head a few times trying to remember. "Things get confused at this point, until the searchlight shone straight on you. I had shot you. The last thing you said was 'You never should have come back." Then some half-naked little boys came pouring out of doors and windows. They were singing something that I recognized in the dream, but not now. Then one said 'What about her?' and pointed to you on the ground. I said, 'She'll be all right, as soon as I go.' So I left, and you got up and asked for lemonade."

Jess gave a small laugh. "Lemonade?"

Sam looked at her as though he wished he hadn't told her the dream. "Don't laugh."

"So you would end everything between us because of a dream! Sam? It's a *dream*!"

Sam put his face in his hands. "Don't make this hard. All those letters. You can't know what it meant to get them, and to write to you. I meant everything I said, but . . . " He looked straight at her.

"Are you saying you don't love me?

"I do love you." Irritation entered his voice. "Damn it, Jess." He stood, and Jess thought he was going inside.

"Don't!" she yelled. "I thought we loved each other, but if your feelings for me have changed then . . . " She took a deep breath.

"Something's shifted," he said. "I don't know what."

"But on the way back home when we stayed at the motel . . . we . . . I mean, I thought we were good."

"I know. But what I'm saying is different . . . "

"Help me understand," she said.

He stood with his back to her, and was through discussing it. "What's to understand?" He sat again on the porch steps, but not beside her. The porch boards creaked when they moved.

They sat for a few minutes looking out at a group of stunted trees. Sam pulled out another cigarette. Jess wished he wouldn't smoke so much. She didn't like the smell of cigarettes. When he took a drag and blew it out, he asked about the trial.

She looked at him privately trying to feel calm. "I don't know what will happen," she said. They studied each other's faces, astonished at how different they were. "I thought we were all right," she said. "When you came to

Lula and got me. I thought we could just pick up where we left off."

He put his arm around her shoulder. "Don't cry."

"But you don't just *stop* loving somebody!" she said.

He didn't answer her.

"Tell me what you want me to do," Jess said.

"Just don't forget me." Sam looked helpless, both loving and unable to love.

"That makes it even harder. I want to forget you right now." Her face looked shiny, oiled in the afternoon light. "When will you be leaving?"

"I'll stay through the trial, Jess; then I'll go. I don't know where."

"Maybe you should leave now," she said.

"I can't." She knew he loved her, but could not look at her. The war, she saw now, was still being fought within him.

September light had started to change to the gold of fall. Soon the whole forest would be lit from within, but, as Jess and Sam sat on the porch steps, early twilight moved over the trees like a weary ghost.

— 39 —

The trial began on Thursday.

At nine o'clock Judge Horn said that the question of guilt or innocence depended upon whether Adam's death was a suicide or if it was caused by "culpable negligence". "In that case," the judge announced, "a defendant can be charged with manslaughter. The key component, though, lies in how much the victim understood the consequence of going into the river." He nodded to the prosecutor, "You may call your first witness."

The prosecutor called Bobby Coe to the stand.

Jess saw Sam sitting next to her father in the second row of the courtroom. Sam smiled weakly. She leaned toward Mr. Strickland to ask who Bobby Coe was.

"He's the man who found Adam's body in the river." Strickland was taking notes.

The man stated that his name was Robert Louis Coe, and said that he had found Adam's body at Sudderth Creek. "I found him on a shoal about a hundred miles downriver. I was walking by early one morning and saw somebody. Looked like they'd washed up onto the bank. His leg was caught on a tree stump."

"What were you doing in the woods that day?"

"I walk that path most every day. I go visit my brother. He's in a wheelchair and needs my help, so I'm always going by there."

"Did you know Adam Finney?" The prosecutor would preclude any chance for Strickland to put suspicion on Coe.

"No, sir. I never saw him before in my life, till then."

"And what did you see, Mr. Coe?"

Bobby Coe described how Adam's hair and clothes were soaked with mud and sand, and his face, he said, "was turned up to the sky with his eyes open. He looked bloated, more like a sack of something washed up on shore, but peaceful, you know?" Jess wanted to close her ears. "I wiped the mud off his face. Looked like he had some bones broken, 'cause he'd been washed over rocks and stuff. I hesitate to tell y'all these things." He looked toward Clementine. "Anyway, I called the police."

The prosecutor asked if it looked like Adam had been hit or struck in any way.

"Couldn't say. He was pretty beat up, but I couldn't say how."

"He looked beat up?" said the prosecutor. "You could say that for sure?"

"Yeah. I can say that. His head looked caved in."

Clementine made a small, high sound in her throat. Everyone heard it.

The prosecutor sat down and Strickland walked quickly toward Mr. Coe as though this wouldn't take long and he wasn't going to waste the judge's time. "Are you saying he looked damaged in a way that was not from normal river damage? Or are you saying he might have been beat up by a person?

"No. I can't say that. I don't know. I'm just saying he'd been washed a lot of miles, and maybe the river rocks were hard on him."

When Mr. Coe left the stand, Jess asked Strickland if Coe's testimony had worked against her. Strickland shook his head to reassure her.

The prosecutor called the medical examiner next. The examiner described the broken bones, the damaged head, the body water-logged and bloated. He named the cause of death as drowning. When Strickland questioned him, the examiner testified to the fact that the absence of bruises on the body meant that Adam was already dead when his head was bashed in. "Since there is no blood flow after death occurs, or drowning in this case, there can be no bruising."

Jess found the medical examiner's formal description of Adam easier to listen to than the testimony of Bobby Coe. She kept seeing Adam lying on the bank, his shirt torn, his arms and legs sprawled into peculiar angles; she saw his mouth and ears filled with mud, his hair flat on his caved-in head. She saw the details clearly, as if she had been there herself, standing beside Bobby Coe. But she had not been there. She had gone far away.

The prosecutor called Clementine Finney to the stand, and she sat straight-backed in her chair, tucking strands of hair under her small hat, her freckles visible in the courtroom light. She wore a gray dress and a jacket with braids at the cuffs and collar. Her waist, cinched with a wide belt, made her look cut in two. Her hands stayed folded on her lap, her legs crossed at the ankles and neatly placed underneath her chair.

The prosecutor asked her to tell them about Adam.

"He was a good boy. His real daddy, Calder Finney, left when Adam was six years old. When the doctor explained to us about Adam's limitations,

Calder decided he had to leave. He just left." She snapped her fingers, one hand rising like a small bird from her lap.

"How did Adam feel about Jess?" the prosecutor asked.

"Oh, he loved Jess. She was real good to him." She pretended to be praising Jess. "Jess could have told Adam to do anything, and he would've done it. She could have told him to drown himself, and he would've done it. Just because she said to." She turned toward Jess, her eyes like burning coals.

"Jess thought you should not put Adam in the Cadwell Institution. Is that right?"

"She made it real clear that she did not want him to go." Clementine's face looked nervous and drawn. "She said he would be better off dead. She said that to me and to Edward Booker." She sighed. "My decision was not easy. I was more afraid of Adam ending up in jail than anything else. I couldn't think about him going to jail. He wouldn't have understood."

"And you believe Jess Booker assisted in Adam's drowning? Even urged him toward that end?"

Clementine looked down into a handkerchief that she kept wadded in her hands. "That's what I'm saying. She could have told him to do anything. He would have done it."

The prosecutor turned the questioning over to Strickland.

"Mrs. Finney," Strickland began. "Or should I call you Mrs. Booker?" Clementine said that, though she and Mr. Booker were married, she had kept the name Finney because it was Adam's name.

Strickland continued. "Had Jess ever urged Adam before this time to do anything that was harmful? To himself or to anyone else?"

"Not that I know of." Clementine didn't look up. "I don't know what she did."

"Why exactly had you decided to send Adam to Cadwell?"

"He was getting out of control. We tried everything. He was bothering little girls at the playground. Scaring them. And their parents."

"Had you ever discussed sex with Adam?" Strickland asked.

"Well, no. He wouldn't understand. I told him what *not* to do."

"Did people in the community report his behavior to the police?"

"A few times they did." Clementine worked her handkerchief with her fingers.

"Have you ever been told that Adam would have the same sexual feelings as any other boy his age?"

"I guess that's true. That's what the doctors told me."

"So it would have been helpful, don't you think, to have explained some of those feelings to him?"

Clementine held tight to the arms of the chair and scooted forward, rising slightly. "I get so tired of people knowing what I should have done with Adam. I loved him. They were going to put him in jail." She began to sob and couldn't stop.

Judge Horn called for a short recess, informing the witness that she would be called back to the stand after ten minutes.

After the break Strickland spoke softly, "Just a few more questions, then we'll be through, Mrs. Finney." He turned away from her. "Adam knew that he would be leaving soon for the Cadwell Institution. Is that correct?"

"Yes, he knew." Clementine braced herself.

"And he knew that his life—instead of being at home with you where he had always been—was going to change? He knew because he had already received several shock treatments at Cadwell?"

Clementine did not answer.

"Is that right?"

"I guess he knew." Her body suddenly looked bent at an angle.

"Did he beg not to go?"

"He had almost stopped begging, but sometimes at night he . . . "

"He begged you not to send him away?"

"He didn't understand, you see. I told him and told him. I said, 'Adam, we don't have a choice.' He never understood."

Strickland leaned in close. "Had you already discussed an operation with the doctors at Cadwell? The castration procedure, I mean. And had you talked to the doctors about the possibility of a lobotomy?"

"Well, it wasn't for sure." She put her handkerchief to her mouth and twisted sideways in the witness chair. She wanted to leave.

"In fact," Strickland urged, "didn't you sign papers giving the doctors permission for whatever procedure they thought best?"

"I had to. I had to sign, or they wouldn't take him." She was whispering.

Sometimes, at night, Jess had seen Clementine in Adam's room, sitting on his bed, her hand on his chest. They were whispering. Adam had told Jess that on those nights his mama could "talk him back to himself." He said that if he got lost in his head, she could talk him back and make him feel good again. She had always done this. But today was the first time Jess had seen how scared she was. She marveled that she had not seen it before.

"So you knew exactly what Adam would face when he entered the Cadwell Institution. Mrs. Finney, did you know that in some states those practices have been declared against the law?"

"I didn't know." Her head rolled on her shoulders. "I told him we would visit him."

"But he knew, didn't he?" Strickland paused. "That he wouldn't come home again."

"Stop! Stop it!" Clementine wrapped her arms around her waist. She began to yell. "We had no choice. Jail or Cadwell. That's all there was." She suddenly raised the handkerchief in mid-air, and shivered like a child.

Clementine tried to stand up, but fell back into her chair. "For me, Cadwell was the only thing to do. Even though . . . even though." She did not finish. She coughed and strangled back a sob, then turned to face the judge. "He was my son, Judge. He was my only boy."

They broke for lunch, and when they returned, at two o'clock, Strickland called Rick Blalock to the stand.

"What is your line of business, Mr. Blalock?" Strickland asked.

"I own Rick's Garage in Goshen," Blalock said.

"And what was your relationship to Adam Finney?"

"Adam got hubcaps from me. Been doing that for years. Most of his collection came from the ones I helped find. If I saw an unusual hubcap, I thought of Adam and took it over to his house."

"You delivered hubcaps to his house?"

Jess wondered where this was going. She turned to look at her father and Sam sitting beside him. He didn't know either.

"A few times. That's what I was doing one day last March when Adam answered the door. He looked terrible and I asked if he was sick. He said he'd been drinking poison."

"He said the word 'poison'?"

"Yes, sir. He showed me the bottle he got from under the sink." Rick Blalock turned toward the Judge. "Cleaner. A bottle of Clorox or ammonia, something. He started vomiting. Right there in the hallway."

"What did you do?" Strickland asked.

"I drove him to the emergency room. They pumped out his stomach." Rick Blalock touched his neck. "His throat was pretty bad damaged, I think."

"Where was his mother?"

"She was at the grocery store. When she showed up at the hospital, she told me I should leave. She said not to tell anybody about it. So I didn't until now."

"Why are you saying this now?"

"Because the poison thing happened in March, a few weeks before he was supposed to go away. So maybe Adam did want to hurt himself. I didn't want Jess blamed for something she didn't do."

Jess had never heard about Adam's emergency trip to the hospital, but now she remembered a day when her father called her at school, saying that Adam had been taken to the doctor for a bad stomach-ache. From her father's choice of words, Jess suspected that he, too, had not known the seriousness of that episode.

James Strickland offered Blalock's testimony as proof that Adam had been capable of taking his own life and that he had tried to do so in this earlier instance. The prosecutor requested a break, so that the prosecution could change the charge from involuntary manslaughter to helping a minor commit suicide, which was illegal in North Carolina. He believed, he said, that even though Adam was twenty years old, he could still be considered a minor—both mentally and emotionally.

Strickland called other witnesses who described a strong friendship between Jess and Adam. Her father testified that Jess had taken care of Adam—how, at first, she had resented his presence in the house, but that after a year they were a close brother-sister team. He claimed that Jess would never hurt him. One teacher mentioned that Jess had brought Adam to a school dance. "She spent all week teaching him basic dance steps, then she urged the other girls to dance with him. Adam said it was the best night of his life."

Then Strickland called Jess to take the stand. She wore a light blue sleeveless dress that hit just below her knees. Her shoes were blue leather with a small heel that accentuated the calves of her legs. Her slim white arms moved gracefully at her side.

Strickland approached the chair. "Did you ever hear Adam beg not to go to Cadwell?"

"Almost every night," Jess said. "Before he went to bed. He begged and cried. He knew he would get electric shock treatments. Once, they put him in a coma. They did these things to get rid of his desire for girls."

"Were his desires getting out of hand?"

"They thought so. But Adam never did anything bad, not really. Still, they were going to operate on him."

"By operate, you mean castration? Was this operation already planned?"

"Yes. Clementine told me she had to sign the papers. I couldn't stand to think about it. They were treating him like an animal."

"Jess, since we already know that Adam had been sexually aggressive toward little girls at the playground," Strickland said, "did he ever behave sexually toward you?

"No, no. We were buddies. At the playground he pulled up the dress of a little girl, and he tried to kiss another, but he wouldn't have hurt them. And he would never have tried to hurt me. My daddy told me that they would have to lock him up if he couldn't control himself. It wasn't fair. He liked to hug people. He even hugged the men at the auto supply places."

"Did you think he would choose death over the life he would have at Cadwell?"

"It wasn't death he wanted. He just didn't want to go to Cadwell. We went to the river on that last day, but Adam went in too far . . ." She paused. "Adam didn't want to go where nobody cared for him. One time when he went for a shock treatment, I went along. I saw people walking in the halls. They were strange and sleepy. I saw one woman tied to her bed. When Adam came out he looked like those people."

"But, in your opinion, did Adam understand the consequence of going into the river? With his clothes on?"

"He wanted to say goodbye to the river. He'd done that before. He loved the river like it was a person."

At that moment Jess saw, in the back of the courtroom, a man leaning casually against the wall. She recognized his hat. The man from the brown and white car. She made a small sound in her throat and Strickland came close. He stood directly in front of her, wanting to block her view. He couldn't tell what she was looking at, but he could see that something had disturbed her.

"Do you think Adam understood what he was doing?" Strickland repeated.

"Yes. I think he understood," Jess said. "Because when he asked me to come into the river with him I said, 'No.' I didn't say anything but 'No.' I think he knew then."

"Did he say he knew?"

"No, but he said he wouldn't have to go to Cadwell now. He said he wouldn't have to wear the helmet that hurt his head. He said he could ride all the way to the ocean."

"All the way to the ocean?" Strickland, as well as Judge Horn, looked puzzled.

"Adam loved the ocean," she said. "He drove us crazy talking about it." Edward smiled slightly at that remark.

When Strickland went back to his seat, Jess could see that the man was still leaning easily on the back wall. Not until he removed his hat did she recognize him from the photo in Adam's room, and saw that this was Adam's father.

The prosecutor approached Jess. His body faced the judge but he looked directly at Jess.

"It was late April, but it was still cold, wasn't it?" The prosecutor paced in front of her. "Could Adam swim?"

"No," Jess said. "He couldn't swim."

"Why did he go in with all his clothes on?"

"He was afraid he might get cold."

"Why didn't you call him to come back out? If he would have done what you said, why not call him to come back?"

"I did, but he had gone too far," Jess said. The prosecutor stopped dramatically in front of Jess. "Did you help Adam Finney commit suicide?"

Jess lifted one hand to touch her face. "We had talked about death before, but I don't think Adam understood what suicide was."

"Do you know if Adam preferred to drown rather than to live at Cadwell? Did he say that to you?"

"I don't know." Tears fell down her face.

"So you allowed Adam to enter the water wearing his clothes because you decided this would be better. Do you have the right to that decision when his own mother, as well as your father and the doctors, believed differently? And, since you let him make that decision, he drowned. Weren't you in charge of Adam at that moment?"

Strickland stood. "Objection, your honor. The prosecution is badgering the witness."

"I wanted him to be in charge of himself," Jess said. "For once in his life."

Strickland tried not to look disappointed at Jess's last statement, which sounded more like an admission of guilt. But since it was almost five o'clock, Judge Horn announced that the trial would resume again tomorrow morning at nine-thirty.

— 40 —

On the second day the prosecutor brought in two doctors from Cadwell, who testified to the positive and soporific effect of certain operations. But Strickland called to the stand Dr. Stanley Oberlin, who had worked for ten years at Cadwell, and had left there under the shadow of controversy.

As Strickland stood to call his witness, Jess turned around to see Calder Finney sitting in the back row. He didn't look at her. Maybe he was here to tell what he saw. Why wouldn't he look at her? She hadn't mentioned him to Strickland. She should have. Sam sat directly behind her and she could smell his cologne. The smell of him calmed her.

Dr. Oberlin took the stand. A small man, about five feet four, he had a neat beard and a long face. His lean fingers laced together in his lap.

"Are you familiar with the practices carried out at the Cadwell Institution?" Strickland asked.

"Yes, sir. I certainly am."

"What's your connection to Cadwell?"

"I was a doctor there from 1940 to 1951. Two years ago I left and since that time I've been working to close the place down. Much of what's done there is illegal."

"Yet when you were a doctor there you carried out the same procedures."

"Yes. I did. I hold myself accountable for what I performed, and I want Cadwell to be accountable too. Those procedures—lobotomies, castrations, hysterectomies—these might be done in particular circumstances, when deemed needed, but most of what was performed at Cadwell was for convenience."

"In what cases would such operations be deemed necessary?"

"For the criminally insane. That's when extreme measures might be taken."

"And for Adam Finney?

"Adam Finney would not be considered criminally insane by any measure. He was merely a young man of limited intellectual abilities." The doctor cleared his throat and wiped his brow with his hand. "But to remove him from a loving home to spend the rest of his life at Cadwell Institution . . . well . . . " Dr. Oberlin paused. He looked directly at Strickland. "There are things worse than death."

The prosecutor objected. The judge sustained.

"Doctor, could Adam have known what he was doing when he decided to enter the river?"

"I don't know what Adam knew. I can't testify to that in any exact way, but I can tell you of another patient. In 1947 I knew a mentally deficient woman who had lived with her parents until she was twenty-eight. When both parents were killed in a car wreck, this young woman was sent to Cadwell. She didn't understand what had happened to her world. She was treated with electroshock and medication, but even with those treatments she was despairing. Within a few months she hung herself in her room. Another patient showed her how, though this young woman did not tie a proper noose. She took a long while to die. The rope finally broke her neck. The woman who instructed her did the same thing a few days later. I could give other examples over the years. That's why I'm here now. That's why I'm working to have these practices declared illegal." He adjusted himself in the chair.

The prosecutor began his own questioning. "Dr. Oberlin, you have admitted to being one of the doctors who performed these so-called 'extreme measures' on your patients. During your ten years at Cadwell, didn't you ever question those operations?"

"I did, many times, but I did not have the power to make a change."

"Do you hold a grudge against the hospital for letting you go?"

"They did not let me go. I left."

"Ah, well, the head administrator at Cadwell has a different story. He says that you botched an operation and they had to let you go."

"They had to let me go because I was leaving anyway. The 'botched' operation, as you call it, was one that I finally refused to perform. A fourteen-year-old boy was masturbating much of the day in his room, and also in the public rooms. It was his only source of pleasure. He had no planned activities that interested him. He made paper airplanes and necklaces with beads. I was told to castrate him and I refused."

Clementine looked as if her insides were collapsed and empty. Her mouth was open and she was moving her head back and forth.

"You have said that you cannot testify to Adam's frame of mind, but you have spent enough years with these patients to know them better than most? Is that correct?"

"I know how confused patients become upon entrance to Cadwell. I know they cry for months, some for years. They finally forget why they are crying, but they do not forget to cry."

Jess heard a rustling in the rear of the room and turned to see Calder Finney walk to the front of the courtroom. He looked determined as he passed a note to an assistant sitting at the prosecutor's table. Jess saw the assistant open the note and turn, then whisper to Calder Finney, who did not return to his seat, but stayed close-by. Jess sighed, more loudly than she meant to, loud enough to make Strickland turn and look at her. Jess had the face of someone who had been slapped.

The prosecutor continued with his witness. "Dr. Oberlin, would you say that you are hated by the staff at Cadwell?"

"I can say that, sir. I am their enemy now."

"You've lost their respect."

"I very much doubt that. My work there was good, competent work, but wrongheaded. Mrs. Finney has protected her son from harm all of his life, I'm sure. And she believed she was saving him from a lifetime in jail." He held his chin in his hand. "But I am fighting for a different way of life for people like Adam."

Jess was taking short breaths. She looked at Sam who was leaning forward in his seat, his face concerned. He wanted to know what was wrong with Jess. She had turned pale and looked as though she might pass out. Calder Finney was waiting, she knew, to be called to the stand. She had everything to lose. The person she wished for right now, wished for the most, was Adam.

Once Jess had told Adam, "You are the real thing. You know that?"

"I am a real thing."

"You are *the* real thing. Let me tell you what I mean. I mean that you don't ever pretend to be somebody else, and . . . "

"I pretend to be a cowboy sometimes, and a Indian."

"I mean that people are always wearing a mask of some kind, not being who they are, but you . . . "

"At Halloween I wear one."

"Adam?"

"What?"

"If I never love anybody else, I love you. Do you know what that means? Love?"

"It means that the person wants you to be happy and they leave a muffin on the table in the morning."

"Yes. That's right."

"And I love my room in the house, and my radio, and Hap, and Buckhead. I love hearing people talk downstairs at night, so I know where they are, and I can sleep."

The prosecutor, after returning to his table, asked permission to bring in a new witness, Calder Finney. "We have a witness who was at the river that day in April," he said.

Strickland objected to the witness and looked questioningly at Jess. Strickland asked for a brief recess, and after talking to Jess told her that an eye-witness could change everything. After the recess both lawyers met in Judge Horn's chambers. When they came out again, Calder Finney was called to the stand.

Clementine looked happy. She believed that Calder had come to help her case, but when he got to the witness box, he did not look at her. After he was sworn in, he said that he was Adam's father and that he had come that day to Adam's home.

"The question we want you to answer, Mr. Finney, is about Jess Booker and Adam Finney on that last day they were together." The prosecutor looked confident. "Did you see the two of them together on April 28th at the riverbank, just before Adam drowned?"

"Yes, I saw them together that day," Calder said.

Clementine let out two short breaths.

"Can you tell us why you were there at the river that day?"

"I was going with them the next day to take Adam to Cadwell. I arrived in Goshen early, because I wanted to see him. I drove to Edward Booker's house, and that's when I saw Jess and Adam leave to go through the woods. I followed them to the river."

"Jess with Adam? Could you could describe exactly what you saw?"

"I saw them talking. Beside the river. Couldn't hear anything, just saw them. Then Jess kissed Adam and waved goodbye."

"She kissed him?"

"Nothing that seemed romantic. Just saying goodbye. She waved. Adam took off his coat and then he went into the water. I figured he was going to swim downriver, meet her there. Nothing seemed to be dangerous about what they were saying. I didn't suspect anything. That's for sure. I thought maybe they were planning some kind of escape together." Calder's breath was heavy. He waited a long moment. He was looking now at Clementine. "I left

Adam when he was a little boy. I've always been ashamed of that. Clementine did everything for him, and I came back when he was ten. I hoped then that maybe I could stay, but I couldn't. And for all those years I hated myself. I loved Adam, you know? But felt so sad when I saw how hard he tried. I came back over the years, sometimes on his birthday. Once Adam came to spend a long weekend at my house, but he mostly wanted Clementine. She sent pictures, and, when I called him, he always wanted to talk to me. Broke my heart to see how he always forgave me."

"What did you see on that day?" The prosecutor wanted to get back to the subject.

"Like I said, I thought she was going to meet him downriver and that they would run away. So I followed Jess, best I could. After a couple of weeks I saw her a few times on Highway 53, then again near Rome, Georgia. But kept losing her. Finally I went home, but after they found Adam's body I knew Jess had run away because she was afraid. After the funeral, I went to look for her again and saw her on State Road 20. That road took me to Lula, Alabama. That's where she was."

The prosecutor interrupted. "Do you think she was responsible for Adam's drowning?"

Calder stopped, sinking into thought. "I don't think Jess would do anything to hurt Adam. Clementine told me what good friends they were. Not at first, but finally Jess became his main caretaker. Took him everywhere. He missed her when she went off to school." Calder turned to the people sitting in the courtroom. "You people around here, you might not remember me, but you knew Jess. And you knew Adam."

Clementine was rocking back and forth in her chair, tears streaming down her cheeks.

"Adam loved everything," Calder laughed, "like those damn hub-cabs all over Edward Booker's garage. You know what?" he said suddenly, "Maybe we try too hard to question the hell out of everything, to put life in a box and label it there. Yes, that's it." Calder rose from his chair, standing now, confused. No one told him to sit back down. "I'm not saying this right."

"What are you trying to say?" Judge Horn asked.

"I'm saying I can't blame Jess for anything. My God, Clementine. *I'm* the one to blame. Blame me. For everything!"

The prosecutor wanted someone to object to his own witness. Strickland had not objected to anything.

"Does anyone understand what I'm saying?" Calder asked again. Judge Horn looked around as though he expected someone to raise a hand.

"Clementine? What are you doing to Jess? Please!"

For a moment no one breathed, then Clementine stood slowly rising from her chair. As the prosecutor returned to the table he touched her arm, but could not stop her.

"I don't want this anymore," she whispered, loud enough for everyone to hear. "This blaming. Adam can't be brought back. It's all over."

Her lawyer conferred with her for a few minutes before he announced that the accusation made against Jess Booker would be withdrawn. "Clementine Finney wishes to drop the charges against Jess Booker," he said.

They returned to the judge's chambers, and when they came back Judge Horn dismissed the witness, and declared the trial ended. The courtroom bustled as people left, and Sam walked beside Jess toward the car, his arm around her waist; her father and Calder followed behind them. Clementine sat alone on the courthouse steps, and Jess peeled away from Sam to sit with her. They leaned forward, both of them, as though observing something down in a hole. The trio of men waited at a distance. When they stood up, Clementine walked in a different direction but Edward called out to her.

"We're going home now," he said. "Clementine, if you want to come by the house for supper, you'll be welcome." A slight wind brushed them as they walked and autumn leaves fluttered down like so many butterflies.

— 41 —

Jess decided not to return to Mt. Chesnee School until January, so she spent fall semester at her old high school with her old friends. She never mentioned Sam Rafferty, so no one else did either; but he had written to her twice, both letters avoiding anything personal. He sounded deeply sad about who he was now. She answered him, writing to him as an old friend.

Clementine had moved back into the house, but at Thanksgiving said she did not want to prepare a big dinner, so they ate with the MacDougals next door. Nothing could make that first holiday right, but Clementine promised Christmas would be special.

In mid-December Jess went back to Lula, Alabama, for Will and Miss Tut's wedding. She stayed five days in her old room. The house was decorated lavishly, the way it had been for the July celebration, minus the fans. Ray and Shooter wanted to be around Jess every minute, and kept introducing her to their father. Rosemary had cut her hair and, though she seemed less concerned with her appearance, she looked prettier. Her need for planning, however, continued to thrive, and, in addition to all the Christmas decorations, pedestals were covered with white cloths topped with bowls of flowers. Swags of lilies draped the hallway. The house smelled like a funeral parlor.

Chairs were set up in the large front room, and, as Miss Tut walked down the aisle, the professor played the piano. Miss Tut wore a lavender dress, and had a wreath of purple flowers in her hair. Will wore his only dark suit. They said their vows before the Presbyterian minister, and Jess cried when they kissed.

Frank sat beside Jess on one side and Zella Davis sat on the other. Frank did not seem as interested in Jess as he had been a few months ago, but he was polite. The boys were ring bearers. They carried rings on small pillows and looked miserable doing it. Ray's ring fell off the pillow twice before he got to the altar. Each time it fell, Shooter mumbled under his breath.

Jess returned home from Lula refreshed and a little hopeful. Christmas day was quiet without Adam, but the house smelled of Clementine's cooking. That, itself, made the day bearable. But it would be New Year's Eve before Jess and Clementine sat alone together. They had not been comfortable around each other, but their lives had found a regular rhythm. Adam's absence still felt palpable, and though they could have a reasonable conversation, Edward was always nearby.

Tonight, even on New Year's Eve, Edward had gone to check out a problem at the downtown store. He promised to be home soon and to bring some noisemakers for celebrating.

"Will you be at home tonight, Jess, or are you going out?" Clementine smiled at Jess, but her smile looked sad. She moved to the couch and patted the cushion next to her, inviting Jess to sit down.

"I'm staying home." Jess wondered what Clementine wanted to say. Her hands trembled and she tried to hold them still.

"I'm glad you'll be here with us." Clementine paused. "I hoped Sam might be here for Christmas." This was her way of asking a question. "He liked my cooking as much as Adam did."

Jess thought of Sam, his sweet breath in her hair, his hand combing her body, those soft nights and mornings in his arms when she moved toward the sleepy smell of his face. "He won't be back," she said simply. A shudder moved through her like a rolling egg.

Clementine leaned to touch her. "Oh Jess, this is so lonesome. For all of us. I just want you to know I care about you, and last summer when I accused you, I was so full of anger." Her face had the look of apology, but her voice took on the rhythm of a wheel wobbling, ready to come off. "I was beside myself."

"I want to say something . . . " Jess began. This was her chance to say it all.

"You don't need to say anything." The tenderness of Clementine's words washed over her.

"But I *want* to tell you . . . " She did. She did want to. She had to tell her.

"No." Clementine sounded firm. "No." She continued, "You know, my life with Adam was hard for so many years, then we came here, and you made him happy, Jess. I saw that. Living in this house made him happy." Light from the table lamp sprayed the room, hitting above and below the shade, but not doing anything to illuminate what was around them. "Listen," Clementine was saying something important. "We all made mistakes. Adam was the only one who didn't make any mistakes."

"I keep thinking I see him in the house or yard," Jess said, turning toward the window. It was dark.

"I know. I know." The two women suddenly leaned to hold each other—to embrace all that could not be said. They looked shy, like children at peace after an argument.

Jess sat, still in the loop of Clementine's words: *I know, I know.* The tension gripping her neck and shoulders softened. She felt almost forgiven, though forgiveness had not been mentioned. She knew that the memory of Adam, his bright face, would pour through her dreams for years, like rain to rinse her in old grief.

— 42 —

Hap still wandered the house trying to find Adam. He looked in every room and made small whining noises; but whenever Jess remembered Adam, two images came to mind: his unkempt body as it had been found that day on the riverbank, and Adam alive, laughing too loud or walking somewhere with Hap.

Before going back to Mt. Chesnee School for winter semester, she went to the river. She had not been back there since that April day. She wore the necklace Adam had made for her in Cadwell. She had not worn it in a long time and the metal felt cold against her skin.

"Want me to come with you?" Edward asked.

"Not this time." She walked alone through the woods to the place where Adam had entered the water. Today was January 3rd, and she could not imagine how the New Year would unfold. This winter day, though, was not cold, but nearly sixty-five degrees—much like April. A few jonquils had already begun to rise up out of the ground. Jess stood on the bank and threw in sticks, watching them float, go under, rise up, and move quickly into the river's current.

On the day she brought Adam here, he had walked into the water, getting his shoes wet, saying his goodbye to the river. When he came out, they sat on the riverbank. Adam looked sad.

"When you think about going away, Adam, what do you think about?" Jess asked him.

"Being dead," he said pragmatically.

"And what is that to you?"

"Layin' down still and quiet-like. Can't talk. Can't run anymore."

"Like being asleep?" she asked.

"Yeah. Like a dream."

"A dream is good," she told him.

"A good dream is good."

"Can dying be a good dream, Adam?" She didn't know what he would say.

"It can be a good thing."

Jess had been sitting very still, but when she heard his answer she stood and began to pace the river's edge. "I don't know." She said to no one.

"I go to Cadwell on Wednesday," Adam said. Then he asked, "When's Wednesday?"

"Tomorrow."

Adam looked hard at the river, listening. Sometimes he thought the river talked to him in riffles and murmurs. He thought he knew the language of rivers. Sometimes he talked about the arm, or the mouth, or the foot of a river, believing it was a real person.

"I could go in the river and let it take me all the way to the ocean."

"But maybe you don't want to," Jess said.

Adam walked toward the river. "I tell them not to hurt my head." He held his head in both hands as though it were hurting at that moment. "They do it anyway."

Jess came close and put her hand on his shoulder. "Come on, Adam." She urged him into the edge of the water that lapped his soles. Water reached his pant legs.

"Adam."

He stopped suddenly.

Her voice grew shaky. "You want to go floating down the river? Like a dream?" She saw no other way. Tears already streamed down her face.

Adam took off his jacket and threw it on the ground. Jess took off her sweater and laid it beside his jacket; then he began to unbutton his shirt.

"Leave your shirt on," said Jess. "Even your shoes."

Adam laughed.

" . . . and you can float away. It's as simple as that. You'll go all the way to the ocean. You'll swallow water like a fish." She looked at him, the beginning of a smile on her face, but no light shone in her eyes.

Adam nodded, and he kept nodding. He didn't smile.

"You're pretty smart, aren't you?" Jess said. "You're smarter than anybody knows."

"And I don't ever go to Cadwell," he said.

"Not ever."

"And you come *with* me?" he asked.

"No."

He looked at her a long moment, his eyes knowing something for sure. "Will you stay here while I float?"

"Yes."

"Don't go away until I'm gone." He understood.

"Yes. I'll stay until you're gone." Her tears could not stop.

"Don't you cry," he told her.

"I won't." She stepped toward him and held Adam tight for a long moment. "Well, maybe a little," she said. Her arms wrapped around his neck and he ducked his head into her hair. She kissed him.

"When you come see the ocean sometime, you see me too," he told her. He moved away from her, her hand slipping like a feather off his shoulder, not quite falling.

"I'll see you there, Adam. I'll see you everywhere." She reached for him again but he had gone into the water. He was up to his waist.

"Adam?"

Adam nodded again and again, and went deeper. His long body brave and alone, as always. "I won't *ever* go to Cadwell. I go all the way to the ocean, like dying." He went into the water. He yelled to Jess that it was cold. She saw his arms trying to swim.

"Are you floating?" she called.

"I'm going fast," he said. "Jess?"

"I'm here, Adam!" She had a moment of panic. She screamed to him. "Adam, come back."

"I'm here," he called. The rim of quiet water was breaking against the bank. Jess waded in up to her waist where she could see only his head bobbing in the middle of the river, until he was gone.

It was as simple as that.

— 43 —

Jess stood on the bank to see the river curve, then curve again, going toward the foot of a mountain not far away. She would take this image with her back to school. Think of it in class, or walking on campus. Speckled light on the currents looked giddy. She could smell the beginning of rain, and saw a wide cloth of showers moving toward her. A drop fell on her arm, then another and another. Jess no longer felt young. She might never feel young again.

High over the mountain, lightning winged at random without sound. Rain poured down and washed her, and, for one moment, an image of Adam in the river came back. Jess did not want to let it go—seeing his head just above water. Her eyes searched for him. If she stared intently at the river current, maybe the dead could rise up, maybe the past and present could move along together. Rain had soaked her clothes. She was trembling.

Then, she heard a sound, something more than the dripping of trees. Water fell from her hair, her tears indistinguishable from raindrops. She turned and saw Hap, his tail wagging, running toward her from the edge of the woods. Then she saw Adam, as clearly as if he were really there, she saw his tall body beneath the trees, his face a map of what they still had together.

He would laugh at the water dripping from her hair. He would say, "You're gonna get wet. You better go home now."

The hard downpour turned to a soft, mizzling rain, and Jess imagined that the rim of night stars, not yet visible, were falling. She squinted, trying to see Adam once more—his head or arms, anything that could loosen the dark strings of her mind. But there was nothing, except for Hap, who stood quietly at her side. They both faced the river.

Adam, I'll keep your hubcaps burning in sunlight on the garage, and leave muffins on the table for Hap to steal. Adam, I will cling to the spirit that sings or talks until your head gets things right, and see you in every moon that rises over the river. I'll grow old for you, and let nothing of you go.

Jess turned to go back home with Hap, when suddenly the sun broke through a low shelf of clouds and made the trees bright with drops. The river roaring by felt like thunder beneath her heart. Then something on the opposite bank broke off, swirling down into a deep socket of water, before rising up. She watched, until it dropped out of sight. Along the water's edge, little pieces of white foam lingered like memory.

Adam

When he steps into the river, his shoes fill up, and his pants suck at his legs. He likes being in the river more than being at Cadwell, but he goes deeper than he has ever been before. Jess said it would be all right. Jess loves him and makes his mind clear as sunrise. She can't come with him.

The river grows cold, but no more burning wires will be placed on his head. Those wires made him dazy like a ragdoll, not able to remember who he was. They tried to make him somebody he was not, but he wouldn't go back there. So now he tries to float, his clothes like balloons on his arms. In the water he feels washed of desire, of need. I'm not scared, he thinks. He is floating, floating; but his pants grow wet and heavy. He calls to Jess and hears her say, I'm here.

Now he can't remember. Maybe the river remembers everything. He becomes soft underwater, tumbling, not breathing. Jess said she would stay there. He is going far away. Don't cry, he told her; then she did. She will see him sometime in the ocean, but it won't be him. And he will never wear the helmet again, or be locked in the metal clamps. And Mama's eyes won't look down when she leads him out of Cadwell, and Papa B. won't drive sad home, and Jess won't cry. And Hap. Hap.

Everything is moving too fast. He sinks down and pulls back up. Underneath, he sees fishes, and mud fills his eyes. Breathe. He can't breathe. He didn't know it would be this hard. He waits for the ocean, wishing it would come soon. He coughs out water, but more water bathes his head. His chest hurts, like knives stabbing. He tries to call out. Hap.

Adam has always known about the word Love; he knows who has it and who does not have it. He is not smart, but he is smart about the word Love. He knows what it means. It means he can live in people's hearts, like they live in his.

Now, he is no longer floating. Now, he is more river than man. The water fills up his clothes and eyes. His legs are water and he has touched the river-floor. If he is gone from the world, he is gone from the world—and nothing will ever be the same.

AUTHOR'S NOTE

This novel truly began with my grandmother's younger sister, Pearl. She went to school for only a short time and never became independent or integrated into society, although no one ever mentioned that she might be "retarded" or "deficient." She was beautiful as a young woman, and sought out the company of men, which caused much concern for her family. At nineteen she fell in love, married a young man, and ran away; but the police found her and brought her home. The marriage was annulled, and Pearl, heartbroken, lived most of her life with her sister (my grandmother), helping her to raise five children. She spent much of her time cooking and cleaning, then in the late afternoon she sat on the sofa to work her "arithmetic."

I knew Pearl only as an older woman who always had brown syrup at the corners of her mouth, which I believed was chocolate, but later learned that it was snuff. I liked to work arithmetic with her. I don't remember if her calculations were correct. I didn't care. I loved being with her and I loved eating her fried chicken and her three-layer lemon cheesecake. I do remember her temper, how she would throw things in the kitchen, and yell.

During the 1950s Pearl, then in her seventies, was sent to the asylum in Milledgeville, Georgia. She died there. I was about ten. To this day, no one in the family has mentioned the word "retarded" in reference to Aunt Pearl.

In the 1960s I got a job teaching Special Education in the public schools. Special Ed. was a new experiment in Tennessee, and this class was the only one of its kind in our school. The class had twelve students: a few had Down's Syndrome, several were brain-damaged, one was a crippled, hydrocephalic teenager, two had severe cerebral palsy, and one boy who never spoke and might have been more emotionally disturbed than mentally deficient. These students ranged in age from eight to nineteen. Each needed individual attention and each one learned differently. If I changed the bulletin board to emphasize images particular to Thanksgiving or Christmas, the brain-damaged children felt displaced and distraught. I learned quickly the importance of stability.

After a few months I noticed that no meanness lived in these students. They could be mischievous and they could misbehave or throw a tantrum, but they appeared not to have the capacity for cruel or deceptive behavior calculated to hurt someone's feelings. I was inspired by the children's determination to learn, reveled in their ability to laugh and joke, and felt calmed by their lack of competitive edge and by their generous ability to help one another. I loved being with them each day and I began to prefer their company to that of other people I knew.

By Christmas vacation I could not bear the thought of not seeing them for two weeks. After the Christmas party with cupcakes, Christmas tree cookies, and ice cream, and as they were leaving, I put my head on my desk and sobbed. They were, of course, excited about leaving the school, but came back to comfort me, gathering around, patting my back, and telling me in halting and unintelligible speech that "it would be all right."

These kids worked harder at their simple tasks than I had ever worked at anything in my life. They possessed patience, persistence, and a kind of acceptance that I had seen nowhere else. Their lives were more emphatically sensory, with a remarkable ability to notice the world around them.

The death of Eunice Kennedy Shriver brought focus, once again, on the plight of the mentally handicapped. Eunice's sister, Rosemary Kennedy, was considered "retarded" or "mentally ill' and, in 1942, because of her tantrums and the fear that Rosemary would become sexually active, her father allowed her to undergo a lobotomy, a practice familiar in those days. The lobotomy was badly botched, and Rosemary remained in an institution for the rest of her life.

During the 1940s, '50s, and '60s, people loosely categorized as retarded, mentally challenged, or mentally ill were often institutionalized and treated experimentally. In many cases, life lived in those early institutions—often in the South called asylums—was hardly a life at all.

This book is an apology to those who lived in a world unwilling to make a loving place for them. Faulkner's Benji was "gelded," Steinbeck's Lenny was shot by the one who loved him most. I give a nod to the literature that focuses on characters not understood by society, and therefore deemed not worthy of a full life. I hope Adam's heart will remain full in the minds of my readers.

ACKNOWLEDGMENTS

I want to gratfully thank those who have helped this book come to light: Marly Rusoff, my agent who was enthusiastic and believed in this novel; Jonathan Haupt, my editor, who read with such intelligence and care; Herb Barks, my brother, who made good suggestions each time he read it; Jill Mc-Corkle, my friend who read through several versions and whose keen eye for character and plot helped me to revise; and Kittsu Greenwood, my lontime friend who read every version of this novel and gave me help the whole way.

I wish to also thank Judy Sternlight, my former editor at Random House, who edited an early version of the novel; Mark Byrnes, history professor at Wofford College, who gave advice about the Korean War; and Dan Barks and Max Hyde, lawyers, who answered questions about court procedure.

For their constant support and encouragement I thank Elizabeth Morrow, Michael Cox, Coleman Barks, Ginger Smith, and Bill Arthur. Without their affirmations, writing would be too lonely.

Finally, thanks are owed to my husband, C. Michael Curtis, who is both my constant and fierce editor and my loving sweet companion.